Sister Seen, Sister Heard

Sister Seen, Sister Heard

Kimia Eslah

Roseway Publishing
an imprint of Fernwood Publishing
Halifax & Winnipeg

Development editing: Fazeela Jiwa
Copyediting & text design: Brenda Conroy
Cover design: Tania Craan
Printed and bound in Canada

Published by Roseway Publishing
an imprint of Fernwood Publishing
32 Oceanvista Lane, Black Point, Nova Scotia, B0J 1B0
and 748 Broadway Avenue, Winnipeg, Manitoba, R3G 0X3
www.fernwoodpublishing.ca/roseway

Fernwood Publishing Company Limited gratefully acknowledges the financial support of the Government of Canada through the Canada Book Fund, the Canada Council for the Arts, the Province of Nova Scotia, the Province of Manitoba and Arts Nova Scotia for our publishing program.

Library and Archives Canada Cataloguing in Publication

Title: Sister seen, sister heard / by Kimia Eslah.
Names: Eslah, Kimia, 1979- author.
Identifiers: Canadiana (print) 20210357576 | Canadiana (ebook) 20210362952 | ISBN 9781773635200 (softcover) | ISBN 9781773635422 (EPUB)
Classification: LCC PS8609.S45 S57 2022 | DDC C813/.6—dc23

To my sister

1

Friday, May 7, 1993

Late Friday morning, Maiheen Ghasemi woke to her husband belting out an Iranian love song in the shower of their Toronto apartment. Mustafa had left the door to the ensuite bathroom ajar, most likely to coax her out of sleep and woo her into joining him. The ballad he sang dated to the sixties and the final stages of their courtship. Soon, they would celebrate their twenty-sixth wedding anniversary, and it pleased her that he lusted for her as much as he had back then.

Maiheen stretched in all directions before she turned onto Mustafa's side of the bed, taking in his lingering scent on the pillow and tucking in the blankets around her, reluctant to rise on her day off from serving and cleaning at the coffee shop. In the vanity mirror, she saw her puffy face and grayed roots. She chastised herself for not keeping up her appearance, and she thought about Mustafa and the importance he placed on his looks. Back in Iran, when they both worked in the same branch of Sepah Bank, Mustafa had always been the best dressed of the managers.

Through the sole window of their bedroom, Maiheen noticed that the sky was a brilliant blue and she smiled with gratitude. She didn't expect it to be a warm day, not in Canada in the month of May, but she was glad it was cloudless. *Maybe I can go for a walk. Really, I should be more like Mustafa. He's so much better at taking it easy.*

Maiheen hoped her two twentysomething daughters would meet men as balanced as their father, though it seemed like an impossible future to ensure. She considered herself friendly and open-minded, and she felt unfairly excluded from their love lives. She scowled at the thought. *They never bring home any of the young men they're dating, as if I don't know!*

She heard Mustafa turn off the shower, and she quickly rose from bed, brushed her hair, and wiped the sleep from her eyes. Spritzing herself with flowery perfume and chewing on a breath mint, she examined her body from various angles. The wrinkles and spots that had appeared in late middle age could be masked with the right makeup and hairdo, but she was daunted by her widening waist and rear end.

Her former coworkers in Esfahan would have teased her about the pear shape she had acquired since moving to Toronto fourteen years earlier. The physical labour involved in working at factories, cleaning offices, and serving in coffee shops depleted her desire to do anything but slump on the couch once she got home. Of course, even those moments were brief and crammed between her own housework and cooking duties. Eating, whether it was donuts at work or candy on her bus ride home, soothed her weariness. Feeling despondent, Maiheen wrapped her silk robe tighter and decided to meet Mustafa at the breakfast table rather wait for his return to the bedroom.

As soon as Maiheen opened her bedroom door, she heard Farah rush down the hall. Her twenty-year-old daughter, looking like a transient with cropped hair and oversized men's clothes, often behaved liked like an impatient child, making demands and responding ungratefully. Maiheen was not impressed by Farah's displays of immaturity, and she often wondered why the girl could not model herself after her older sister. Maiheen conceded that Farzana was not perfect, especially with her inclination for secrecy, but at the very least, she was composed. If Farzana was still water, Farah was a whirlpool.

"Mama, do you have the deposit cheque?" Farah asked before her mother stepped out of her bedroom.

"Good morning, Mama! Good morning, Farah-*jaan,* dear! How was your sleep? Good, thank you. How was yours? Good, thank you for asking." Following her performance, Maiheen pursed her lips and walked past Farah to the kitchen.

"Oh, sorry." Farah followed behind closely and spoke without pause. "Good morning, Mama-*jaan*. How was your sleep? I slept well. Thanks."

"Farah, can I get ready for my day first?" Maiheen asked rhetorically as she grabbed instant coffee and a mug from the cupboard. She had prepared the cheque the day before and placed it in the top drawer of her dresser. It was tempting and easy enough to direct Farah to its location, but Maiheen refused to reward her daughter's bad behaviour, especially since soon she would have fewer opportunities to instill the right values in her daughter. Maiheen's own mother would have been horrified by Farah's direct and demanding disposition, having taught Maiheen to use diplomacy, compassion, and flattery to achieve her goals.

Farah tried to sound unhurried, "Yeah, of course. I'm just making sure that ..."

"*Medoonam*, I know, Farah," Maiheen interrupted without looking up from the cup of coffee she was preparing. "You're excited. I understand. I just need ..."

"I'm being organized. See, just like you said," Farah whined. "I'm making sure that everything is ready and I've covered all the bases. Like you told me to."

"I also asked you to calm down and take things one at a time," Maiheen added, looking desperately at the timer on the microwave, willing it to go faster.

"That's not fair," Farah complained. "I'm supposed to be, like, responsible but when I try to get stuff done you tell me to, like, calm down."

The microwave beeped, and Maiheen took her cup to the counter to stir in cream and sugar. She tried to remain composed in spite of her desire to throw a nearby banana at her daughter's head. She inhaled and exhaled deeply before she replied. "I'm happy to see you being responsible, but I wish you would take into account everyone else's experience."

"What does this have to do with other people?" Farah continued, flustered, pacing in the tight space and gesturing wildly with her hands. "Why is this, like, such a big deal? I just need a deposit cheque. You already said you'd give it to me. This conversation totally doesn't make any sense."

"None of this makes any sense to me," Mustafa complained as he entered the kitchen from the other end. He kissed Maiheen on the lips and discretely patted her rear with a conspiring grin.

"No, no, no!" Farah stomped her feet. "Baba, we've already agreed. There's nothing to explain. We've agreed!"

"I didn't agree to anything," Mustafa said with a shrug. He took a sip of Maiheen's coffee and grimaced. "Too sweet," he declared and returned the mug to Maiheen.

"Mama! This is not fair," Farah pleaded with her mother. "Baba, stop it! This is not funny."

Maiheen sighed, "Mustafa, you're making it worse. Can you please leave it to me, my love?"

She encouraged him towards the dining table, and Mustafa complied. Maiheen rewarded him with her smile of appreciation, and then she continued her lesson with Farah about the merits of delicacy and diplomacy.

☽

From the dining room, Mustafa heard his wife extoling Farzana's interpersonal skills and then his younger daughter giving a frustrated moan. This was a lecture Maiheen had delivered many times before, and he wondered why she bothered to repeat herself. Teaching Farah etiquette wasn't a lost cause, but she needed to learn her lessons the hard way, through consequences. She had been obstinate since early childhood, always speaking out of turn and saying too much, and Mustafa blamed the examples set by Canadian children, whose culture lacked subtlety and refinedness. Whereas Farzana spent her preadolescent years in Iran learning decorum from relations and teachers, Farah grew up in Canada and adopted mannerisms that would be considered uncouth by even the lowliest of Iranian society. Like her tendency to inject herself into conversations without an invitation and her inability to stand down or allow others to save face. *Maiheen's just wasting her time. The girl is too stubborn to listen to anyone.*

To distract himself, Mustafa turned his attention to the best part of the newspaper, the sports section. Athletics was the realm of gods and miracles, and he had felt destined to be in that sphere since he was a boy. He wasn't fast enough for football, strong enough for weight lifting, or agile enough for wrestling, so he pursued a business degree in hopes of opening a training gym that rivalled the world-class gyms of Moscow and Brussels. The managerial position he accepted at Sepah Bank, at age twenty-five, was intended to provide the funds to purchase and renovate a facility.

These days, his life bore little resemblance to the past. The tailored suit and corner office had been replaced by coveralls and long days cleaning cars. What remained, day-in and day-out, was sports. He had installed a satellite dish on the balcony so he could watch football matches from around the world, but he was also dedicated to hockey and baseball, having declared his allegiance to the Toronto home teams almost on arrival in the city.

Hearing Farah interrupt Maiheen repeatedly irked him, and Mustafa cast aside the newspaper and injected himself in their conversation without waiting for a pause. "I just don't understand why you need to pay someone else when you have a room here," he challenged Farah from one end of the kitchen, looking past Maiheen who stood in the middle.

"Baba, we've already talked about this," Farah whined from the other end of the kitchen.

Her crossed arms and pouting lip reaffirmed Mustafa's opinion that Farah couldn't think clearly, unemotionally.

"So, you know the reasons. Tell me again," he responded coolly, trying to set an example.

"Mustafa, my love," Maiheen pleaded, handing him a cup and saucer of hot fragrant tea.

She looked tired but not angry. His wife rarely became angry. He placed the cup and saucer back on the counter, kissed Maiheen's hands in show of appreciation, and prepared for a routine faceoff with Farah.

"I mean, really. What's the point of wasting money? I'm not a bank manager anymore. I clean cars, and it takes a lot more time and effort to earn money. So, why am I paying for three places? I mean mathematically, this is nonsense." He ended with his arms crossed and his head cocked to receive her attack.

"You don't," she snapped back. "You *and* Mama pay for my stuff. Farzana pays for her own place."

Farah held his gaze in a show of defiance. Her mother had taken her coffee into the dining room, making space that Farah filled by widening her stance and placing her hands on her hips, elbows wide.

"Is that what you think?" Mustafa asked with a smirk. "We pay for a lot more than you know, and I'm tired of it."

With unmatched daintiness, he picked up the cup and saucer and joined Maiheen in the dining room. When Farah followed, he knew he had weakened her defences.

"Baba!" Farah started with a drawn-out whine. "We've already talked about this. I need to be closer to school, downtown."

Feeling in the lead, Mustafa retorted, "Why?"

He wasn't sure about his endgame, but if it was possible to discourage another one of his daughters from moving downtown, he would continue trying. Farah had yet to place a deposit on the one-room rental.

"You've been bussing downtown all this year, and it's been fine."

"Not fine," Farah rejoined, sounding less angry than fraught. "I had to take the bus and the subway for an hour, five days a week. Twice a day. You don't know what it's like. You drive everywhere."

She was nearly in tears now. To sustain his resolve, he diverted his gaze to the newspaper and spoke from behind its pages.

"I drive to work, to earn money, to pay rent. Three times, if you had your way."

When Farah didn't respond, Mustafa snuck a peek from around the paper. She was sitting on the couch, adjacent the dining table. From her rigid posture and clenched fists, Mustafa knew Farah was fuming.

Apprehensively, he glanced to catch Maiheen's reaction. Since the girls were young, it had been Maiheen who signalled the right approach and led him to victory. But she wasn't in sight and Mustafa felt out of his league.

☽

On the couch, Farah stared at the oversized aquarium that occupied one wall of their living room. She sat with her arms crossed and her lips firmly set. The one remaining bubble-eye fish swam slowly about the tank, mouthing any small floating debris that crossed its path. Farah silently cursed its mediocre existence.

Years earlier, her father had spontaneously bought the fifty-gallon tank and three dozen assorted fish. As he assembled the aquarium, he had described the goldfish in the pond at his childhood home. Farah, who had longed for a pet she could cuddle, had accepted the fish in lieu. She and her father weren't fluent in the same language, embedded in the same culture, or of one mind about any matters close to the heart, but they could care for the fish together.

Pathetic. Absolutely pathetic. She fumed as she observed the lone surviving fish. The others had died in a slow massacre that could have been avoided if her father had researched beforehand. The betta fish and cichlids dominated the tank, eating all food flakes before the goldfish could swim to the surface. The discus fish died within days because the temperature didn't suit them. The barbs nipped at the angelfish and the angelfish bullied the guppies.

Farah was past caring about the fish. Their demise was a testament to her father's disregard in the one bond they could have shared. She resented the last fish, and she wished it would die and bring the whole affair to an end. *He doesn't care about me or what's important to me. He's power-tripping like the macho Neanderthal he is.*

Farah glanced his way to examine her father's expression, but the newspaper hid his face. It didn't matter. This situation was all too familiar, and Farah knew her parents' expectations. It was the same old bullshit about attracting flies with honey, not vinegar. *Fuck that. Flies are attracted to shit, not honey.*

She refused to be manipulated into behaving like someone she wasn't, specifically her older sister, the good daughter. She loved Farzana, whom she considered to be her best friend, but Farah had long ago tired of being measured by the standard her sister set.

"You let Farzana move downtown for school," Farah started.

With dramatic flair, her father lowered the paper and replied knowingly, "And how did that go? Four years renting a room and now she lives with some fast friend. They should both be living with their families and saving for the future, not throwing away their money on rent."

Farah squeezed shut her eyes and emitted a guttural sound. *There is no way to reason with this man.*

"Mustafa, my love," Farah heard her mother entreat. "Let's leave Farzana out of this. She's doing just fine."

Farah opened her eyes to see her mother stroking the nape of her father's neck. She planted a kiss on his forehead, and his grimace transformed into an adoring gaze, one that followed her mother even as she returned to the kitchen.

Her father's softened expression relieved Farah. Typically, it meant an end to their argument, with all likelihood that the deposit cheque would be in her hands soon. Subduing others with entreaties as a way of handling conflict was her mother's specialty. Farah intuited that her mother had used this particular conflict to reinforce her lesson about influencing others with charm.

Deflated, Farah leaned back and unclenched her fists. Her gaze fell again upon the lone fish, which gobbled a piece of floating debris and spit it out again, recognizing it as inedible. Next, she admired the expanse of clear sky and the view from their eighteenth-floor apartment. In the far distance, she could see the top half of the needle-like CN Tower, demarcating downtown Toronto and signifying her new life as an independent woman. *Partially independent, I guess. I still have to rely on them for rent.*

From the kitchen, her mother returned with a platter of fried eggs, enough for four people, and another platter of warmed pita bread, all of which she set on the dining table. Once she had transferred buttery eggs onto a plate for her father, her mother took a seat on the couch next to Farah. From the pocket of her robe, she retrieved a folded cheque and silently placed it on Farah's lap.

"*Merci,* thank you, Mama," Farah said quietly, tucking the cheque into the back pocket of her jeans. She was grateful for the money, but she refused to ingratiate herself to her mother, especially with her father covertly observing their exchange. *Why can't this be a cut-and-dried exchange? Why do we need to make everything about pleasing each other?*

Before she rushed out of the room, Farah kissed her mother once on the cheek to avoid seeming ungrateful. Over her shoulder, she informed her parents, "Oh, and I'm staying at Farzana's tonight."

"What's this?" Her mother asked as she rushed to the hallway, where Farah slipped on her army boots and prepared to leave.

"After school, I'm meeting Farzana at the subway station. Then we go to the landlord and do all the lease stuff, you know, 'cause Farzana is my co-signer. After that, she's letting me stay over, finally."

In a half-whisper, to avoid attracting her father's attention, her mother narrowed her eyes and leaned in to ask, "And when I call Farzana's tonight, you'll be there?"

"Of course," Farah replied resolutely.

"And your exams next week?"

"They're fine," Farah perked up, glad to move on to another topic. She counted off her exams on one hand. "I have four. Monday, Tuesday, Wednesday, and Thursday. Then the semester's done. And the exams are all based on assignments, so I can do them in my sleep." She offered another pleasing smile and added, "Okay, I've got to go now. The bus."

Before Farah could unlock the front door, her mother asked, "I thought there weren't any more classes. Why are you going to school?"

Farah sighed and dropped her shoulders. She was still facing the door, and she made sure to plaster a smile on her face before she turned to her mother and answered. "There's a meeting for one of the clubs."

"What club is it?" Her father asked as he stepped into the hall and took his place behind her mother.

To sustain her momentum and avoid further delays, Farah kissed each parent farewell as she answered. "It's a women's club. The meeting's at twelve and I've got to catch the bus ..."

"Oh," her father interrupted, "I thought you said it takes an hour to get downtown. It's already nearly eleven. How're you going to make it to this meeting?"

Before he finished asking his question, Farah had walked out and the door had closed behind her. She was halfway down the hall, towards the elevator, when she heard her father call for her.

"I have to go, Baba," she pleaded.

"I know, I know. You're a very busy person," her father teased her.

He ambled down the hall, and when he reached Farah, he pressed a twenty-dollar bill in her hand. "This should cover your expenses tonight." He winked knowingly.

Farah realized that her father had overhead her plans to spend the night at Farzana's. Mildly vexed by his covert games, she offered a small smile and thanked him for the money.

"I really have to go now."

"Go, go!" He urged her jovially. Then, he turned back toward his apartment, where his wife stood in the open doorway.

From the landing in front of the elevators, Farah heard her father say, "Maiheen, none of this makes sense. You understand, yes?"

"Yes, my love. I do," her mother answered before she shut the door.

Farah had the elevator to herself during the ride down to the lobby. That wasn't a surprise since it was late morning on a weekday, and everyone who had to be at school or work would have departed hours ago. She crammed the twenty dollars into her back pocket, along with the cheque, and prepared her portable cassette player for the hour-long commute downtown.

As she stepped off the elevator, Farah heard a commotion in the concrete room at the rear of the lobby, near the double doors she used to access a shortcut to the bus stop. Except for moving days, when tenants used the rear entrance for loading and unloading furniture and boxes, the room was a quiet space.

One corner of the room was sectioned off by a floor-to-ceiling chain-link fence. Inside the fence, two dozen bicycles were locked to a set of heavy-duty bike racks. Farah's bike was among them, stripped of its front and back wheels and long forgotten. The bicycle locker offered little protection against theft since the four-digit code of the combination lock was common knowledge.

As Farah neared the concrete room, she heard the static of handheld radios that signalled the presence of police. At the doorway between the lobby and the concrete room, she paused to inspect the scene. The double doors that led to the loading area and visitors' parking lot were propped open, and Farah spotted three police cruisers parked at odd angles, several officers jotting notes, and police tape cordoning off an area of asphalt half the size of a basketball court.

Farah was accustomed to police activity in her neighbourhood. In a crammed corner of her dilapidated high school, there existed an office for the resident police constable. At the start of every school year, the principal reminded students that the officer served in the capacity of a guide and advocate, not a monitor or mole, but the kids didn't trust the principal or the officer, neither of whom lived in their neighbourhood. She knew police officers to be short-tempered bullies who targeted Black boys at her school and protected only their own reputations.

From experience, Farah knew that the police didn't concern themselves with her. Often, they didn't acknowledge her existence. Somehow, being young, brown, and female was disarming, and her features made her invisible to police officers.

Fine with me, she thought every time a constable looked through her as if she didn't exist.

She was about to change her plans and leave by the front doors when she spotted Michael Selkirk in the bike locker. Dressed in black from head to toe in his customary outfit of oversized trench coat, loose shirt and jeans, scuffed sneakers, and tattered cap, Michael knelt in front of a bicycle that Farah knew wasn't his. Michael lived with his parents and younger brother in the apartment building identical and adjacent to hers, which is where he also stored his beat-up bike.

What is he doing? Farah could have stood there watching Michael for a long time. With his too-pale skin and prematurely thinning hair, Michael wasn't anyone else's idea of a dream boy. To others, Michael appeared malnourished, if not jaundiced, and his lanky posture under the threadbare trench coat gave him the air of a delinquent, but Farah felt that she knew him better than anyone else, and she knew that Michael was harmless.

His pale skin, which barely concealed the network of blue-green veins, was the result of his sleeping all day, working in the back room of a shoe store until closing time, and staying up late into the morning to smoke cigarettes and play cards with his friends at an all-night coffee shop.

When a flurry of activity started among the officers, Michael leaned far to the right to inspect the commotion. Absentmindedly, he placed his hand on a bike seat to lean farther and his weight caused a series of bikes to topple over. The officers stopped talking and turned in his direction with concerned expressions. One of the officers approached the bike locker.

"Is everything okay?" The constable asked with a grimace. "What are you doing in there?"

Farah took the opportunity to ingratiate herself to Michael. She rushed into the concrete room and called out to him. "See, they took both my wheels."

Pretending that she just noticed the constable, Farah acted surprised and asked him, "Did you come about my bike? Someone stole both my wheels. See." Farah pointed to her bike, one of the many that Michael had knocked over.

The constable said sternly, "This area is part of a crime scene. I need both of you to leave, immediately."

"Okay," said Farah, as she stepped back from the bike locker. She looked at Michael and suggested, "Maybe you can help me later?"

Michael nodded silently. He slung his black knapsack over one shoulder and exited the bike locker, making sure to shut the chain-link door behind him. The two walked through the double doors and into the lobby without looking back at the constable.

Farah felt the rush of adrenaline that surged through her body when she was in close proximity to Michael. She smelled his menthol aftershave and nearly swooned. Once, after having sex in his bedroom, she had concocted an excuse to borrow his shirt. She slept with that shirt for several nights, burrowing her face into its thin fabric until his scent had been replaced by her own.

She wanted more of Michael, more than casual sex and a borrowed shirt, but he was content with the arrangement they'd maintained for two years. Sex, no strings attached, and the occasional hour spent smoking cigarettes and watching music videos. Farah had convinced herself that this arrangement would eventually lead to a romantic relationship since neither of them was dating anyone else, but time was running out, especially with her imminent move downtown, an hour away from him and out of range for last-minute calls to drop by his place.

"What were you doing?" Farah asked in a teasing tone.

"Trying to find out what happened," Michael replied coolly.

"What did happen?" Farah asked as she recalled the section of the parking lot that was cordoned off by police tape. Her memory of the crime scene had been compartmentalized at the sight of Michael in the bike locker.

"Are you serious? You didn't hear the sirens?" Michael scoffed as he walked to the front doors and lit a cigarette as he exited the building.

Trying to remain unperturbed by his frosty demeanour, Farah followed slowly, not submitting to her desire to rush Michael and kiss him deeply until he declared his affection for her.

Outside, the weather was a mixture of spring sunshine and chilly winter air. Farah zipped up her hooded sweatshirt and stuffed her hands in its pockets. Michael had readjusted his black cap to cover his eyes and raised the collar of his trench coat to shield his neck. Slightly hunched over to block the wind, he shuffled along the paved path leading from her apartment building to his own. Farah stepped in stride next to him though the path led her away from the bus stop.

"I'm on the eighteenth floor. I don't hear much up there," she explained plainly.

Michael had never seen her apartment since her parents would have embarrassed her with their formality. Farah cringed at the thought of Michael sitting on their overstuffed couches, her mother offering fruit with delicate plates and knives and her father reciting the previous day's sports scores.

Michael did not use delicate plates or watch sports. His apartment and his family could be described as informal in every respect. No one cooked, and with the intrusion of cockroaches that scattered every time Farah opened a cupboard, it made sense. Meals came out of cans or the freezer, and their family ate with plates on their laps in front of the television.

The apartment was cluttered with piles of knitting and scrapbooking projects and stacks of electronics waiting to be repaired. The smell was most disturbing of all, a mixture of cat urine and spoiled milk. Farah could just imagine what Michael would think of her and her family if he ever stepped foot inside her parents' pristine apartment. *Uppity, vain, self-obsessed.*

She didn't want him to judge her or to assume that she judged him.

"Oh, yeah. I forgot. You live in the penthouse," Michael teased and poked her side.

She interpreted his teasing as a friendly gesture, so she stepped closer and decried, "Uh, Michael, the penthouse of a rat's nest is still the penthouse of a *rat's nest*."

"Yeah, but it's still the *penthouse*," Michael joked.

They both chuckled and Farah felt confident about their bond. She didn't understand why Michael opposed their dating, and she wondered whether he was embarrassed by her, or possibly he was interested in someone else and Farah was keeping his bed warm until he convinced the other woman to go out with him.

Farah noticed that they had reached the end of the path, at the front door of his apartment building. She wanted to kiss him but she knew that he didn't display affection publicly. Instead, she stalled for more time to look into his eyes.

"So, what happened? The police and all?" she asked.

Michael took a drag from his cigarette before he answered. "Remember Sheena, with the long hair, the really long hair? And, the chunky heels ..."

"Shireen," Farah interrupted. "Sheena is Ali J.'s ten-year-old sister."

"So you know her? Shireen?" Michael asked, lifting his cap to reveal his hazel eyes.

"No," Farah answered distractedly, preoccupied by Michael's nearness. "I never talked to her. She's, like, five years older than us. Her dad worked at the same place my dad works, like, a long time ago."

"Yeah, well, Shireen jumped." Michael informed her, following a long deliberate drag from his cigarette.

"Shit! How do you know it was her? Is she going to be okay?"

She crossed her arms to feel safe and warm, but the chill that overcame her refused to relent.

Nonchalantly, Michael exhaled a plume of smoke over his shoulder before he answered, "She's dead, Farah."

"Shit. That's crazy," Farah whispered, shocked by the news. "Did you see anything?"

"No. They'd already taken her away when I got there. I think it happened really early."

Michael took a final pull of his cigarette before dropping it to the ground and crushing it with his sneaker. His tone had grown solemn, possibly influenced by Farah's severe reaction to the news. He wasn't a sentimental person, and Farah knew that he distrusted emotionality. Jokingly, Michael's mother likened him to a zombie because of his dispassionate reactions, and Michael suggested that the cold-blooded nature of a vampire was more fitting to his character.

With his hands tucked into the pockets of his thin trench coat, Michael turned toward the front doors of his apartment building and gestured with a nod that invited Farah to follow.

I'll catch the next bus, she assured herself as she trailed behind Michael.

In the empty lobby, Michael leaned on one shoulder near the elevator doors but he didn't press the button. Farah stood steps away, biting her lip and wondering where this was leading.

"I heard from the super that they took her dad away too and that her apartment's got tape across the door," Michael added while he toyed with his plastic lighter.

"Shit. That's crazy," Farah replied, shaking her head in disbelief.

She had known of other kids who died, like Thomas Frey's older brother who was killed in a drunk-driving accident and the sixth grader who got sick with meningitis and died overnight, but she had never heard of a kid committing suicide. *So why was her dad taken away?*

She didn't pose the question to Michael because she feared that he might reply cynically or make a sarcastic joke, and Farah wasn't interested in humour just then. Shireen was only an acquaintance to Farah; still, it seemed unfeeling and callous to judge or mock a dead girl.

"Yeah, crazy," Michael said, still playing with the lighter but eyeing Farah. "Sorry about your friend," he added when Farah remained quiet.

"Oh, I didn't know her," Farah explained, concerned that she seemed overly affected by Shireen's death. "A lot of people worked at the same place as my dad." *Did that sound bad, snobbish? Did I just snub a dead girl?*

"That's cool," Michael shrugged. He pressed the button for the elevator and casually asked, "Do you wanna hang out? No one's home at my place."

Michael didn't attempt to seduce Farah with a look of longing or persuade her with charisma. He remained his usual aloof self, shielding his desires and discouraging intimacy. His gaze rested on the dial overhead, which indicated that the elevator was descending from the fourteenth floor.

Within the next minute, Farah needed to decide whether she would join Michael for their routine of sex, junk food, and TV, all of which would consume at least a couple of hours. Or whether she would head downtown to campus, where she was expected at a meeting. The elevator had descended to the fifth floor, and for the first time since they began sleeping with each other, Farah considered declining his offer. *Taari is expecting me.*

During her first year of university, Farah had connected with only one person, Taari Hadva. When Taari suggested that Farah join her at the women's studies' meeting, she agreed readily, if only for the opportunity to chat with Taari outside of class. Farah desperately wanted a friend at school, someone to hang out with during breaks, maybe have a beer together at the on-campus pub that she had been too intimidated to enter alone. It had been easier for Farah to make the honour roll than to make friends.

Unsettled, or possibly surprised by her delayed response, Michael responded, "It's cool."

Just then, the elevator door chimed open and an elderly woman walked out pulling a collapsible shopping cart that had been lined with cardboard. Michael stepped aside to let her pass and Farah smiled briefly at her, out of respect. Then, Michael stepped into the elevator, pressed the button for his floor, and leaned against the back wall, facing Farah.

He offered a tightlipped smile and said, "Catch ya later."

As the elevator door closed, Farah replied, "Bye."

She watched the dial as the elevator ascended to the tenth floor, Michael's floor. She sighed, bit her lower lip, doubting herself, then put on her headphones, turned on her music, and started for her original destination.

Farah walked the sloping sidewalk that led from the cluster of deteriorating high-rise buildings on the hill to Don Mills Road, the throughway that carried cars, trucks, and buses north to the suburbs and south to downtown Toronto. The road was three lanes wide in each direction, and walking across its intersections was a fatal act for a handful of people each year. Left-turning cars preoccupied with oncoming traffic and right-turning cars inattentive to pedestrians regularly threatened Farah.

To top it off, weather made the commute just as difficult. In turns, the blustery winds of winter and the scorching heat of summer depleted her energy. On wet and slushy days, she feared being soaked by a passing vehicle as its tires drove through a pool of dirty water in the ubiquitous potholes. If Farah never took the No. 25 bus again, she wouldn't miss it at all.

At the traffic lights, Farah crossed the road to wait at the deserted southbound stop. The three inner corners of the narrow plexiglass shelter were littered with used coffee cups, cigarette butts, and potato chip bags. Farah gingerly stepped through the small opening to avoid contact with the grimy walls that were marked with graffiti and streaked with spit.

After examining the two-person bench for wetness, Farah sat and held her knapsack on her lap. The music from her headphones drowned out the racket of traffic, and Farah assumed the universal mindless stare of commuters waiting for the next bus.

Presently, a thirtysomething white woman dressed in office attire entered the shelter, stepped past Farah and stood to her left, facing the direction of the impending bus. Farah studied her covertly and imagined what it would be like to dress in a skirt and blazer. Soon after, two East Asian women arrived. The younger of the two was middle-aged and dressed like Farah's mother, in floral print blouse, chunky cardigan, pressed black slacks, and sensible walking shoes. Her companion was a much older woman, hunched over and dressed in a long gray wool coat, knit hat, and tightly wound scarf. They moved slowly towards the grassy strip behind the shelter and away from the traffic.

Farah considered offering her seat to the two women but she couldn't bring herself to start a conversation. She continued to stare ahead, into the middle distance, and concentrate on her music.

Moments later, she spotted two young Black women crossing the street and approaching the bus stop, one of whom she recognized as an acquaintance from high school, Terry Henderson. Farah assumed the younger woman, possibly fourteen or fifteen years old, was Terry's sister. They shared a resemblance but they had also donned similar stylish track suits and wore their hair tied back in small high buns. Farah smiled to herself when she noticed that the sisters even walked with the same confident gait, and she wondered if she and her sister walked alike.

Farah remembered how much Terry had been liked in high school by teachers and students. Terry was friendly, athletic, and smart, someone Farah admired for her ability to fit into any crowd. She knew that Terry lived in one of the high-rise buildings in their neighbourhood, but their paths hadn't crossed since high school.

She probably doesn't even remember me.

Hoping to avoid an awkward situation, Farah decided to keep her eyes cast leftwards, in the same direction as the office worker. Shortly, Terry and her sister entered the shelter. The younger sister sat to the right of Farah, and Terry stood facing her sister. Farah's music blocked out their conversation but she could see they were talking excitedly.

Tired of staring at the oncoming traffic, Farah squinted to see the front page of the newspaper in the box chained to the nearby lamp post. It was the picture of a white man, dressed in a suit and tie and sitting in the back of a police cruiser. From the nightly news coverage, she recognized him as Paul Bernardo, a serial rapist and murderer, a predator who had been attacking women in East End Toronto for six years before he was caught.

In a pamphlet on campus, she had read that one in four women is sexually assaulted in their lifetime. This information staggered her. Farah considered the five women waiting for the bus at that moment, and she wondered if any of them were already a statistic. One disturbing question led to another, and she pondered what percentage of men were rapists and sex offenders.

Presently, a black pickup truck pulled up alongside the bus stop even as traffic continued to speed through the intersection. Farah couldn't hear the two young men who had crammed their torsos out of the passenger-side window but she could tell that they were yelling.

A quick glance at the frightened expressions on the faces of the women on each side of her informed Farah that these men were strangers hurling insults and threats. She made to remove her headphones to hear the men with their bulging eyes and flashing teeth, men young enough to be teenaged, but what happened next shocked her into paralysis.

One minute she was removing her headphones and the next she

was shielding her head and face from speeding projectiles lobbed from the truck. A series of loud thuds reverberated inside the plexiglass walls of the bus shelter, followed by yelps from each side of her, and then Farah heard the squealing of tires as the truck peeled away.

She opened her eyes, and after confirming that the truck was out of sight, she exhaled the breath she had been holding. *What the fuck was that about? Who were those guys? Why would anyone do that?*

A dark gelatinous substance covered the outer pane of the glass wall directly in front of her, and from its viscous motion as it travelled down the glass Farah guessed that it was pudding. *Was that supposed to be a joke, hurling pudding at strangers? They have a truck, so they can get away with it?*

To her left, the office worker looked startled, her knuckles white as they clutched her leather handbag to her chest. On Farah's right, Terry rose from having draped herself like a human shield over her sister and knelt to the side of the girl to whisper reassurances.

Adrenaline pumped through Farah, and she noticed that her hands were quivering. She wanted to say something, anything, but no one was looking her way. Instead, she scanned the grassy area behind the bus shelter for the middle-aged woman and her elderly companion.

The two women were slowly approaching the red and white bus-stop pole, avoiding the thick globs of brown that had splattered the pavement. A moment later, the office worker stepped past the bench and joined the two women at the pole. Farah could see that the bus was two blocks away but she didn't want to leave Terry and her sister, who were still in their protective huddle.

"Is she okay?" Farah asked softly.

Terry looked up and nodded. Then she whispered something to her sister and rose from kneeling. The young girl's lower lip was trembling, and she wiped her face repeatedly with the sleeve of her track suit.

Arm in arm, the sisters joined the others in line, and Farah followed close behind, scanning all lanes of traffic for the black truck. *Is it over? Are they gonna come back and follow the bus?*

Once she retrieved her bus pass, Farah glanced at the soiled bus shelter and the burst containers of pudding on the pavement, their plastic dented from the impact against the glass. *Is this when I'm supposed to be grateful for not getting hurt?* she wondered cynically as her adrenaline dissipated and her anger surfaced.

On the half-empty bus, Farah noticed that all five women sat near the front, though none of them acknowledged the others or their shared experience.

Terry and her sister sat side by side in the first set of forward-facing seats. Terry's arm was wrapped around her sister, who sat by the window and stared off into the distance with an expression that was hard to read.

Farah chose the side-facing seat directly in front of them, her legs perpendicular to theirs. She wasn't sure why she sat in such close proximity. It might have been the comfort of being near Terry Henderson, someone familiar and formidable, someone who reacted to distress by offering reassurances.

What the fuck just happened? Farah needed someone to explain what had happened and why it happened at all, but the world around her had moved on, without explanation.

The bus bumped and rattled in the pothole-ridden right lane of Don Mills Road, stopping every couple of blocks to pick up riders, some carrying backpacks and satchels, others pulling shopping carts, each adding their scent to the mélange of odours trapped by the closed windows of the bus.

Usually, she listened to music to pass time during her commute, but it felt unsafe to disconnect from her surroundings, to miss the cues leading to imminent danger, and to be caught off guard again. Instead, Farah watched the pairs of shoes walk by as each new rider passed her to find a seat, she studied the ads for radio stations and community colleges posted overhead, and every few minutes she scanned the faces of the five women who had also been present at the bus stop.

At the intersection of Don Mills Road and Lawrence Avenue, a densely populated neighbourhood packed with a bustling shopping mall, a high school of two thousand students, and several mid-rise medical buildings, the bus all but emptied. Farah pulled her feet under her seat to avoid the rush of riders filing out the front doors who were too busy peering through the windshield for connecting buses to avoid stepping on her as they passed. She noticed Terry and her sister whispering to each other and then hugging briefly before the younger sister squeezed past and disembarked.

Farah watched the young girl join the other students at the corner, all of whom were waiting to cross to school. She wondered if Terry's sister would describe the disturbing event at the bus stop to her friends and what she might relay. *These guys in a truck yelled at us. Then they threw pudding at us and drove away.*

It sounded ridiculous, almost comical, and Farah imagined listeners laughing at the scene, unable to empathize in the absence of an altercation, broken bones, or bleeding bodies. How could she describe what had occurred in a way that expressed her horror at being targeted, her fear of escalation, and the sustained confusion and anxiety?

The bus started again southbound on Don Mills Road, filled to capacity again with students, seniors, and mothers with young children. Terry moved over one spot into the window seat, and a large white man in a grey suit and tie immediately took up the vacancy. He arrived with a suffocating cloud of cologne that stung Farah's eyes and caused her to turn away to take shallower breaths. While his broad shoulders and heft filled the seat, his thick limbs occupied space in the aisle on his left and pressed against Terry on his right.

Terry adjusted her position to regain distance from the man but what space she created he filled quickly by relaxing his posture and expanding his domain.

When he spread his knees farther, bumping into Farah's own, she expected him to say something to acknowledge his transgression. He said nothing. Instead, he pulled out a folded newspaper from under his arm and opened it before himself so widely that his elbow hovered near Terry's left ear. Farah was exasperated by the man's arrogance and disregard, and from Terry's narrowed eyes, she knew she wasn't the only one.

Unsure about what to do, if anything, Farah glanced at Terry and met her gaze. Both women rolled their eyes and shook their heads in disgust, cracking the tension, and they erupted in chuckles.

The man lowered his paper and eyed the two young women with disdain. With greater contempt and added dramatics, Terry shifted her body away from him and turned to face the window. Farah bit her lip to suppress her smile. It felt good to deride the man, entitled and arrogant as he was, and it felt great to detest him in league with Terry.

Should I say something, or push away his knee? Her heart beat rapidly at the thought of confronting him, and she decided against taking further action. It seemed risky to call him out for his bad manners, being trapped on the bus and unable to make a hasty retreat if he were to lash out. Farah didn't trust the bus driver or anyone on the bus, except possibly Terry, to defend her against a big white man in a suit. To them, she probably looked like a rowdy brown teenager with a chip on her shoulder. *Enough conflict for one day.*

The bus pulled into Pape Station, and both sets of doors opened for the rush of riders descending to the subway. Terry was somewhat trapped in her window seat, and she waited for the man to refold his newspaper and heave himself to standing. Farah chose to wait too though there was room for her to join the line of disembarking riders. She felt protective of Terry and wondered whether the man might choose this period of commotion to berate the young woman. As he rose and walked to the door, the women glanced at each other and laughed out loud.

"Farah, right?" Terry asked as they disembarked. Her smile was as endearing and intelligent as it had been in high school. "Mr. William's physics class," she said, reminding Farah of their last shared class.

"Yeah. Terry Henderson," Farah replied and immediately regretted using Terry's last name. She thought it made her sound uppity or formal but Terry smiled and nodded.

They walked against a tide of riders ascending the stairs from the subway and rushing the platform of buses that were prepared to depart. Farah thought about this commute and the jumble of bodies pressing one way and another, running for trains and buses, rushing to claim seats, and refusing to move farther down the bus, the subway car, and the platform.

It was exhausting to travel this route twice a day, and it brought a smile to Farah's face to count down the remaining number of commutes until she lived downtown, when she could walk to campus and avoid the perils of bus stops and busses.

"You going east or west?" Terry asked when they reached the landing one floor above the train platform.

"West," Farah said. "You?"

"East," Terry answered. "'Kay, see you around, Farah."

"Bye, Terry." Farah gave a small wave at shoulder height.

She walked the dingy hallway to the stairs, which led down to the westbound platform. Upon hearing the door chimes of a train, she imagined herself speeding down the steps and hopping on. Then, she saw the tide of people coming up the stairs, leaving no room for her to descend, and she sighed, bracing for the onslaught. *It's almost over.*

☽

Taari Hadva rooted through her overstuffed carpetbag, her right arm in up to her elbow and her right hand stinging from the small cuts caused by the sharp edges of her binders. The lounge in the Humanities Building was nearly empty, except for a couple necking on the couch tucked behind a pillar and a trio dressed in collared shirts and sweater vests working frantically on a presentation, their papers strewn about adjoining tables in the centre of the lounge.

An hour earlier, she had lain on the shabby, stained loveseat that she positioned against the floor-to-ceiling windows of the lounge's eastern wall. Taari was still recovering from the previous night, when she had stayed up late with Natalie, one of her new roommates, drinking wine from coffee mugs and sharing tales of misadventure.

Pain relievers had deadened her headache but her stomach refused to be soothed. When it gurgled and Taari burped, she emitted a sour, pungent odour of rotted fruit, the fumes of cheap wine. She cringed at the stench but she refused to regret her drinking; it had brought her so much closer to Natalie, the only other female in a house of seven roommates. Taari considered regret to be a disguised form of self-hate and self-doubt, and she was finished with demeaning or diminishing herself. She was twenty years old, and it was time for her to be her own person, no regrets.

She stopped searching her bag momentarily to chew on half a piece of fennel gum, a brand Natalie had turned her on to, which was sold at a nearby health food store and cost more than Taari thought was possible for a packet of gum. The flavour was overwhelming for the first couple of minutes, but it mellowed into a pleasant taste that reminded Taari of the licorice allsorts her Sinhalese-British grandparents kept on hand.

Ambient light from an overcast sky filled the lounge, and she pondered the view into the sunken courtyard, the flowerbeds edging its perimeter dotted with crocuses and bits of litter. Taari wished springtime would speed up, or better yet, be skipped altogether and summertime could bring warmth and colour back to the bleak landscape and gray skies. *I'm so done with all this cold and rain*, she inwardly bemoaned as she returned to searching her bag. *I just want some sun.*

Earlier that week, she had traded in her wool sweaters and scarves for delicate cotton blouses, bohemian skirts, and leather sandals. It was too early for this thin clothing, she knew, but she needed a shift in perspective, away from the cocoon-like existence of winter garb. The change in wardrobe had improved her disposition slightly, even if others expressed dismay at her bare arms and toes. *My body, my choice.*

On the walls of her windowless bedroom, once the storage room of a grand century home in the West End of Toronto, Taari had posted her other favourite quotes, words which encouraged her to trust herself and which prepared her to defend her ideals. The quote she had most recently taped up was written in large, neat print, without flourish. The words came from bell hooks, a black feminist Taari studied in her introductory women's studies course, "I will not have my life narrowed down. I will not bow down to somebody else's whim or to someone else's ignorance."

In that quote, and in the rest of hook's writing, Taari saw herself depicted and her thoughts detailed in a way that ignited her sense of self and purpose. She refused to have her life narrowed by parents and grandparents who continued to be governed by the ideals of the same white colonial powers that had disenfranchised and subjugated them in Sri Lanka, England, and Canada. She refused to bow down to the hopes and dreams of others, no matter their good intentions.

In the past year, Taari had recast herself as an activist against misogyny and racism and as an advocate for the rights of women of colour, and the first task on her new agenda was the reconstruction of the women's studies program.

Taari withdrew her hand from her large bag and sucked on the stinging cuts that were imperceptible to her eyes. She shook her hand as if to cast off the pain and finally conceded to emptying the bag. She was certain that her quarry was located in its depths, not forgotten under the piles of clothes on her bedroom floor or left behind in her childhood bedroom at her parents' home during her weekend visits to wash laundry and stock up on essentials. No, it was in the bag, she was sure.

Taari withdrew one item after another, placing each belonging on the stained cushions of the loveseat. She proffered a collection of goods that typically never leave a person's home, like a wrinkled potato, a pint jar of turpentine, and a cardboard jewellery box filled with the broken wings of moths and butterflies. *It has to be in here. I know I packed it.*

☽

Before Farah could catch her breath, she was explaining her tardiness to Taari. "Hi, I'm really sorry I'm late. It's just the bus and then the train. It was kinda crazy this morning. I'm really sorry."

Taari stood up and leaned forward to hug Farah. This act caught Farah off guard since she only ever hugged her parents and sister. In high school, everyone maintained a socially acceptable distance, and the only people who hugged were the ones who also necked.

She leaned in and the smell of Taari's patchouli and body odour enveloped her. In an effort to appear comfortable, Farah placed her palms on Taari's shoulder blades but when their chests touched, Farah pulled back, embarrassed by the intimacy of the moment.

"No need to apologize," Taari brushed off the concern. "I'm just chilling."

"Oh," Farah said, looking around Taari at the spread of belongings on the seat.

When she saw a lacy blue bra, Farah turned away, pretending to look for a seat behind her.

"You wanna sit here?" Taari offered the spot next to her. "Don't mind my domestic artistry. I'm just trying to find something. I think my bag ate it."

Farah smiled at the joke self-consciously and answered, "No, it's cool. I can pull up a chair."

"You sure?" Taari asked, sitting back down and spreading out her long skirt.

"Yeah, besides, it's so late now, shouldn't we be going?" Farah asked.

She pulled a plastic chair close to the loveseat and sat with her knapsack on her lap and her arms wrapped around it. From the subway station, she had run to campus to meet Taari, and the anxiety about being late refused to dissipate in spite of her friend's non-judgemental and relaxed attitude.

Taari had returned to emptying the carpetbag, not bothering to conceal the opened box of tampons or the bottle of salicylic acid with the caked rim.

"Um, yeah, sure. We could go. I just want to find this one thing," Taari answered distractedly, nearly entering the bag head first.

"Cool, okay," Farah said, not sounding cool or okay.

She focused on her breath to calm herself and match Taari's nonchalant manner, but after a few breaths, she found herself rocking and tapping her foot impatiently.

"So, what're you looking for?"

"A hammer," Taari replied, not looking up.

"Pardon?" Farah asked, thinking she'd misheard.

"A hammer," Taari repeated as she removed several binders and a heavy technical textbook. "I know it's in here."

A hammer? Farah wasn't sure whether or not to laugh. Her impression of Taari had been forming gradually over the term, during their small parcels of time together in a women's studies class, but Farah wasn't confident she knew Taari well enough to know when she was joking.

For the most part, Farah had heard Taari speak passionately, though not always eloquently, in response to their professor's lectures about gender equality and barriers to opportunities for women. Of the fifty or more students in their class, Taari was the one who offered her opinions and answered questions most often. Sometimes, Taari posed her own provocative questions to the professor, Dr. Marie Holland.

During one of Dr. Holland's last lectures, Taari had asked the professor to discuss white feminists' disregard for the experiences of women of colour. She cited the 1970 Royal Commission and the 1990 scholarly critiques of the commission, both of which neglected to distinguish the experiences of women of colour from those of white women.

Taari's lengthy question had caused several students, including Farah, to flip quickly through pages of bound course notes and loose-leaf lecture notes in a frantic effort to find a reference to the topic, a topic that might appear on the upcoming final exam. The 1970 commission and the 1990 critique were covered extensively in their lectures, but there had been no discussion about differences between white women and women of colour.

Farah felt foolish recalling that her first reaction had been, *What's the difference? Women are women.*

As Farah remembered it, Dr. Holland hadn't responded to Taari's question. Instead, she had addressed the lecture hall and informed the students that this question would not appear on the final exam, setting off a round of sighs and cheers. To Taari, she suggested that they could discuss the topic during office hours to avoid using class time for special interests and causing confusion about exam topics. Taari had just shaken her head in disappointment.

Now, Taari was searching her sack for a hammer and Farah didn't know what to say. Her new friend seemed mature and worldly, and Farah worried that asking questions might give Taari the impression that Farah was naïve and inexperienced. Scattered about already were a jar with clear liquid, a box, three hairbrushes, tampons, a bra, an old potato, binders, pencil nubs, and a deformed textbook. *How did a hammer fit into all of this?*

"Ah! Here it is," Taari exclaimed, holding up a slim hammer like a trophy winner. "Trapped in a binder all along."

"Great," Farah said, having returned to her restless rocking and foot tapping.

"Yup," Taari answered happily, placing the hammer in her lap and returning the items to her bag. "Now, just have to get everything back in."

Taari positioned and repositioned the items in the bag until everything fit, and then she placed the hammer on top of it all and closed the bag.

"Okay, let's go. The meeting's in the last seminar room."

Their footsteps squeaked on the vinyl flooring as they weaved through the labyrinth of empty halls in the Humanities Building. Taari's excited chatter about her new housemates bounced off the walls, and Farah smiled and nodded silently for fear of amplifying the sound.

Discreetly, Farah glanced at her watch. It was a quarter past noon, and she wondered how they would enter a seminar room, a space of four hundred square feet, without disturbing a meeting that had started fifteen minutes earlier. She had hoped to linger and observe from the back, without drawing attention to herself.

"... and you should totally come," Taari finished saying.

Farah had been distracted by her anxiety and hadn't heard the first half of the statement.

"Uh, sure," Farah said softly. "Today?"

"No, it's tomorrow, like, nine-ish. It's BYOB but there'll be plenty to share, so no worries," Taari said, smiling. "It'll be fun. My roommates are so cool, especially Natalie, the one I was talking about."

A party! She's inviting me to her place for party! This was exactly what she had longed for, a friend who wanted to hang out, someone fun and smart.

Playing cool, Farah answered, "Sure thing. Thanks. Can I bring anything?"

"Just your awesome self," Taari said earnestly. "Oh, here it is."

Taari stood in front of a set of closed doors, on which a letter-sized sign was posted. Over her friend's shoulder, Farah read, Annual Open General Meeting of the Women's Studies Program. It sounded mundane and important at the same time, and Farah realized she had no idea what to expect. Was it possible that she might fall asleep listening to the inane details of an academic program?

Farah heard Taari inhale and exhale deeply before opening the door. The two young women entered the meeting, one carrying a hammer.

☽

Farzana had cycled to the Bedford Road entrance of St. George Station to meet her younger sister. After locking her bicycle to a signpost, she rushed inside the vacant subway station to wait. Outside, the sky that had been sunny and promising when she left home that morning had turned overcast, and a sharp wind pierced the gaps of the station doors and stung her bare skin.

Dressed in a dark red bodysuit, a black skirt, and cowboy boots, she was as fashionable as she was cold. She tugged at her thigh-high skirt and rubbed her forearms to rid herself of goose pimples. If she weren't admiring her own newly waxed legs, she might have regretted wearing the skimpy outfit in the fickle month of May.

I'll be home soon enough. This shouldn't take long, Farzana assured herself regarding their appointment with Mrs. Castalano, the landlady at the rooming house. She eyed the delicate silver watch on her wrist and decided there was time for a smoke.

From her miniature knapsack, she procured her plastic lighter and an extra-long menthol cigarette. Along with her smokes, wallet, and keys, the bag was crammed full of cosmetics. She wore every kind of makeup and spent the majority of her expendable cash on lipstick, lip liner, blush, eyeliner, mascara, eyeshadow, foundation, toner, and bronzer. Her mother complained that Farzana was naturally beautiful and only required a fraction of that makeup to bring out her features. To appease her mother, Farzana wore only a small amount of lipstick and eyeliner when she visited her parents once a week.

That morning, she had preened to her own standards: the sexy outfit to flaunt her legs, full makeup to accentuate her eyes and lips, and a thorough dousing of CK One perfume, her most recent acquisition. Puckering her lips to avoid removing her expertly applied and overpriced lipstick, she lit her smoke. With eyes closed, she inhaled, exhaled, and felt the immediate release of tension.

Farzana loved to smoke, and if she could afford it, a lit cigarette would sit between her manicured fingers all day long. Taking another pull with her O-shaped mouth, she wondered how she ever managed to get through her day without smoking. The first cigarette started almost immediately upon waking and continued while she sat on the toilet and then made a cup of instant coffee. The next cigarette was lit on the sidewalk outside her apartment, a less-than-leisurely smoke that kept her company on her fifteen-minute bike ride to work at the call centre.

She didn't smoke again until ten-thirty, when everyone at the office took a ten-minute break and the smokers rushed to the sidewalk en masse. Farzana enjoyed this smoke the least because it was complicated by small talk. She could have snuck away to smoke in private but Farzana didn't want to offend her coworkers. Instead, she smoked silently among them and avoided attracting attention.

This level of interaction was sufficient to exhaust her. Debilitating anxiety, a remnant of the harassment she had suffered at the hands of two shop clerks at her last job, Parsa's Quality Garments, still plagued Farzana. She wasn't ready to open up or make friends but she looked forward to a different future.

In the span of six months, every aspect of her life had transformed. The job at the call centre, where she solicited donations for the World Wildlife Fund, was a welcome change from the toxic environment at Parsa's. And moving in with Soreyah felt like a huge step up from living among strangers in a rooming house. Then, there was her relationship with Amir, Soreyah's older brother, which had unexpectedly transformed from physical attraction into a love affair.

Farzana had filled multiple journals detailing his acts of devotion, his quirky mannerisms, and of course, every aspect of his hunky body. She knew it sounded cliché but when they locked eyes, there were pangs in her chest and she had to keep herself from crying. Of all the men she had dated, he was the most beautiful.

"Amir," she whispered just to hear his name. "Amir."

Tears sprang to her eyes and she chastised herself for making a difficult situation even worse. Quickly, she dabbed the corners of her eyes with her knuckles to keep her mascara from running. Weeks earlier, she had resolved to end their relationship, a fling that wasn't supposed to take root and mature, and tonight she intended to break it off with Amir. He didn't know it was coming, and she was certain he wouldn't accept her reasons.

Farzana assumed responsibility for carelessly cultivating their relationship. If only she had gone through with the abortion by herself, without confiding in him and allowing him to accompany her. Then, maybe he wouldn't have had the opportunity to demonstrate his love for her well-being and they wouldn't have become as intimate as they were.

Her eyes stung. She blinked away the tears and took another drag of the cigarette. Her shoulders relaxed slightly.

"You can't smoke in the station," came a warning from the overhead speakers. "Put out the cigarette or step outside."

Farzana looked up and around the empty space. No one else was present, not a ticket agent or another rider. In the upper corner, a CCTV camera blinked a red light in her direction. Farzana grimaced at the camera but still walked out to the sidewalk and into the cold.

"Assholes," she muttered. "What do they care, anyway? Who am I bothering? There's no one else there!" She turned and gave the finger to the doors.

Just then the doors opened and Farah walked out smiling widely, "What'd those doors ever do to you?"

"Hey!" Farzana cheered, her irritation instantly dissipating.

With Farzana holding her cigarette out to one side, the two sisters embraced. Playfully, Farah rocked them side to side, nearly tipping them over, and then she squeezed Farzana a little harder before releasing her.

The sophisticated exterior Farzana presented to the world fell away when they were together. Farzana considered it Farah's superpower, a magical disarming that offered relief from the rigidity of social conventions.

Since birth, her family had treated Farzana like a precious ornament, to be presented, admired, and detailed with the refined mannerism and accomplishments of a respectable young woman. Every family gathering and personal introduction included announcements of Farzana's achievements: her top marks, her award-winning calligraphy, her perfect recitation of Sufi poems, and her obedient disposition. She had even overheard other mothers and her own aunts pressure their children to be more like her, entreaties that exacerbated Farzana's social anxiety.

Then, along came Farah, a free spirit who seemed immune to the prescriptions and admonishments of their parents. Farah was the little girl who talked non-stop, the child who kicked back, the one who turned away from kisses, and the one whom no one revered, no one except Farzana, who refused to admonish her little sister publicly.

She recognized Farah's acts of disobedience as expressions of sovereignty, and though Farzana considered Farah's assertiveness over the top and counterproductive, she also didn't want Farah to betray herself. *She just needs to sort out her priorities and she'll be set.*

Her twenty-year-old sister stood before her grinning, a young woman who resembled an army cadet in her loose hooded sweatshirt, khaki cargo pants, and scuffed army boots. Farzana rubbed the top of Farah's head, the hair clipped short and fringed by gelled spikes. It was a style the hairdresser called a Chelsea and their mother referred to as The Worst Thing a Daughter Can Do to Her Mother. Underneath the tough façade, Farzana still recognized the rosy-cheeked toddler who cried every morning when her older sister left for grade school without her.

"Okay, ready?" Farzana asked, taking another drag.

"Are you still smoking menthol?" Farah looked disgusted. "They taste awful."

"Yes, and that's why I smoke them." Farzana replied, smiling. She blew a plume of smoke toward the sky. "I know people won't mooch off me."

"Wrong!" Farah yanked the cigarette from between her sister's fingers and took a long pull. "Beggars can't be choosers, you know."

"Uh-huh," Farzana said, giving up on her stolen smoke. "So, you ready?"

"Yup, see," Farah replied. She pulled out the deposit cheque from her back pocket. "Cha-ching!"

"Okay. This way." Farzana turned down Bedford Road.

They headed toward the rooming house where Farzana had lived for four years during her time at university and where she had arranged for a room rental for Farah. The predominantly white, residential neighbourhood with its stately trees and Victorian homes dated to the late nineteenth century. Farzana loved biking its picturesque streets and reading under poplar trees in its small parks, but she was put off by the cold stares of its privileged white residents. Initially, she presumed that she was being overly sensitive to the curiosity of others. *It's their neighbourhood, after all, and they're naturally concerned.*

Then, she heard other residents of colour complain about scowls and intrusive questions from white neighbours, and her sentimental attitude about the historic neighbourhood changed.

Having lived for two seasons on Bloor Street West, in a two-bedroom apartment above a commonplace restaurant, surrounded by low-income families and newcomer Canadians, Farzana felt commonplace herself, no longer an intruder. The sidewalks were lined with grocers, travel agencies, bookstores, and thrift shops that offered something from every part of the world. Jewellers sold jade and twenty-four karat gold, considered too soft for Western shoppers. Herbal stores, whose windows were lined with unlabelled jars of loose teas and roots, released their pungent odours onto the street. Fruit sellers offered discounts on overripe figs, persimmons, and carambola, and Farzana made a habit of returning home with a piece or two of an unfamiliar fruit, just to know the scent and flavour that lay beneath its skin.

Of course, her happy days in the neighbourhood were numbered now that she was ending her relationship with Amir. It was unlikely Soreyah would want a roommate who had broken her brother's heart. Besides, Soreyah and Amir had the same group of friends, young Iranians who regularly hung out at the apartment. In fact, even before they started dating, Amir was at the apartment nearly every evening, usually arriving with takeout from his job at the pizza parlour. His steady presence contributed to the making of their romance. It was unreasonable to expect him to stop visiting his sister because it was too hard for Farzana to share space with him.

Farah disrupted her sister's thoughts when she asked, "Where is she meeting us?"

"Mrs. Castalano said she'd be on the porch," Farzana replied with a sigh, making the last left turn before they reached her old residence, and then she returned to her older-sister role. "You'll want to ask her any questions now. She'll be hard to get a hold of later. She disappears unless you owe her money."

"Okay," Farah replied, unworried.

"Farah, do you have any questions?" Farzana stopped walking and asked pointedly. "This is important."

"I know," Farah assured her. "I just don't have any questions. Do you have questions?"

"No," Farzana said, "but I'm not the one moving in."

Farah shrugged and grinned widely at her sister. Farzana couldn't help but return her smile. It was obvious that Farah was too excited to be thinking critically about anything.

"Okay," Farzana conceded.

She started walking and Farah followed with a spring in her step. Before long they had reached the house on Cartwright Street, and a middle-aged woman in a grey plaid pantsuit and severe haircut stood at the top of the stairs looking down on them over her clipboard.

Farzana introduced Farah to Mrs. Castalano, and soon her former landlady and her little sister disappeared inside the three-storey mansion which had once served as a family home and now housed twelve tenants in one-room units.

On the sidewalk, Farzana awaited their return, willing herself to hold off on another smoke until the viewing had ended.

Farah walked with confidence alongside her sister as they retraced their steps to retrieve Farzana's bicycle. The meeting with her new landlady had been a success. The lease was signed and co-signed, a receipt for the deposit was in her pocket, and she had a move-in date, the first day of August, in less than three months' time. Suddenly, the day was brighter and the world held more promise. Very soon, she would be living downtown, on her own, and free to come and go as she pleased.

"So, what did she say?" Farzana asked as they rounded the bend toward her locked bicycle.

"Not much," Farah answered. "Just showed me the room and the kitchen cupboards that'll be mine."

"Did she tell you the rules?" Farzana asked with less patience.

"Uh, yeah," Farah said, though she didn't remember hearing any rules.

"Like, no hot plates, no parties, no pets," Farzana offered as she knelt to unlock her bicycle from the signpost.

"Yeah, yeah," Farah repeated with more confidence. She wasn't interested in talking about rules and constraints. This was her big day, or her biggest day until her move-in date, and she didn't want to be treated like a child and pestered about policies. Farah was ready to celebrate.

"So what do you want to do now? Food? Pizza?" she asked, tapping her fingertips on her chin.

Farzana straightened her posture and gave her sister a stern look.

"What?!" Farah exclaimed.

"Farah, this is important. I need you to focus on the details," Farzana pleaded.

"What details? It's sorted out," Farah whined, dropping her shoulders and tilting her head.

"Yeah, like the café job?" Her sister retorted as she wheeled the bicycle westwards towards her apartment.

Farah, who shuffled beside her, objected at the reminder. "No, not like that at all. Plus, I already apologized about that. I didn't know they'd want me to clean." Her pitch rose and her lips curled at her memory of the shift manager handing her a toilet brush. "I wouldn't have taken the job if I'd known they wanted me to clean."

"It's a coffee shop," Farzana stated plainly. "Of course you had to clean."

"You said it was a café, so I thought it'd be a ..." Farah paused to consider her words. "Like, a posh place. Not me washing cups and mopping floors. That's what maids do."

"That's what people do when they work at a café," her sister rebuked.

"I get it!" Farah raised her palms in surrender. "It's not like I'm the only one who's picky about her jobs. You quit yours at Khanome Parsa's store, and all you had to do was hang up clothes and fold stuff."

Farah's mentioning Khanome Parsa's store unsettled Farzana, and she nearly walked her bicycle into a fire hydrant. She protested, "That's different. My schedule at the call centre made it impossible to take shifts at the store."

"That's not what Khanome Parsa said to Mama," Farah said with an apologetic shrug.

Farzana glanced at her sister, signalling her to tell all.

Farah had heard Khanome Parsa complain to their mother about Farzana suddenly quitting her position as a store clerk without a call or a conversation. Indignantly, the store owner had decried, "I'm not a charity, you know, Maiheen. I have to be able to count on my staff. I'm really very disappointed in Farzana. Such a bright and beautiful girl, and to leave me in a lurch like that."

Their mother had offered sympathy without taking sides, which caused Farah to resent her even more. Of course, Farah wouldn't divulge the details of the conversation she'd overheard. She didn't want to upset Farzana, whom she considered tenderhearted.

"She said you didn't want the job," Farah summed up the story.

"I didn't," concluded Farzana. "Anyway, speaking of jobs, Annette is ready to meet with you. They hire call centre reps on Fridays, so you need to get your resume ready. Oh, and don't even think about asking for any special treatment."

Giddy with good news, Farah hopped on and off the sidewalk as they meandered through residential streets to avoid the congestion of pedestrians, cyclists, delivery trucks, and cars one block south, on Bloor Street West.

"What are you talking about? I'll be great on the phones," Farah grinned and assumed the voice of a radio announcer. "Hello, Mr. Smith. I'm calling on behalf of the World Life Wife Fund. Did you know ducks are dying in Denmark and turtles are used as sleds by privileged poachers? You can help!"

The two women burst out laughing and spooked a dog walker ahead of them.

"So, in the interview with Annette ..." Farzana began a moment later.

Farah interrupted her, "Is Annette starving? 'Cause I am."

She made a beeline for a hot dog cart at a busy intersection and yelled over her shoulder for Farzana to follow. This was a momentous day in her life and she was in no mood for mundane lectures about job interviews. She was going to celebrate this occasion all night long, starting by stuffing her face with a fully loaded Italian sausage.

☽

"Thanks for lunch, or is it dinner?" Farzana said as she wiped the remaining mustard from the corners of her mouth. She checked her watch. It was coming on four o'clock and she expected Amir at her place after ten, following the end of his delivery shift.

"You're welcome," Farah replied, and then followed up with a loud burp. "Whoops, sorry!"

Farzana grimaced incredulously but didn't comment outright. Instead, she prepared for an after-meal cigarette, one of her favourite times to smoke.

They were sitting on the low stone wall that surrounded St.

Joseph's Church and separated its front lawn from the bustling sidewalk of Bloor Street West. Passersby weaved among each other and between cars as they crossed the two lanes of traffic. Farzana watched people dodge cyclists and cars, and she listened to Farah describe a meeting which she had attended at school. Her thoughts were mostly elsewhere until Farah mentioned a hammer.

"A hammer? She brought a hammer to the meeting? Why?" Farzana felt angry, though she wasn't sure why she cared at all.

"It's symbolic, see. Like dismantling the system," Farah explained, excited that her sister was engaged in the conversation. "Taari said it was reference to an Andrea Lorde quote. No Anne Lorde. An important feminist."

"And you believe in this? Bringing a hammer to a meeting?" Again, Farzana heard anger in her voice.

"Yeah, totally. Taari knows her stuff. She's not posing," Farah said with confidence as she turned to face her older sister.

"What does feminism even mean? Like how can a program about women's studies even be against women?" Farzana questioned disingenuously. She wondered why they were talking about this topic at all.

"It's about representation," Farah answered defensively. "It's 'cause the whole program is about white women. There isn't even one course that talks about what it's like to be black or brown."

"This sounds like a lot of nitpicking. Isn't it good enough to have a women's studies program? Does it have to be perfect?" Farzana asked, blowing smoke away over her shoulder.

"Why are you so against this? It's not even your program." Farah frowned.

"It's not yours either," Farzana retorted. "I thought you were doing economics. You are still doing economics, right?"

"Whatever," Farah said in a defeated tone and turned back to face the street.

As a measure of goodwill, Farzana offered her pack of cigarettes to Farah. Her younger sister smiled for a moment and took a smoke, but refused Farzana's lighter, proffering her own. The argument rattled around Farzana's head and she wondered why she had started the fight. There was far too much conflict in her life already, and it was nice to have one relationship that wasn't marred by disagreements.

Farzana pinched the bridge of her nose as a headache developed and she thought about the night ahead. Inwardly, she practised her lines, just as she had written them in her journal. *You're a great guy but this is not going to work. I need to focus on the future. This has been so much fun but it's better to stop now.*

She knew it sounded hollow and meaningless but she couldn't hurt him with the truth. *Uh, Amir, my parents want me to marry someone with a business degree. Sorry, better luck next time.*

No, that explanation placed all the attention on her parents and made her sound like a child under their control. It wasn't an accurate account of why she needed to end their relationship, just a summation.

"What's wrong?" Farah asked with genuine concern. "Headache?"

"Yes," Farzana accepted the easy answer. "Ready to be home. You?"

"Yeah, I'm good to go."

The sisters collected their belongings and joined the throngs of pedestrians.

☽

Farah awoke in the middle of the night, groggy and nauseous. A fleecy throw blanket fell about her waist when she propped herself to sitting, stretching her neck and back, which were cramped from sleeping on Farzana's lumpy couch. Her knees knocked against the coffee table, cluttered with a full ashtray, a bowl of potato chip crumbs, smeared highball glasses, and the contents of Farah's pants pockets, her wallet, keys, lighter, and bus pass. *Water. I need water.*

Accompanying the cottony feel of her tongue and the sour taste that lined her mouth, a headache was developing behind her right eye. She squinted in the dark room to locate the kitchen before she rose and shuffled with eyes half-closed from the couch.

The counters were covered with empty liquor bottles and dirty dishes, and Farah couldn't think clearly enough to find a clean cup or to wash one. She opted for running the tap and leaning under to drink directly from it. Water splashed her face and ran up her nose, startling her awake, before she managed to drink her fill.

From down the hall, she heard soft voices and spotted light under Farzana's bedroom door. Farah squinted at the microwave clock, two in the morning, and she considered knocking on her sister's door. *Is Farzana talking to Soreyah?*

Farah felt slightly jealous at the possibility that they had continued chatting after she passed out. She recalled their evening in fuzzy snapshots. A Julia Roberts movie, then a Patrick Swayze movie, and Soreyah had started a drinking game early on. She remembered stumbling about in the bathroom, not being able to unlock the door from the inside and needing Farzana to talk her through it. *Oh, I must've made an ass of myself.*

The ache behind her right eye threatened to spread throughout her head, and Farah pressed her eye with the heel of her hand to no avail. From her place leaning against the kitchen counter, she could see through the dark living room, down the hall past the bedrooms, and to the bathroom.

It seemed likely that pain relievers were among the mess of bottles, tubes, jars, and cans stacked precariously on the narrow shelves above the toilet. Her nausea had subsided, so she wasn't worried about being sick on the way to the bathroom, but she feared making a racket and drawing attention to herself. She was embarrassed enough for having fallen asleep before the others, tucked in by her sister like a little kid at a sleepover, and if Farzana and Soreyah were still awake, then Farah didn't want to face them until morning.

Silently, she shambled through the living room and down the hall, past the yellow glow that crept out from under Farzana's door, and into the cramped bathroom, lit by a cracked plastic night light. With undivided attention, Farah closed the bathroom door without a click or squeak.

The search for a pain reliever was less complicated than she had feared. A family-sized bottle of acetaminophen sat atop the ledge of the medicine cabinet, its bright red lid a beacon for every desperate soul seeking out relief from behind narrowed eyes. Farah dispensed one, then two, of the white tablets and swallowed them without water, afraid of alerting the others to her presence by turning on the tap.

"It's not that easy," Farzana's voice carried through the vent that connected her bedroom to the bathroom.

Farah frowned reflexively upon hearing the distress in her sister's tone. *Is Farzana in trouble? Is that why she was so distant last night?*

She recalled Farzana's preoccupied manner while they watched movies with Soreyah, her frequently checking the time on her wristwatch. Farah assumed that her sister was disinterested in the feel-good storylines of the romantic comedies Soreyah had rented, since Farzana had always preferred the weightiness of dramas and foreign films. Now, Farah was ashamed of having drunk herself to sleep instead of inquiring about Farzana's pensiveness.

She crouched by the vent and listened closely to her sister's weeping, and then she heard another voice, a man's voice. He spoke softly but it startled Farah nonetheless. *There's a guy in there. What the fuck?!*

"That's okay. I can handle it," he contended.

"You don't understand. They're not ..." Farzana's voice caught with emotion, and the sound brought tears to Farah's eyes. "They don't just change their minds," Farzana continued.

"That's okay, too. We can live our lives, and we'll wait for them to come around," the man maintained.

Farah settled on the bathroom floor and leaned closer to the vent. Tension in the adjoining room tugged at her sense of agency, and it took all her willpower to remain in place, to resist the urge to intervene and put an end to the tears. Observing conflict with detachment or treating differing perspectives as equal was a waste of time to Farah, who perceived actions and opinions in two contrasting forms, wrong and right. Doing right made sense and doing wrong made her angry, especially when wrongdoing caused her sister distress.

Who is this guy? Why is he making her cry? She thought about putting an end to their conversation. *If Farzana's unhappy with this guy, why doesn't she kick him out? I could kick him out.*

"You don't know them. You don't understand," Farzana said, followed by her demure sniffle. "They won't change their minds. It's not like them. They're not going to change their standards."

"Standards?" the man asked in a hurt tone. "And you? Do I meet your standards?"

"Yes, of course," Farzana assured him. "Amir, it's not about me."

Amir? Who the fuck is Amir? Wait, isn't that Soreyah's brother?

"How can that be possible?" Amir asked with disbelief. "This is about your life."

"No, well, yes, but ..." Farzana tried to explain her circumstances. In a weak voice, she continued, "They came here so that I can have a better life. They expect me to get a good job, like being a business manager, and they want me to marry someone who's the same, or ..."

Amir interrupted her, still sounding more anguished than angry, "Not a pizza delivery guy. Not someone with just a high school diploma."

"No, well, yes," Farzana conceded. "They want me to buy a house, like a big one where they live with me and my husband and my kids.

That's their dream, Amir. They want me to be well off and they want a son-in-law who's well off too."

"I make good money," Amir defended himself. "You don't need to have a business degree to make money. Besides, that's what my parents wanted too but they got over it. Yours will get over it too. They might be mad for a while but they'll come around."

"No, Amir, it's not going to work. They're not like your parents, and I'm not you. You have so much freedom. Your mom thinks you're a god. You don't even have to do anything and they're proud of you. It's not the same for me."

"So, you're giving in," Amir retorted. "You're letting them get their way. Anything they want, they get, right?"

"You don't understand. They came here for me. They left everything behind for me," Farzana pleaded.

"So did my parents," Amir persisted. "But they don't lord it over my head. They don't act like martyrs."

"It's not like that. They love me. They want the best for me," Farzana entreated.

"And I'm not the best for you. You know what, Farzana? It sounds like you don't think I'm good enough for you either."

The series of sounds that followed were easily identified by Farah. Amir rose from the creaking bed and went out of Farzana's room. Farzana followed him into the hallway but remained silent. The front door opened and closed as Amir departed, and then Farzana returned to her bedroom, closing the door behind her. Back in bed, Farzana could be heard whimpering into her pillow. When light stopped emanating from her sister's room into the bathroom through the vent, Farah stood up from the tiled floor and returned to the couch.

Snuggled under the throw blanket and positioned to avoid the springs of the thrift store couch, Farah reflected on the conversation she had overheard. She wasn't sure how to feel or what to think about

Farzana's predicament. Strangely, she felt sympathetic towards Amir even though she hadn't met him. His statements struck a chord, and his sentiments were reminiscent of Farah's own feelings about her parents. *Why doesn't Farzana just stand up to them? It's about time.*

She fell back into a restless sleep, frustrated by the complexities of other people's lives.

2

Saturday, May 8, 1993

Saturdays began early for Maiheen because she opened the coffee shop at seven o'clock, giving the other full-time server a reprieve from the task. When she left home, it was breaking dawn and the sky was shades of pink and yellow, a striking scene which she admired while she waited for the bus. On Don Mills Road, a few cars sped past; otherwise, the street and sidewalks were deserted, too early for shopping or leisurely strolls.

Maiheen enjoyed the peacefulness of the setting, rare in a bustling city, but she didn't like to be alone because a lone woman was easy prey. In her handbag, there was a large kitchen knife, which she carried on such occasions. The blade was dull but it was wide and long enough to create distance between her and an attacker. So far, she had never used it to defend herself, but several times she had held its handle while it remained sheathed in her handbag.

By ten o'clock, she had served two dozen customers, brewed four pots of coffee, tidied the washrooms, made two pots of soup, and prepared enough plastic-wrapped sandwiches to feed a mob. A handful of customers lounged with their newspapers; others gazed out the windows at the foot traffic, and Maiheen joined them. Three hours more to the end of her shift, and two hours more until another server arrived to help with the lunchtime rush.

"Thanks, May!" A regular customer called out to Maiheen as he ambled through the two sets of glass doors and onto the sidewalk.

"Bye, Frank," Maiheen replied with a polite smile and wave.

Her expression didn't reveal her slighted feelings about being called by another name. *May? When did I become May?* She looked down at her name tag which read Maiheen, and she shook her head at the discourtesy. *How about I call him Fran?* The silly idea made her smile, and she returned to looking out the wall of windows that faced the sidewalk.

Coffee Express was a one-storey eatery near the busy intersection of Don Mills Road and Steeles Avenue. Since its construction in the late seventies, it had served as a diner in one form or another, and none of the owners, past or present, had renovated the rundown interior. A stained and seared Formica countertop ran the length of the space and separated the prep area from the seating area. The mustard yellow linoleum flooring was chipped and peeling, and the exposed subfloor that had been painted to mask the disrepair was the wrong shade of yellow. All the equipment was outdated, noisy, and prone to failure, and the bathroom fixtures were too damaged and ugly to be improved by rounds of cleaning. After five years, Maiheen had stopped looking closely and thinking too hard about the shabbiness; she had made her peace with the condition of the place.

"*Salaam*, hello," said a friendly face. "Lost in thought?" Dressed in a vibrant and summery outfit, Yasmeen crossed the room to greet Maiheen with kisses on her cheeks.

"*Salaam, salaam!* I was wondering if I was going to see you today," Maiheen said. Immediately, she prepared Yasmeen's usual order of a black coffee with one sugar, and she wrapped up a honey cruller out of affection for her friend.

"*Dast-et daard nakoneh!* My deepest gratitude!" Yasmeen accepted the takeaway cup and placed it on the counter to proffer her wallet.

"Put that away!" Maiheen insisted and slid the brown paper bag with the cruller across the counter.

"Are you sure?" Yasmeen asked as she continued to search her handbag for her wallet.

"*Hatman*. Of course. Now, sit, talk. Are you working today?"

Yasmeen found her wallet, removed a five dollar note and placed it in the tip jar. In an instant, Maiheen reached for the jar to return the money to her friend, but Yasmeen sucked her teeth in disapproval, and Maiheen stopped midway.

"*Merci*, thank you. You're too generous." Maiheen slipped a second honey cruller into the bag and explained with a wink, "This one's for Ahmed. Now, tell me, are you working today?"

"Oh, the life of a real estate agent! When am I not working?" Yasmeen replied. She placed her wrist on her forehead and grinned at Maiheen. "Saturdays are great for realtors. Clients have more time, and I can usually manage to schedule a bunch of viewings before running an open house."

Enamoured by Yasmeen's enthusiasm and confidence, Maiheen rested her elbows on the counter, placed her chin on her palm, and leaned in to hear more. Yasmeen's professional life was invigorating, a breath of fresh air compared to the stale atmosphere of Maiheen's work. It felt good to hear from an Iranian woman who was living her dream, even in Canada.

"Maiheen-*jaan*, dear, I have the perfect place for you and Mustafa," Yasmeen started.

"Yasmeen, you know we don't have money like that, not with Farah's tuition," Maiheen reminded her sheepishly.

"Wait, let me finish. It's perfect for two, now with the girls moved out, and the mortgage rates are much more reasonable than you'd expect," Yasmeen continued.

"Thank you, Yasmeen-*jaan,* dear. I really appreciate it but I'm sorry, we don't even have enough for a down payment," Maiheen apologized.

"Well, that's where these come in," Yasmeen replied, placing her red leather briefcase atop the counter and removing a set of coil-bound books, which she spread out for her friend to examine.

Maiheen lowered her forearms and leaned in to read the titles: *Becoming a Mortgage Broker, Basic Mortgage Concepts, Property Ownership in Ontario, Insurance in the Mortgage Industry,* and *Contract Law*. The pages were slightly curled at the edges from use but in good condition otherwise.

"Ahmed won't need them now that he's passed his licensing test," Yasmeen continued. "They're all yours. The next round of classes starts in two weeks."

"Oh, Yasmeen, I don't think so," Maiheen said as she tidied the books into a pile. "I was just talking before. I don't think I could actually do this."

Yasmeen examined the cracked vinyl covering of a stool before she sat, resting her elbows on the counter, interlacing her fingers, and arching one perfectly shaped eyebrow at Maiheen. "I figured you'd say something like that. So, I've come prepared," she began in a diplomatic tone.

"Yasmeen-*jaan*, I really appreciate these but it's not in the cards for me," Maiheen explained. She produced a damp cloth and wiped the clean countertop.

"I hear that you think you're not ..." Yasmeen hesitated on the next word.

Maiheen pounced on the moment. "I'm not young. My life has already taken shape and I can't change that. There's no way I could even pass this test, you know my English, and besides, who would hire an old woman like me?"

Yasmeen, who had been shaking her head throughout the spiel, leaped to answer, "You can hire yourself, work for yourself like Ahmed, or you can work for any of the brokerages up and down this block. They'd be lucky to have you. Besides, Maiheen, you're the same age as Ahmed, a young fifty, and you know your English is better than his. He still calls it *the bitch* when we drive up to Wasaga Beach."

For a moment, Maiheen paused her nervous tidying and smiled, then her shoulders drooped, her expression grew somber, and she sucked in her lips to keep from crying. Yasmeen reached out to hold her hand, and Maiheen allowed her friend to comfort her, all the while ready to present the same smile that made her the favourite server among the customers.

"It's five Sundays and an exam," Yasmeen beseeched. "Ahmed and I can help you, really. It'd make him feel like a big man, and you know how they are."

Maiheen nodded, she knew all too well what men were like. She didn't want to say it about Mustafa, not to Yasmeen or anyone, but this would be too much change for him and it would create too much distance between them. Right now, they both worked menial jobs without any opportunity for growth. He was happy at the car wash, and in the decade he'd been working there, he had never sought after a different position, one with more responsibility.

Most supervisory jobs required him to improve his written English skills and learn how to use a computer. Now at age fifty-five, Mustafa considered studying to be a waste of time. Intellectually, he had retired after they emigrated from Iran. Maiheen couldn't see him warming up to her pursuing a new career.

"Listen," Yasmeen continued, releasing Maiheen's hand, "just take them home and look through them. No harm in that."

"Yasmeen-*jaan*, I'm not you," Maiheen said softly. "You have time and energy. Your whole life is ahead of you."

Yasmeen replied with concern and authority, "Maiheen, that's not true. You're unhappy because this ..." and she waved a hand behind her in reference to the coffee shop, "this is not making you happy. I have energy because I love my job. I loved it in Tehran and I love it here, too. You know, my father jokes that I was born with a

For Sale sign in my hand. Now that's a rough delivery."

When Maiheen smiled, Yasmeen continued with gentle regard, "You are good with people. You are good with numbers, and you'll look so good rolling in the money. Then, you can buy a big house for you and Mustafa and the girls, and their families, too. I'll sell it to you!"

Maiheen was smiling but it was a sad smile. She spotted a customer coming in and put up a finger to pause their conversation while she served coffee and a donut. When she returned to her friend, she changed the topic for respite from the turbulent feelings that had stirred within her.

"Tell me, how are your boys?" Maiheen asked, pouring herself another coffee and tearing into an apple fritter.

"You know what it's like," Yasmeen sipped at her coffee. "Majeed wants to be a pilot but he doesn't want to study, and Babak is too busy with his friends to look for work. You know, some days, I think I was too easy on them. They have no drive, no ambition. My worst nightmare is waking up at seventy and finding my middle-aged sons still on the couch playing video games and smelling like a bus seat."

"I know what you mean," Maiheen replied, popping another piece of the fritter into her mouth. The sugar and spice flavours distracted her from the ache she felt each time she caught sight of the stack of books.

Incredulously, Yasmeen exclaimed, "What! No, no, no. Your girls are nothing like Majeed and Babak. Farzana has already completed her degree, and Farah's well on her way."

"Yes, but Farzana seems to have stopped looking for work in her field. I thought with her last job at Khanome Parsa's she might get some business experience and possibly work up to a manager's position, but she quit the job just a few months in. Then, she takes a job at a call centre. A call centre, Yasmeen! Where's that going to lead her?"

Yasmeen emitted a sympathetic sigh and waited for her friend to continue.

"I tried to talk to her but you know how she is ..." Maiheen paused for a knowing look. "She says everything I want to hear but she doesn't take the first step to change anything. I mean, what's the point of a business degree if you don't use it. I don't know what to do. And, Farah ..." Maiheen paused again, this time to shake her head. "She contradicts me at every turn, acts as if she raised herself and I don't have a brain in my head."

"Oh, Maiheen-*jaan*, when will they learn?" Yasmeen said with another deep sigh.

"On their own time," Maiheen replied.

Yasmeen glanced at her friend with a quizzical look, "Say that again? Who are you? Sally Jessy Raphael?"

Maiheen chuckled, "That woman knows a thing or two about difficult people but I prefer Donahue. He gets straight to the point."

"On their own time? Ha! My mother told me what to do every moment of my life." Yasmeen laughed at her own joke. "She even told me when to get pregnant."

"Mine, too. When to get pregnant, when to marry, when to cut my hair," Maiheen recalled. "I didn't always like it, but I did it. I mean, her advice made sense. Good luck convincing my girls that I know what I'm talking about." She harrumphed for effect.

"Right! My boys are the same. They act like going to school or getting a job is a new concept, something I don't understand. I've done it, twice, in two different countries. For shame." Yasmeen sucked her teeth again.

"My mother said not to suck your teeth, it causes wrinkles," Maiheen jeered playfully.

"My mother said to mind your own business, it also causes wrinkles," Yasmeen said with a boisterous laugh.

After catching up on other news, Yasmeen invited Maiheen and

Mustafa over for dinner to celebrate Ahmed's passing the licensing exam. Maiheen insisted that Yasmeen allow her to contribute to the meal, and Yasmeen agreed, joking that Maiheen's dishes were superior to hers, and Ahmed would appreciate an Iranian dish that tasted authentic, like his mother's cooking.

Yasmeen left to meet her clients, and Maiheen returned to wiping a clean counter, however stained and cracked. Under the counter, Ahmed's books were stacked in a tidy pile. Yasmeen had refused to take them with her. Maiheen glanced at them every so often, and she wondered what her elderly mother would say about her becoming a mortgage broker.

☽

Nearing noontime on Saturday, Farah awoke to a striking stillness. Farzana's apartment was devoid of sound and movement, and Farah wondered if she was alone. She stretched to alleviate her throbbing head and cramped muscles but the movements exacerbated her aches and pain. Looking around the corner of the living room wall, she saw the open door of Soreyah's bedroom and the closed door of Farzana's. The conversation she had overheard last night came to mind and she thought to look in on her sister. *Water, first.* She headed to the messy kitchen to procure a clean cup, or even a bowl, any vessel that could hold water. She settled on a souvenir shot glass, which Farzana and Soreyah seemed to collect given the inordinate quantity in one kitchen cupboard. The one Farah chose bore an illustration of Niagara Falls. It reminded her of a family trip to the natural wonder ten years earlier, of her father finishing two rolls of film with photos of mist and poorly lit tunnels, and of herself clinging to Farzana and crying as her older sister led them through the darkened halls of a haunted house attraction.

She refilled the shot glass several times to quench her thirst, and on her last gulp she heard a door shut down the hall. The stillness of the apartment was wearing on her nerves, and she had the discomforting sensation of looming misfortune. She placed the shot glass on the counter among the other dirty dishes and returned to the couch. When she heard the toilet flush and the bathroom door open, Farah sprang to her feet and began folding the throw blanket.

"Hey," Farzana said on her way to the kitchen, still dressed in nightclothes with her long hair in a loose bun.

"Hey," Farah replied, refolding the blanket and dropping it to the floor. "How're you doing?"

"Good, and you?" Farzana asked with her back turned.

"Okay. Sorry about passing out last night," Farah said with a nervous chuckle. "I guess I'm a lightweight."

"No worries. Coffee?" Farzana called out.

"Sure, thanks," Farah said. "Is Soreyah still asleep?"

"No, she's gone for work," Farzana said.

A few minutes later, Farzana returned to the living room, handed a mug of steaming coffee to Farah, and nodded in the direction of the balcony. Farah joined her on the concrete slab that was shorter and slimmer than her single bed. Farzana lit a cigarette and offered Farah a drag. They leaned on the metal railing and observed the traffic-lined lanes of Bloor Street West, its sidewalks crowded by café seating, fruit stands, and weaving pedestrians.

"Did I tell you that I'm almost a shoo-in for the department's scholarship? The head looked over my application and said it was 'very promising,' " Farah said with a professorial accent. "Of course, I still have to ace these exams but that's not a problem."

"Hm, that's good. Congratulations," Farzana said with a short-lived smile that never reached her eyes. "I hope you get it."

"Thanks. Me too," Farah said.

Farzana's downcast expression and her indifferent tone rekindled Farah's agitation. *What can I do for her?*

Farah didn't want to admit to eavesdropping on a private and painful conversation. Surely, that would upset Farzana even more.

On the other hand, Farah wondered why Farzana hadn't mentioned Amir during their frequent phone calls. *Why'd she keep Amir a secret? Why didn't she tell* me *about him?*

Farah could sympathize with Farzana not confiding in their parents since they ignored personal boundaries, but she was Farzana's best friend, or at least she thought she was. *Maybe she doesn't trust me? Why keep secrets from me?*

"Is everything okay?" Farah asked as casually as possible.

"Yup," Farzana answered without pause. "Do you know how to get to the subway from here?"

"Yeah, I remember. Aren't you coming to Mama and Baba's?" Farah asked.

"Uh, no, not today. I'll come tomorrow. I have some stuff I need to do here," Farzana replied.

"Okay, can I help?" Farah offered.

Another smile crossed Farzana's face, briefly, "Thanks, Sis. It's not much. I wanna do it myself."

"Are you sure everything's okay?" Farah asked again.

"Yup, just drank too much, hm," Farzana said as she tossed her cigarette in a coffee tin filled with brown water and floating butts.

"Okay," Farah said and dropped the subject.

Shortly thereafter, Farah entered Ossington Station and took the eastbound subway towards her parents' place. An hour had passed by the time she stepped off the No. 25 bus and walked up the winding hill towards the cluster of high-rise buildings. She took the shortcut across the grassy hill that led to the back entrance of her building to check out what remained of the scene of Shireen's death. As she crossed the visitors' parking area, she noted that nothing looked amiss. There was no sign of police or any evidence of an untimely death. Farah stood in the spot where she figured Shireen must have landed on the asphalt, and she glanced up at the building. *Which balcony was Shireen's? Did she live on the tenth floor?*

Farah looked at the balconies overhead, her pointer finger moving as she counted to ten. She was startled to find a young girl, possibly eight or nine years old, looking down at her. Farah didn't know whether to wave or smile or to pretend she had been looking elsewhere. *Is that Shireen's sister? She's so young.*

Farah didn't get a chance to react. A voice called out from above and the young girl retreated into her apartment. She shivered at the thought of her own sister's death. She wondered if Shireen's family would move elsewhere, or if it mattered where they lived when they awoke each day to her absence. *It wouldn't matter. It would be hell no matter where I lived.*

Inside the back room, Farah eyed her disabled bicycle in the locker and remembered Michael crouching to listen in on the constables. Just thinking about him caused her to flush, and she hoped he wasn't upset with her for declining his offer yesterday. He didn't seem upset but he was difficult to read. She thought about inviting him to the party at Taari's that night but decided against it. It would hurt too much if he rejected her invitation. Besides, she doubted that he would enjoy himself at a house party. He seemed to prefer hanging out with people he knew more than meeting new people.

Farah was about to cross the threshold into the lobby when she heard her father's voice. Her wristwatch read two o'clock, the time when he returned from his half-day shift at the car wash. She took a step back and listened to him, not expecting to hear anything of interest but not wanting to enter his conversation either.

"It's the way of the world," he said. "You let your daughter dress like that and it's bound to attract the wrong kind of attention."

"I agree with you wholly, my friend," another man replied. "The softer we are on our children, the more danger we place them in."

Farah couldn't think who the other man was, but his accent resembled her father's. Upon hearing the tone of their conversation, Farah resigned herself to waiting them out.

"She had a boyfriend, did you hear?" the other man asked. "She was pregnant; that's why she killed herself."

What?! Was that true? Why she killed herself?

"Hm," her father said.

"You used to work with her father, right?" the other asked. "Jamal? Or Javeed?"

"Javeed, yes. He was at the car wash for just a few months. That was a long time ago."

"Sure, sure," the other agreed. "Such a shame for him. Imagine, you bring your family here only to have your daughter ruin her life and then destroy any possibility of future happiness."

"Hm," her father said. "I wouldn't know about that. My girls are good girls. They don't dress like whores and jump from bed to bed. They respect themselves, their mother and father. I am a lucky man."

"Most certainly, Mustafa. You've kept them on track, set rules. I'm the same, none of this 'do as you like' ideas they have here. Young people need discipline, especially girls. They're so naïve about the world. It's not all makeup and clothes."

Farah felt like screaming at this man; his comments were grating, provoking her anger. To keep herself from interrupting them, she clamped on her crooked index finger.

"You are right. It's not a nice place, and they have no idea how bad it is," her father said with a deep sigh.

A pause followed and Farah listened for footsteps but there were none.

"Well, my friend, I must be heading off," the other man said. "Another day, another dollar, as they say."

"Yes, yes, well good luck to you. And, why don't you come by sometime with Aditi? And bring your children. I am sure my youngest could entertain them."

"You are too kind, thank you. I will tell Aditi. And please send my best to Maiheen."

"So long," her father said.

"Yes, good bye," the other man's voice trailed off.

Aditi, is that the hairstylist on the fifteen floor? Mama can't stand Aditi. She calls her a gossipmonger. Baba invited her to our place. Idiot! He is so clueless.

The elevator's door chime played, and after Farah heard the door close, silence followed. She waited another moment and peeked around the corner to see the landing was deserted. The dials indicated that two elevators were located at the lobby and the third had ascended to the penthouse, her floor. Her father had returned to their apartment and Farah was certain to encounter him.

Ugh, fucking idiot! Why does he say shit like that?! "Dress like whores." As if he knows Shireen. He's talking shit, acting big. Idiot!

Farah punched the elevator button and the doors opened instantly. On the ride up, her outrage deepened and she composed a lecture to berate her father for his narrow-minded comments. She wanted to reduce him to tears and apologies, to make him acknowledge her moral superiority, and when she finished, she wanted him to promise to keep his big mouth shut forever.

By the time she got to her apartment door, Farah was livid and then promptly relieved to hear her father singing in the shower. She had fifteen minutes to grab a snack and disappear into her bedroom. She could avoid him until this evening, when she planned to leave home close to nine for Taari's party downtown.

In between her crossed arms, Farah piled plastic-wrapped cheese slices, hot dog buns, a can of pop, and a bag of chips. She dumped her cache onto her bed, locked her door, and nestled among her blankets to eat, journal, and listen to her headphones.

☽

Mustafa wished Maiheen had arrived home before Farah so they could have enjoyed a quickie. He wasn't opposed to having sex while their daughter was home, but Maiheen didn't relax and enjoy herself unless they had the apartment to themselves. *I guess that's one benefit of Farah moving out.*

Maiheen had announced herself upon arrival, pushing open the heavy front door with her backside because her hands were full with heavy plastic bags. Mustafa dashed to her aid, taking three bags from her and kissing her juicily on the lips.

"What's this?" He asked as he set the bags on the counter. "Aren't we grocery shopping tomorrow?"

Sunday grocery shopping at Knob Hill Farms, the terminal-style supermarket where they could buy produce and meat at wholesale prices, had been their routine for years. When they'd first immigrated, the girls would come along to help bag produce and read labels for Maiheen, so she didn't inadvertently buy the fat-free or low-sodium version of the foods he liked.

"Oh, of course. You think I'd buy lamb at Dominion if I didn't have to," Maiheen rebuked. "This is for Yasmeen's tonight."

"No!" Mustafa jumped back from the bags as if they were on fire. "No, no, no! Please, Maiheen, please, no!" He clasped his hands before his chest and pleaded. "Not so soon. It's only been ... I don't know but it's too soon."

"Mustafa, grow up!" Maiheen said.

She refused to look at his dramatics and busied herself by unpacking the groceries onto the counter.

"She's my friend, and Ahmed is a really nice man. He likes you, you know."

"He's so boring, Maiheen. All he talks about is interest rates and financing," Mustafa whined, plunking himself on the nearest dining room chair facing Maiheen.

"Of course, he's a mortgage broker. He just passed his test, and we're celebrating with them," Maiheen said.

Mustafa groaned and slumped in his seat but he stopped complaining. From years of experience, he knew that Maiheen could only tolerate so much bellyaching. *Why me? Why can't I get to spend my Saturday night with someone, anyone, who knows a thing or two about football, hockey, even basketball?*

"Come on, sweetheart," Maiheen entreated, bringing a box of dates to the table and offering to feed him one. "Yasmeen is my good friend. Do it for me."

He wrapped his arms around her waist and pulled her down onto his lap.

With a fresh date melting in his mouth, Mustafa said, "Yes, of course. Anything for you."

They kissed deeply, and Mustafa took the opportunity to slip his hands under her work shirt and massage her breasts. Maiheen moaned and writhed in his lap, and when their lips parted she produced the date pit from her mouth. They chuckled and remained wrapped in each other's arms.

"Is Farah home?" Maiheen asked.

"Yes, she's holed up," Mustafa said as he nuzzled his face into her underarm. "I think she's become nocturnal, like a hedgehog, hiding under a rock during the day."

"Come now," Maiheen said. She kissed his forehead and rose from his lap. "She's just touchy. It'll pass."

"She didn't even say hello. Straight to her room. Check the fridge, I bet she took the roasted chicken in with her."

Admiring his wife's figure, Mustafa stood and adjusted himself before he trailed her back to the kitchen to help. Maiheen was kneeling in front of the opened fridge with a bundle of produce in her arms.

"No, chicken's still there," she remarked with a grin.

They chuckled as Mustafa unpacked fruits and vegetables, playfully tossing them to Maiheen to store in the fridge. It felt terrific to frolic and joke together, to see Maiheen's features unshrouded by melancholy, however briefly. Not outings, gatherings, nor gifts dissipated the gloom in her eyes for more than a day. He had broached the topic, determined to remedy her sadness, but at first she denied feeling unhappy, and later on, she admitted to not knowing the source of her sorrow.

"I think you got someone else's bag," he joked when he came across the plastic bag filled with books. "I guess it's high in fibre. You always say we need more fibre."

"Oh, that's ..." Maiheen faltered, no longer smiling. "Here, I'll take that." She grabbed the bag from the counter and zipped out of the kitchen.

Perplexed by her sudden shift in mood, he followed her slowly, careful to not spook her. He found Maiheen in their walk-in closet, shoving the plastic bag behind a set of suitcases in the corner. Maiheen had never been one for secrets, aside from the white lies she told when she didn't want to be rude or hurt someone's feelings. It was obvious that she was hiding the bag from Mustafa, but what reason could she have. He sat on the edge of their bed and waited for her to reappear in the bedroom.

"Maiheen?" He prompted her.

"Yes," Maiheen said between short breaths as she recovered from her swift movements.

"What was that about?" Mustafa asked gently.

"Nothing, Mustafa. Nothing," Maiheen replied. "Can we just leave it for now?"

He knew better than to demand answers of her. Maiheen worked on her own schedule, and if she didn't want to talk about something, it would be disastrous to pressure her. Yet, before he submitted to her will, Mustafa wanted to gauge her resistance to confiding in him.

"Leave what?" Mustafa asked.

"Mustafa," Maiheen said resolutely, "please, just give me some space. I don't ask for much but I want some space."

Her rigid posture and decisive tone said more than her words, and Mustafa cautioned himself to not push his luck.

"Okay, you have space. I'm here when you want to tell me … whatever you want to tell me," Mustafa conceded.

He kissed her forehead, and as he left the room, Mustafa heard his wife exhale.

☽

Farah woke from an extended nap nearing eight o'clock. Her mother had tried to wake her earlier with enticements of lamb stew and buttery rice. Farah, who had been enjoying a lust-filled dream about Michael professing his love, had thrown a hissy fit and disappeared under the blankets in a desperate attempt to fall back asleep.

Now, she was famished and ready to eat an extra-large serving. She practised an apology speech intended for her mother, some excuse about being unable to think straight when she was half-asleep and possibly another excuse about being cranky from sleeping badly on Farzana's lumpy couch. Her apology might not win an award for best composition or acting, but it would go some way to repairing the damage she had likely caused by her childish tantrum.

She found their apartment vacant and lit solely by the setting sun. On the desk by the front door, her mother had written a note.

It read, "My dear Farah, I hope you had good rest. There is plate for you in fridge. We are at Yasmeen Khanome house. Call if you want come. I love you my dearest, Mama."

Farah groaned with guilt. *I'm an asshole, a run-of-the-mill asshole who treats her mom like shit.*

Without heating her food, Farah devoured the rice and stew while sitting cross-legged in the living room and watching the beginning scenes of a Goldie Hawn movie. Her mother's dishes were delicious and satisfying beyond compare, and Farah realized she would miss her cooking every day that she lived on her own. *Still worth the privacy. Besides, Farzana still gets homemade meals from Mama. That I can handle.*

After polishing off the last ice cream bars in the freezer, Farah turned off the movie and considered what to wear to Taari's party. She was emboldened by her parents' absence and the knowledge that they'd be sleeping by the time she returned home that night. Her father's words crossed her mind, and she wondered if any of her clothes gave him the impression that she dressed like a whore. She considered the relative definition of that word and its inherently negative implication. *I hate that word, whore. What does that even mean? Who decides what's whorish? Did anyone ever use whore as a compliment?*

Farah dressed and undressed, checking her reflection from varying angles. As she assembled her outfit, she listened to her favourite grunge band at the maximum volume and hollered the chorus to every song with eyes squeezed shut. At last, she appraised her choice of low-ride jeans, ripped in multiple places, a crop top that she wore without a bra and which revealed her belly button ring, and an oversized plaid shirt, unbuttoned and hanging from one shoulder. To top it off, she applied dark red lipstick, donned a flat cap backwards, and sculpted her sideburns to points.

"Is this whorish?" Farah asked her reflection with a wicked grin. "Fuckin', eh!"

It was another hour before Farah arrived at Taari's place, a few blocks from campus. The residential neighbourhood was a mix of yellow-brick triplexes and red-brick semi-detached houses. She could tell the student housing from the family homes by the number of bicycles attached to the porch railings and whether a piece of indoor furniture, like a plush loveseat or recliner, was housed outdoors.

Coming her way, the foot traffic consisted of middle-aged people meandering with their dogs and couples walking towards Spadina Avenue, where pubs and takeaway places catered to the student crowds with cheap pitchers and greasy food.

Farah hoped her sweating wasn't detectable. This was the first party she had attended as an adult. Prior to this, parties had been glorified hangouts in the ravine. Like her, all of her high school friends had lived in apartment buildings, so there wasn't a basement or garage they could commandeer. Every party was held outdoors — sometimes in their own neighbourhood and at other times they bussed to Etobicoke or Scarborough to smoke and drink with friends of a friend.

You're going to have fun, she thought as she discreetly sniffed her underarms. *Okay, not bad.*

Just like the house parties in movies, there were people drinking on the porch of Taari's place and at least one couple getting to third base against the brick wall. From the sidewalk, Farah took in the sight of the lit three-storey house, its windows curtained with gauze and occupied by silhouettes changing shape and size.

A cloud of marijuana smoke descended from the porch and Farah watched the red tip of a joint pass hands between the four people sitting on the couch. The skunky odour drew her along the short path and up the creaky steps. Smoking-up had been common in high school but not with Farah's crowd, who preferred to get wasted drinking liquor fast and straight from the bottle. On the few occasions she had smoked weed, she'd experienced the irrepressible glee and optimism that she associated with childhood, feelings that sharply contrasted with the melancholic effects of drinking into the night.

"Hey," a young man greeted her from his seat.

"Hey," Farah replied, possibly too quietly to be heard from the top step. She eyed the front door. *Do I just go in? Should I ask for Taari? I am so lame.*

"Hey," said the only woman on the couch.

"Hey," Farah said with more confidence.

"You want a hit?" The woman asked, her bangled arm extended to Farah with a lit joint between her thumb and forefinger.

Farah looked behind herself to confirm that she was being addressed, not someone standing directly behind her, someone who knew these people and had a good reason to be included.

The group chortled in response, laughing in the way stoners laugh when they have witnessed the funniest thing in the world. It occurred to Farah that they thought she was making a joke, that she wasn't so clueless and insecure that she would question whether they were offering her a blunt.

Farah smiled and accepted the joint. She took a drag and inhaled deeply, then held out the blunt for the next taker in line.

"You a friend of Taari's?" The woman asked in a raspy voice, her eye lids drooping heavily.

"Uh, yeah," Farah said, confused and surprised by her correct assumption.

"Cool," the woman said dreamily, and then as if she had read Farah's mind, added. "Taari said she'd invited someone from school. What's your name?"

"Farah," she answered with a bashful smile.

"Cool. I'm Natalie, I live here, too," Natalie nodded, mostly to herself. With thumbs pointed to her left and right, she named the others, "Scott, Jeff, and this is Larry but we call him the L-Bomb because ..."

Larry interrupted Natalie, "No need to go there. She doesn't need to be corrupted like you all."

The group erupted in laughter about some inside joke, and Farah smiled and shrugged to indicate no hard feelings on her part.

"Guess I'll go in," Farah said and made towards the front entrance.

"Cool. Taari was in the kitchen last time I saw her," Natalie said over Scott's head. "Help yourself to whatever's in the fridge."

"Cool, thanks," Farah replied but the quartet had returned to razzing Larry about the origins of his nickname.

Before she entered, Farah lit a cigarette. The weed had gone a long way in relaxing her but a smoke served a different purpose altogether. A cigarette busied her hands and mouth, and when she smoked she could feign being all-consumed by the task and she felt less like a loner standing silently among other people's friends.

Fortified by her smoke, she walked into house and spotted the kitchen directly at the end of the front hall. She registered the staircase on her left and the dimly lit living room filled with people on her right, but Farah kept her eyes on the end of the hall. Finding Taari in the kitchen was her mission, and having a mission kept her confidence afloat.

Three hours later, Taari found Farah sitting on the kitchen counter, drinking a bottle of hard lemonade.

"Hey!" Farah greeted her and then turned slowly to address the other five people in the room, "I told you I had a friend here. She's my friend."

Farah tried to lean back against the wall but she came up against the overhead cupboards. She narrowed her eyes and glared at the cupboards before breaking out into laughter.

"I thought you were a no-show," Taari said, crossing the room to lean against the counter next to Farah. "Are you having a good time?"

"Yes! These are the nicest people at the party," Farah declared, and the five others gave a round of whoops. "Do you know them?"

Without waiting for Taari to answer, Farah pointed and named each person sitting at the rickety kitchen table, "Jessie, Brad, the other Jessie, Tim, and Charles."

She smiled to no one in particular, proud of having recalled their names.

"Hi," Taari said and gave a friendly wave. "Brad and Tim I know, 'cause I live with them," she grinned at Farah. "Jessie, other Jessie, and Charles, nice to meet you."

The conversation around the table reconvened. Tim and the two

Jessies debated the merits of capital punishment, and as Brad sealed the joint he was rolling, he mumbled a list of Canadian convicts who'd already be dead if they'd been sentenced in Texas.

Farah couldn't follow their discussion but she enjoyed the convivial atmosphere. She leaned to her left and pressed her ear against the top of Taari's head. The weed and booze had loosened her emotional constraints and she pondered whether she loved Taari, really loved Taari.

"You are so lucky, Taari. You have the best roommates," Farah crooned. "But Charles is the best one of all. You know the fridge?"

"The fridge?" Taari asked, sounding amused by Farah's softness. "Yes, this one?"

"Yes, that one," Farah said earnestly. "It's full of beer and hard lemonade," Farah raised her bottle as evidence, "all because of this guy."

She pointed at Charles, a round-faced man in a checkered blue shirt and rolled up sleeves, who raised a red plastic cup at Farah in a salute.

"That's cool, thanks. I was about to get one," Taari said to him.

She reached in the fridge, grabbed two bottles of beer, and offered one to Charles.

"No, thanks. I've got a drink," he said and pointed to his cup.

"Oh, cool. What're you drinking?" Taari asked Charles as she replaced the second bottle in the fridge.

"Soda!" Farah answered louder than she intended. Then in an exaggerated whisper, she added, "Charles is working tomorrow. He doesn't want a hangover. That's what I'll have tomorrow. Again."

Taari raised her brows at Charles, who turned at that moment to decline Brad's offer of a lit joint.

"I'm into that!" Farah leaped off the counter and landed in a crouching position. "Gimme a sec."

When she neared Brad, Farah extended her thumb and forefinger to receive the joint but she miscalculated the distance and pinched the air. This mistake caused her to laugh uncontrollably, and she flapped her hands in the air in an attempt to stop. *I love this house. Taari is so lucky.*

☽

Maiheen wiped the makeup from her face with a practised hand, all the while daydreaming about a different way of life. She was reeling from the lively dinner conversations at Yasmeen's home, a three-bedroom unit on the twenty-third floor of a new condominium within walking distance from Coffee Express. In addition to Mustafa and herself, Yasmeen and Ahmed had invited two other couples, both recent Iranian immigrants.

Sara and Ervin, an amiable couple in their forties, were licensed pharmacists in Iran. While they earned their incomes as a house cleaner and taxi driver, they were pursuing re-accreditation and planned to open their own shop. Maiheen appreciated their quiet affection for each other and resisted the urge to openly adore their holding hands on the couch.

Jaleh and Behman were a different sort of people all together. Jaleh, an animated woman in her sixties who owned a catering business, was prone to breaking into song, mostly joyful standards that were popular during Maiheen's childhood. Behman, a long-retired academic professor, was equally high-spirited and started one conversation after another about world affairs.

"That Jaleh was something, huh?" Mustafa asked as he turned off the bathroom light and splayed out on the bed, folding one arm under his head. "She knew all the songs. How old do you think she is?"

"What does that matter?" Maiheen teased him. "You plan to run off with her? I think Behman might trip you with his cane."

"He had a cane?! He's older than I thought." Mustafa laughed and started humming a tune from earlier that night. "I mean, she's still working, and it doesn't sound like they need the money."

"I think she likes to work. I mean, she's not cleaning houses like Sara. She runs her own catering business," Maiheen said.

She examined her face for any streaks of eye liner or foundation she missed. When she was satisfied, she headed to the bathroom to wash with cleanser. In the mirror of the poorly lit bathroom, she considered the deepening wrinkles around her mouth and the enlarged pores of her cheeks and forehead. Maiheen recognized the same features on Jaleh's face, despite the heavy layer of makeup the older woman had worn. *Are my lines just as visible as hers? What's the point of makeup if it can't conceal properly?*

"Yasmeen told me that she doesn't even cook, she hires people for that," Maiheen added while she applied a small amount of an expensive cleanser to her palm and produced a foamy lather with her fingertips.

"Why bother?" Mustafa queried. "She should be relaxing, enjoying life, being with her kids. That's the other thing I don't get. Why are they even here? Why not live with one of the kids?"

Maiheen washed off the cleanser and gently patted her face. She knew that Mustafa was working up to something, and she preferred to let him get there on his own. The questions he posed were rhetorical and offering probable answers was a waste of breath.

"Why does Behman even put up with all this nonsense?" Mustafa adjusted his position and continued. "I'd tell her to close up shop, permanently, so we could travel, you know, take turns staying with each kid. That's the life; that's what people want to do when they get old."

"Hm," Maiheen replied as she brushed her teeth. *What nonsense! Vacationing isn't living; it's a break from the ordinary. And, what's wrong with liking your job and wanting to work? The woman raised four children. Can she finally get a decade to herself?*

She hoped that a partially closed door and a toothbrush in

her mouth prevented Mustafa from detecting her rising temper. After she rinsed her mouth, Maiheen remained in the bathroom a moment longer to regain composure. She had no interest in arguing with Mustafa because that was no way to change his mind. *Change his mind? Is that what I want to do?*

Maiheen looked at her reflection in the mirror, past the lines and spots, and directly into her eyes. There was a woman, smart and ambitious, hardworking and canny, a woman who was ready to start a new chapter in her life.

Upon witnessing Sara's drive to re-establish as a pharmacist, Jaleh's dogged independence, and Yasmeen's confidence in Maiheen's business acumen, she had experienced a sea change. The future that lay ahead of her was unknown, but she was certain that it would be markedly different from the day before. *Convincing him will take time. First, I need a plan, how best to cajole him.*

When she opened the bathroom door, her husband was sprawled naked on the bed, grinning and flaunting his erection.

"We have the apartment to ourselves ..." Mustafa purred. "Why don't you come here and sit on my face?"

Immediately, the gap between her thighs was wet, her body reacting seconds before her mood changed.

Taari wasn't naïve about men. Nor did she consider herself to be jaded, as her mother implied, and not a ball-busting dyke, which her younger brother called her. She had examined the facts: men held power in society and they demonstrated negligible intent to divest their power, and she took these facts into account in every interaction with every man, including her five male roommates and the clean-cut stranger who had arrived at their house party with two cases of alcohol that he had no intention of drinking.

"Paul Bernardo," Brad called out. "That guy should be first on the list."

Tim and the Jessies nodded their heads in agreement. They were talking about convicts most deserving of the death penalty. Bernardo had been indicted for murder as well as a dozen charges of rape. The press had dubbed him the Scarborough Rapist and the Schoolgirl Killer, and coverage of his arrest had monopolized the media for weeks.

Taari read between the lines when columnists and pundits described Bernardo as the boy next door. They meant the white boy next door, the well-dressed and well-spoken white man next door. It implied that Bernardo was an anomaly, that generally rapists were dark-skinned men, unattractive and ill-mannered.

Bernardo's whiteness, his tidy haircut and collared shirts, surprised white audiences, and Taari could read their thoughts. *A good-looking man like him could have his pick of girls. Why rape anyone? He had a pretty wife, a job, a house, and a car. I don't understand why he would do such a thing.*

Taari sneered at the ignorant ideas printed and broadcast. *As if rape is ever about sex.* Paul Bernardo was a serial rapist, a stranger to nearly all his victims, but most women were raped by someone they knew, someone they trusted, not a man hiding in the bushes. Most likely a friend, a date, a lover, a teacher, a relative, or a coworker, any one of the millions of men socialized to consider his gender superior, his demands primary, and his agenda non-negotiable.

"They should cut off his dick," Tim suggested. "That'd teach him a lesson."

"Ew! Gross!" Farah recoiled and nearly tripped on her own feet.

The men laughed at her unrestrained reaction, and Farah stuck out her tongue at them.

"I know a girl who died," she said, apropos of nothing. "In my building. Well not in but outside. She jumped, from the ... really high up."

Taari frowned at this strange news. The death of a person, even a stranger, struck her as inappropriate chitchat. Farah turned towards her, as if to confirm Taari had heard, and she saw that there were tears welling up in Farah's eyes.

"I'm sorry to hear that," Taari offered her condolences.

Farah sighed. With a shrug, she added, "I didn't really know her, you know. She was older."

"She was in the paper today. I read this article," Jessie One contributed, passing the joint to Jessie Two. "Her dad was arrested. They think he threw her over."

"Oh, a Paki girl, right?" Jessie Two said, pulling on the blunt and holding it out to Charles, who refused quietly.

"Whoa!" Brad protested. "What the fuck, dude? Do you use the n-word too?"

"What?" Jessie Two put up his hands in surrender. "What's wrong with Paki?"

"Are you serious?!" Brad exclaimed. "That's not cool."

"The word you're looking for is Pakistani, Indian, Sri Lankan," Taari started, her expression stoic. "Or, if she's from the Middle East, then it might be Afghani, Irani, Saudi, Turk, Lebanese, Egyptian ..."

"Okay, okay, I get it," Jessie Two interrupted with a chuckle.

"No, I don't think you do," Taari said.

"I meant that she's from somewhere else," Jessie Two defended himself.

"We're all from somewhere else," Taari rebuked. "Unless you're native, your people came from somewhere else."

Brad, Tim, and Charles had lowered their gazes but Jessie One was snapping his fingers in Jessie Two's face and quipped with a grin, "Dude, you're being schooled."

"Fucking cut it out, Jessie," Jessie Two waved away his friend's hand. "Listen, what I meant was that this girl, her family, they're ... they like, they think different. I mean, did you read the article?"

He posed the question to Taari, and all of them turned to her.

She stood with her back against the counter, her arms crossed. Her eyes were narrowed and her head shook with the smallest of movements. Generally, she enjoyed an exchange of ideas, but this wasn't a discussion; it was an education in the form of a conversational train wreck.

"Well, okay," Jessie Two said, trying to gain traction. "Her pops was all like religious and stuff, and so he was like really crazy, and all up in her business. So like, he like killed her 'cause of that."

"And you think that he killed her because it's part of his religion?" Taari asked. "Like, his religion made him do it?"

"Well, I mean, it's possible. You can't say it's not possible," Jessie Two said, looking around the table for support.

Taari didn't wait for one more foolish remark. She laid into him, "That's fucking bullshit. It has nothing to do with his religion or where he was born. Men everywhere kill women. They kill their daughters, their wives ..."

"Whoa, whoa," Jessie One began. "I think we need to calm down."

"Yeah, that sounds good. Anyone want a beer?" Charles asked the room.

Taari rolled her eyes at the typical stopping point. No one wanted to hear the truth about why men kill girls and women. They wanted to believe that it was just a handful of sociopaths or religious fanatics who committed these crimes. Never the boy next door, even when it was on the cover of a national newspaper, staring them in the face.

The pleasant buzz from earlier, when she'd sipped red wine with Natalie and her work friends, was replaced by foreboding and angst. She decided on a change of atmosphere and took the opportunity to grab a bag of pretzels and a two-litre bottle of pop and led Farah into the hallway and then outside.

On the vacant porch, the two women slumped on the couch and looked out onto the street. They passed the pretzels and soda back and forth in a session of binge eating, alternating sweet and salty until the pretzels were gone and the bottle was empty. Farah studiously licked the salt from her fingertips, and when Taari released a loud burp, Farah stopped to applaud.

Presently, Taari lit a cigarette and offered it to Farah. After a few minutes of smoking silently, Farah turned to Taari.

"I really like your friends," Farah cooed. "I really like you. You are so nice."

"Thanks," Taari said. "You are so nice, too."

"Let's be best friends," Farah said, releasing a mouthful of smoke upwards.

"Okay, best friends," Taari said.

Farah waited on the porch couch while Taari went inside to get something. She had drunk and smoked too much to remember what Taari was retrieving, so she thought about other things to pass the time. The spring night was getting uncomfortably cold for a tank top and a cotton shirt and Farah considered returning indoors to warm up. The only problem was that she couldn't find the strength to hoist herself out from among the plush cushions of the low couch.

"Hey, you," Charles said, stepping onto the porch.

"Hey, me!" Farah replied and chuckled at her own joke.

"You doing alright?" He stepped closer but remained facing the empty street.

"Yeah, happy," Farah said. "I really like this house."

"Yeah, it's a nice house," Charles agreed. He paused briefly and continued, "I'm heading out now. I thought you might want a ride?"

"Aw, you are so sweet," Farah said. "I live, like, really far away. Like on another planet almost."

"That's cool," Charles said. "It's no problem."

"No, like, really far away," Farah said in a low voice to exaggerate her point.

"That's what cars are for. I swear, it's no problem," Charles said.

He knelt close to the couch and gave Farah a gentle poke on her arm.

"Uh, well, that's really nice. I mean, I was gonna take the late bus but that's always full of weirdos."

"Good, then it's settled. Let's go," he stood up and offered her a hand.

"Wait, I have to wait for Taari," Farah said.

She looked in the direction of the front door, expecting Taari to walk through that moment.

"She went to bed," Charles replied.

"She did? Oh, but she ... I was waiting for her," Farah explained.

"Guess she got tired," Charles offered.

He extended his hand again for her to take. Farah gripped his one hand with both of hers and lifted herself from the couch. Looking back in the direction of the front door, she wondered if she'd mis-remembered her conversation with Taari. *Weird. I must be really wasted.*

Charles took her arm and helped her descend the steps, walk a half-block, and get into his metallic blue sedan. Farah leaned back in the passenger seat and enjoyed the warmer climate inside. As they drove past the house, Farah thought she saw Taari on the porch but she decided it must be someone else.

The distance that consumed an hour each way by bus and train turned out to be a pleasant twenty-minute drive. It helped that there were few cars on the road at two in the morning. The parkway from downtown to her parents' place in North York was almost empty, and Charles required scant directions to navigate to the clusters of high-rise buildings on the hill.

"So what do you do?" Farah asked politely.

Her stupor had been lifting since binging on pretzels and pop with Taari, and it seemed that she was seeing Charles close up for the first time. The man was older than she had assumed. Earlier, she thought he was a similar age to the other guys around the table, possibly in his late twenties. Sitting a foot apart, she noticed the wrinkles around his eyes and mouth and the white hairs protruding from his collar. Farah realized he was closer to middle-age, possibly twenty years older than her.

"I work in sales," Charles said. He flashed a smile her way and returned his attention to the road.

"Cool," Farah said.

"So, you have a boyfriend, Farah?" Charles asked, keeping his gaze ahead.

She recognized his query as a question of her availability. Farah fumbled to compose the right answer, the tactful reply that would communicate her complete disinterest in a relationship with him without offending him. Every relationship column she'd ever read stressed the importance of letting a man down easily, of safeguarding his ego. *The guy is nice, but old, like by a lot, like too old for Farzana, and not even good looking, like Denzel Washington or the James Bond actor.*

"Uh, well, not really. I mean, I'm focusing on school, so ..." She tried to a sound convincing but she came across as uncertain.

"Smart," Charles said with an amused expression.

His reaction got Farah laughing and her anxiety lessened. "Yeah, thanks."

"So which building's yours?" Charles asked in a change of subject as they approached the dozen apartment buildings.

"One-ten. It's on the left. I can get out here, though." Farah made to take off her seatbelt when they stopped at the crosswalk near her building.

"I'll drive up, it's easy enough," he insisted, making a left into her building's driveway.

Charles parked directly in front of the entrance, turned off the engine, and left the keys in the ignition. As the keyring swung in place, an engraved silver keychain sparkled brilliantly in the light of the street lamp but Farah was focused on the second keychain, the one that was white and furry. He must have noticed her staring because he pulled the keys out of the ignition and held them out to her.

Farah opened her palm to receive the keyring but recoiled when he said, "It's a lucky rabbit's foot."

"Oh!" She gasped, disgusted. Then, embarrassed, she added, "Oh, sorry. I ... Cool. So, like, uh, thanks, again. For the ride."

Eager to escape the awkward moment, Farah fumbled with her seatbelt latch, uncomfortable under Charles's persistent stare.

"My pleasure," Charles replied unhurriedly. "Maybe I'll see you at the next party?"

Farah paused, unsure about the hidden meaning behind his question. She held open the passenger side door, preoccupied by her proximity to becoming free of his piercing gaze, and settled for an ambiguous answer.

"That's possible," she said as she stepped onto the curb and smiled back, mostly out of relief for her escape.

"You're really fun," Charles said, bending across the passenger seat to catch her eye.

"Thanks," Farah said weakly. "You, too."

She wanted to shut the car door and walk away but his face was too close to the opening. Then Charles reached into the glove compartment, grabbed a scrap paper and pen, and offered them to Farah. Farah accepted the paper and pen before she could think twice.

"Gimme your number and I'll call if I'm going to the next party," Charles explained.

"Uh, well, uh," Farah mumbled.

She paused and hoped that Charles would hear the hesitation in her voice and retract his request. No such luck. He looked at her expectantly, not breaking eye contact. It occurred to her that she could write an incorrect number, just one digit off would be enough. She placed the scrap paper on the roof of the car and began to write.

Seven digits later, she realized she had recorded the number of a popular pizza chain, and then it seemed hopeless to scratch out one number and replace it with a different one. Frustrated by her error, Farah dropped the paper and pen onto the passenger seat.

"Okay, bye," she mumbled as she walked away, feeling worn down and not bothering with the passenger side door which remained ajar.

In the lobby, while she searched for her keys, she spotted Charles watching her from his parked car. *I could've turned the six into an eight, or the seven into a two. Why didn't I ask for his number instead?! Fuck!* Farah chided herself during her elevator ride up. *I should've just taken the bus.*

3

Sunday, May 9, 1993

On Sunday morning, Farzana spent an hour in the bathroom blow-drying her hair straight. Then, she dressed in an outfit that her parents would appreciate: a pressed and collared shirt, a knee-length skirt, nylon stockings, and small pearl studs. Her face was almost bare, except for a layer of pink on her lips and mauve on her eyelids. *If I tie a red bandana around my neck, I'd look even more like a flight attendant.*

Farzana didn't like dressing according to other people's preferences, but she recognized the importance of playing a part when she wanted to have her way. Dressing like an uppity businesswoman affected her parents like an intravenous morphine drip, abating their anxiety about how she conducted her life. She needed a subdued audience, one who would accept her decision to move out of the apartment with Soreyah without questioning her reasons. Of course, like any businesswoman worth her salt, Farzana had fabricated an explanation that would bring her parents' scrutiny to a full stop. *We have to move out. The landlord needs the apartment for his family.*

It was ten-thirty and her parents expected her to arrive in half an hour. That was not going to happen since the commute was an hour long, at a minimum, and she still needed to buy Mother's Day flowers. *At least I'm dressed and ready to leave.*

As Farzana gave herself a once over in the full-length mirror in her room, she heard Soreyah's bedroom door open for the first time that day. Then came the shuffling of her slippers and closing of the bathroom door. Farzana considered rushing out of the apartment while Soreyah was indisposed.

She wasn't certain that Amir had informed his younger sister about their breakup on Friday night, but it was likely, given their close relationship. On Saturday, Farzana had made herself scarce, moving from the park bench to the public library to a greasy spoon, and returning to the apartment when the lights, and Soreyah, were out.

Today, she planned to be at her parents' place until late. Tomorrow, she would work all day, but she had no plans for the evening or for their remaining days together. She needed to move out as soon as possible; that was her escape plan. Until then, she didn't know what to say to Soreyah, if anything needed to be said. *She must hate me for hurting Amir like this. Probably thinking of how fast she can get me out.*

It was agony to think about. Farzana treasured their friendship, her first adult friendship with another woman. It had taken two years for Farzana to lower her guard, nurture their intimacy, and finally accept Soreyah's offer to become her roommate. They had bitched about dead-end jobs, lamented the ease of student life, cried over broken hearts, and most recently fretted about piling debts. They were a team, and the only team Farzana had been a part of in years, not since she was eleven years old and the eldest of five girl cousins, all of whom lived within a block of each other in Esfahan. *I messed it all up. It's over now. Stupid, stupid.*

Farzana's eyes began to well with tears, and she cursed herself for ruining her makeup. With her first knuckle, she dabbed the corners of her eyes to catch the tears. The shower started, and Farzana took the opportunity to grab her purse and leave the apartment discreetly.

Maiheen had no delusions about Farzana arriving by eleven or about Farah waking before noon. Her daughters were predictable, if nothing else. By ten, Maiheen had eaten breakfast and washed the dishes, touched up her roots, showered and dressed, composed a grocery list, and prepared *salad-e-Olivieh* for their family lunch, a household favourite made with shredded chicken, boiled potatoes, a generous amount of mayonnaise, and topped with green olives. Soon enough, Mustafa would wake, and the two of them would leave for their weekly run to the supermarket.

Sunshine bathed the living room in a warm glow and captured her attention. Maiheen marvelled at the expanse of blue sky and allowed her gaze to rest on the sparkling office towers of the skyline. She knew that each floor of the faraway skyscapers was dedicated to professionals steadily crunching numbers and completing reports, handling clients and holding meetings. She grasped the procedures and pressures that governed their work because she had been one of them for twelve years, the most fulfilling years of her life. Head teller at the most profitable branch of the most prestigious bank in Esfahan and recognized by the district manager for her exceptional service. *Was that really me? Can I go back to that?*

Glare prompted her to look away, and insecurity struck her like a cane whipping the backs of her legs, bringing her to her knees. Her old life felt like a dream about someone else. She slumped into her usual spot on the couch, facing the television. *Am I even cut out to be a mortgage broker? Who'd trust me with their loan?*

She heard the hiss of the shower in the master bathroom. Mustafa was awake, buoyant and singing, unaltered by the weight of their domesticity and the burden of his daily physical labour. *Why can't I follow his suit? He doesn't mope and complain.*

Located at her feet was a basket of folded laundry, and atop the heap was her Coffee Express uniform, brown, white and pressed. Tomorrow, she would return to serving and cleaning at work, an extension of serving and cleaning at home. It had been fourteen years of persevering for the sake of her family, each day more monotonous than the last.

Growth had become the province of others, like her daughters, who were young, and Yasmeen, who was ambitious, not an old woman like her who had enjoyed her time in the sun. Yet, the thought of passing another day, another year behind the coffee shop counter, or cleaning offices, or stocking shelves, caused her chest to ache. *What am I supposed to do? This can't go on. Soon, I won't be able to get out of bed.*

The shimmering office towers were a symbol and by no means a solution. Their prominence in the cityscape, a scene that met her gaze every morning, represented a constant yearning for more, much more than she had presently. Those offices were collective pursuits, complex systems, and capable people making order from confusion. That was her calling, to convert the incomprehensible into the digestible, to produce simple explanations about complicated transactions, and then present them to customers in a tone that gained their confidence. *I don't want to work in those buildings, but I want to do that work.*

How to explain her longing to Mustafa? Financial stability had been their standard since they arrived in Toronto, and the wellbeing and education of their daughters had been their sole pursuit. Mustafa had dedicated himself to their plan, but now the girls were women and they were out in the world, pursuing their own dreams, and Maiheen felt foolish for wanting the same for herself. Whereas Mustafa was counting down the years to retirement, she was hungering for the opposite. She wanted to study, set up a business, scout for clients, and set herself apart from her competitors, make a name for herself.

A new career would take her away from him, she knew. He wouldn't like her working long hours, even if she was working for herself. The privileges of punching out had grown on Mustafa, and he considered it bad form to bring work home or sacrifice time with family for a larger paycheque. He would question her priorities, wonder whether she loved him less, and wither at the prospect of being home without her present. He wanted her to be available and to choose him above all else. Maiheen pursuing a career would be analogous to having an affair, and it would break Mustafa's heart. *How can I do this to him? How can I justify driving a wedge between us?*

Just then, Mustafa arrived in the living room with his arms outstretched, "Happy Mother's Day!"

☽

Farah awoke to the persistent sound of the downstairs buzzer. Her alarm clock read 12:22. She stumbled out of bed, her eyes narrowed and her head throbbing, again.

"Doesn't anyone hear that?!" she exclaimed at the threshold of her bedroom door.

It took a moment to realize that she was alone in the apartment. She sighed and shuffled to the intercom in the hall.

Farah pressed the Speak button and asked gruffly, "Who is it?"

She pressed the Listen button for a response.

"It's me. Open the door," Farzana demanded in return.

Farah groaned to herself and pressed the button to open the door to the building's front entrance. She unlocked their apartment door for Farzana to enter and began her return to bed.

Again, the buzzer sounded. Farah swore at the intercom and pounded the button to open the door. As she walked back to her room, the buzzer sounded again.

She growled into the intercom, "What?!"

Then, she pressed the Listen button to hear Farzana, "It's not working. Come down and open the door."

Farah's head lolled and she pitied herself immensely. She thought about telling Farzana to wait until someone else came along or berating her sister for always forgetting her keys. All of those options required her to talk and at that moment, she wanted to return silently to sleep.

"Coming," she managed to answer.

After pulling a sweatshirt over her pajamas and grabbing her keys, Farah made her way downstairs. In the vestibule, Farzana stood with two plastic bags at her feet, holding a bouquet of flowers in one arm and pressing buttons on the keypad with her free hand. She stopped punching the keypad when she saw Farah.

"Who are you harassing now?" Farah said, leaning on the door to hold it open for Farzana as she gathered her bags.

"What took you so long? I was calling you, in case you went back to sleep," Farzana complained.

"Why don't you find your keys? Or make new ones?" Farah asked.

Farzana was already around the corner and pressing the elevator button. Farah leaned in to read the handwritten note from the superintendent about the broken contraption that opened the door. The reflection of a vehicle caught her eye and she turned to see a metallic blue sedan, identical to Charles's, parked at the end of the driveway, near the street.

"You coming?" Farzana called out.

Farah squinted to examine the person in the driver's seat, but there was too much glare and her head ached from concentrating. *Coincidence?*

She turned and trailed her sister into the elevator. Back in the apartment, Farah shuffled first to the bathroom to take a couple of pain relievers and then to her darkened room and the comfort of her bed.

"You're not going back to sleep, are you?" Farzana asked, standing in the doorway with her hands on her hips.

"Close the door!" Farah cried and pulled the covers over her head.

"Lazy ass," Farzana said as she retreated, shutting the door to Farah's cave.

☽

Mustafa drove south on a scenic route along Leslie Street, a winding two-lane road that butted against the lush greenery of three prominent city parks. New leaves had filled the canopy and the sidewalk was a parade of all ages enjoying the warm spring air. On the car stereo, Mustafa played Andy's "Dokhtar-e Irooni," a pop tribute to Iranian women, and serenaded his wife with the playful chorus. Maiheen smiled his way and even leaned over at a red light to receive his kiss, but he sensed that her mood was even gloomier than before. *Could she be regretting her decision to let Farah move out? Is this about Farzana's prolonged absences?*

No matter the cause of his wife's melancholy, Mustafa was determined to make her Mother's Day a joyous occasion.

"Where are we going? The supermarket is that way," Maiheen said pointing left as their car turned right onto Eglington Avenue.

"We'll go shopping but I wanted to take you somewhere first," Mustafa said and flashed a winning smile.

"Where?" Maiheen asked, less than amused. "I'm not dressed for going anywhere except the supermarket."

It was true that Maiheen was dressed in casual attire, a cotton shirt, cardigan, and waist-high jeans, but she looked beautiful nonetheless. Her hair was pinned up neatly, her makeup was fresh, and her scent was the embodiment of spring and love. Mustafa said as much but Maiheen batted away his compliments, only slightly less perturbed by the sudden change of plans.

They drove farther east on Eglington Ave, past the neighbourhoods of Leaside and Forest Hill, where wealthy professionals added extensions onto their sprawling brick houses set far back from quiet streets without sidewalks, and they arrived in Uptown Toronto, several blocks of posh clothiers, gourmet grocers, and refined French bistros. Nearly everyone who came in and out of the stores and restaurants was white, and the people of colour were typically in uniforms or commuting.

"Why are we here?" Maiheen asked.

"You'll see," Mustafa said.

He patted her thigh to reassure her and she rested her hand on top of his, suppressing a sigh. He parked on a side street and led the way back to the main strip, arm in arm with his wife. In front of Café de Flore, a popular patisserie with bay windows flanking a brilliant red door decorated with stencils of black and white poppies, Mustafa paused and raised his brows.

"Here?" Maiheen asked.

Without leaving her spot on the sidewalk, she peered in the windows to examine the place.

"Yes, here," Mustafa replied, palms exposed and arms open wide in a magician's pose. "It has petit fours in every flavour, just like the bakery on Khiaban-e Chahar Bagh."

Historic Khiaban-e Chahar Bagh, the promenade bordered by centuries-old gardens, was their weekend destination for evenings in the fresh air, among other families. Mustafa was certain that Maiheen would appreciate the memories stirred by these edible works of art. He smiled knowingly at her, willing her to join his enthusiasm for a slice of the past.

Maiheen crossed her arms and asked, "You've been here?"

"No," Mustafa said, lowering his arms. "Hossein told me about it. I thought you'd like it. It's like old times."

"You brought me to a coffee shop on my day off," Maiheen spelled it out for him.

"But it's not a coffee shop. It's a café. Come on," Mustafa encouraged her, even opening the red door with dramatic flair. "I'm sure you'll like it."

Maiheen didn't budge, and Mustafa let the door shut. He faced her but she refused to meet his gaze.

"What's wrong? I thought you'd like this," Mustafa said. "Something out of the ordinary, and they have sweets. You like sweets."

This observation didn't impress his wife, and she turned back towards the side street where he'd parked the car. Disinclined to discuss the matter in public, even if speaking in Farsi offered them some privacy, Mustafa silently followed his wife as she weaved through the crowded sidewalk.

Back in the car, Maiheen turned away from him and stared out the passenger side window. He started the engine and drove in the direction of the supermarket. The stereo was playing Andy's greatest hits and Mustafa ejected the cassette without comment.

What is the matter?! Why is she so upset? Why can't we enjoy a nice time like other people? Mustafa was disappointed in himself for choosing the wrong place, for being out of touch with Maiheen's desires. He used to know everything about her, and these days it was like living with a stranger. Worst of all, she didn't confide in him the way she used to. It was easy to know her wants and needs when she offered these details readily. Now, her inner thoughts were mysteries, and any effort on his part to gain insight was met with resistance and deflection. How long would this go on? Was there some recourse that eluded him?

He looked to his wife, who continued to stare off into the distance with a solemn expression. It was obvious that she didn't want to talk, whether or not she was upset with him. She didn't speak until they pulled into the driveway of the supermarket parking lot.

"Can you please go to the hardware store to buy a box of lightbulbs and a new mop?" Maiheen asked in a neutral tone. "I'll meet you back here in less than an hour."

With that his wife departed for the supermarket entrance.

Mustafa didn't suggest that they buy those items at the supermarket. He knew well enough that she didn't want him around.

☽

Farzana didn't begrudge her sister returning to bed. There were so many thoughts rattling her mind that she was happy to be left alone in her parents' apartment. She placed the Mother's Day flowers, red and white carnations circled by baby's breath, in a glass vase that she positioned in the centre of the coffee table. In matching glass dishware, she laid out two boxes' worth of delicate, pastel Italian sugar cookies, making an attractive pattern of blues, pinks, greens, and yellows. In the fridge, she spotted the *salad-e-Olivieh* and prepared the table settings to match the lunch menu. In small dishes, she set out pickled carrots and cauliflower, as well as sliced onions and sprigs of mint. On a glass platter, she placed a heaping stack of pita bread, neatly cut into triangles for scooping the salad.

Once the dining table was set for lunch, Farzana rested on the couch. She didn't feel pleased with herself or excited about celebrating the day with her mother. Preparing the flowers, the cookies, and the table settings were tasks performed out of devotion to her mother, not due to personal desire. At that moment, all that Farzana desired was to crawl back into bed like Farah and sleep eternally, or at least long enough for Amir to find a new love, time enough for the suffocating tightness in her chest to subside.

That morning, as she was sneaking quietly out of her apartment to avoid Soreyah, Farzana found an envelope tucked under their front door. The unadorned letter-sized envelope was sealed, bulging with folded sheets, and addressed to her in handwriting that she recognized as Amir's. Her name in his cursive script was as intimate and stirring as every spirited time they made love. This was the first letter he had ever written to her, and from the thickness of the envelope, she knew it contained every reason and rebuttal she had refused to hear the night she broke it off.

Although the commute north to her parents' was lengthy enough for her to read the letter several times, she didn't trust herself to remain dry-eyed. *Besides, what's the point? It's over. What difference will one letter make? My parents will never accept me marrying a pizza delivery guy. Marrying?! Where did that come from?*

Farzana tried to be honest with herself, as she did when she journalled. Fibbing and masking the truth were mechanisms to protect her hopes and desires from others but she wanted to be truthful with herself. The truth was that she did want to marry Amir, or at least she had contemplated it for some time. When she became pregnant a couple of months into their relationship, some truths surfaced readily. She was certain that she didn't want to become a mother, not at that time, and she realized she was madly in love with Amir; she wanted him in her life forever. *But not at the cost of alienating my parents. I love them, first and foremost. They're my family.*

"*Salaam!* Hello!" Her father called from the hall. "Anybody up?"

Farzana jumped to her feet and rushed to greet him at the front door. In his large hands, he gripped several overstuffed grocery bags, and under one arm was a dented two-litre plastic bottle of pop.

"Hello, beautiful." Her father greeted her with a trio of kisses on her cheeks.

"*Salaam*, Baba. *Hal-e shoma chetor-ast?* How are you?" Farzana replied.

"*Khoob-am, azziz-am*. I'm good, my dear," he said.

Farzana reached for the bags but her father urged her to grab the plastic bottle before it burst under pressure. They piled the bounty on the kitchen floor and Farzana rushed into the hall to help her mother with the remaining bags.

Father, mother, and daughter worked fluidly to put away the groceries, and Farzana was comforted by their cohesiveness. Despite the numerous secrets she kept from them, her parents meant the world to her. They had nurtured her self-esteem and sense of belonging during the years following their move to Canada, a period defined by its virulent blend of hormones and homesickness.

Whereas six-year-old Farah had leaped into Canadian culture and never looked back, the tear-stained pages of Farzana's adolescent journals attested to her turbulent adjustment and her parents' constant support and ongoing compassion.

It wasn't until the last plastic bag was scrunched into a ball and tucked away that Farzana sensed the tension in the room. She examined her father, who had filled three glasses with ice cubes and cola, and he smiled in her direction but it was a quick glance, uncharacteristic of his doting ways. Her mother slouched as if she was still carrying thirty pounds of groceries.

"*Khoob-asti?* You doing alright?" Her mother asked with a waning smile.

"*Bale, hatman.* Yes, of course," Farzana said with feigned cheeriness, worried that her mother might detect her inner turmoil.

"*Khoob, khoob.* Good, good," her mother replied in an exhausted tone. "I'm going to lie down for a while. Feel free to start lunch without me."

"Here," her father said, offering her mother a glass of fizzing cola.

Farzana noticed that her mother accepted the drink with a quiet expression of gratitude but without eye contact or a smile. This was unusual for a woman who emphasized the importance of seeming genuine.

"We can postpone lunch for bit. I mean, Farah's still sleeping," Farzana said.

She had expected her observation about Farah to incite banter between her parents — possibly a give and take about whose side of the family Farah took after, a playful interaction that might lead to a tale about an especially lazy cousin or a mischievous schoolmate.

Instead, her mother shrugged and said, "As you please." Then she disappeared into her bedroom.

Her father left the galley kitchen from the other doorway, and Farzana heard him switch on the television to a sportscast. She didn't know which way to turn, whether to comfort her mother or question her father. She grabbed her drink and made for Farah's bedroom.

☽

Farah groaned and turned toward the wall and away from her sister and the intruding daylight. It was too early to wake up and too early for conversation.

"Move over," Farzana instructed in a whisper.

When Farah didn't budge, her sister lay on top of the blankets next to her and nudged her toward the wall.

"Listen," Farzana said urgently, "it's time to wake up."

Farah emitted another groan, followed by a pathetic whine, "No."

"I mean it. It's time to wake up. Something's weird with Mama and Baba," Farzana insisted.

"And you just noticed?" Farah asked sardonically.

Farzana poked her side in response, and Farah squealed, butting her sister with her backside to knock her off the bed. The two tussled playfully and returned to their positions, side by side on the narrow bed.

"Seriously, though," Farzana continued, "I think Baba did something and Mama's really ... not mad but maybe upset or sad or something ..."

"He's a caveman, a male chauvinist," Farah proclaimed, remembering the conversation she had overhead between her father and the neighbour, disparaging Shireen.

"Can you get off your soapbox for a sec? This isn't about you," Farzana said, turning on her side to continue with a stern face. "I'm worried. They're ... I don't know. Mama's in bed, and she doesn't even want to come out for lunch."

"Lunch," Farah said and her stomach responded with a gurgle. "Is it lunchtime?"

"You're like a little kid," Farzana derided.

Only slightly hurt by the comment, Farah pouted at her sister and asked, "What's for lunch?"

"Farah!" Farzana chided her. "I'm serious. Can you go to Mama?"

"You go, you're the favourite," Farah replied, knowing that she sounded even more childish.

"True," Farzana joked. "But only because I get up before the evening news, and I don't eat like a vacuum."

Farah chuckled and sighed, "Why me?"

"Because she thinks I'm a spy for Baba," Farzana stated. "And, she knows you don't care about anything but food."

"Ah, the perfect cover for a secret agent," Farah added. "Okay, I'll do it. What's my payment?"

Without missing a beat, Farzana said, "The satisfaction that your sister won't leave you in bruises."

"Ah, the usual payment," Farah said.

Ten minutes later, and following a trip to the bathroom to wash up, Farah knocked lightly on her parents' bedroom door. From inside, she heard her mother give permission to enter.

"Hi, Mama," Farah said.

The blinds were drawn and the room was darkened. Farah walked to the mound on the queen-size bed where blankets covered her mother head to toe. She lifted the edge of the blanket and peered at her mother's face.

"Hi," Farah said sweetly. "I heard the cops were looking for you."

Her mother smiled but remained silent.

"Something about making a killer *salad-e-Olivieh*," Farah continued.

She wasn't certain whether her mother understood the play on words, but she seemed to appreciate Farah's attempt to lighten the mood. With one arm, her mother raised the blankets in a gesture to invite Farah into her arms. Farah crawled under and inhaled the flowery scent as she curled against the curve of her mother's body and allowed her plump arm to pull her closer.

Maiheen Ghasemi was an intimate stranger to her youngest daughter, and as Farah matured, she realized that she knew so much and so little about her mother all at once. While university had made her wise to the experiences of women worldwide — her formidable essays garnering the department head's conditional endorsement of her application to a sizable scholarship — there remained a blind spot in Farah's perception of her mother as a woman, like others. Her mother existed in relation to herself: her caregiver, financier, and next of kin.

"Did you have a good time last night?" Her mother asked as she stroked Farah's back in circles.

"Hm, yeah," Farah said, growing drowsy from the warmth. "You?"

"*Bale*, yes," her mother answered. "Yasmeen Khanome insisted that you come next time."

"Hm, yeah, next time," Farah said, noncommittally.

"Are you hungry?" her mother asked.

"Yes, starving," Farah groaned.

"Go eat, then," her mother said. "There's plenty in the fridge."

"You come, too," Farah whined. "Farzana won't let me eat without you."

Farah turned onto her back and nestled her head under her mother's chin. She realized she was behaving like a child, but it was far too comforting to stop. Her mother's sweet scent, the softness of her skin, and the way she rubbed Farah's back and stroked her head without prompting reduced Farah to her much younger self.

"I'm coming," her mother said in a tone that implied there was never any question about the matter. "You go get dressed, maybe a shower, hm?"

Her mother squeezed Farah's shoulders encouragingly and pulled back the blankets, exposing both of them.

"Shower?" Farah whined. "No showers on Sundays."

"It'll feel good," her mother assured her, giving Farah one more nudge to get her out of bed.

Farah grunted her reluctance and then stood and replied, "Eating *salad-e-Olivieh* from the bowl would feel good."

"None of that," her mother scolded lightly. "Go!"

☽

Mustafa observed his wife during their Mother's Day lunch, and she seemed to have recovered from her earlier malaise. He sat at the head of the dining table as Maiheen and Farzana laid out the prepared dishes. Farah didn't arrive at the table until they were ready to eat.

"It's Mother's Day, Farah. You should have been helping your mother," he chastised his youngest as she took a seat across from Farzana.

"I was taking a shower. You should've been helping Mama," she retorted with a glare.

Before Mustafa could berate Farah for her disrespectful behaviour, Maiheen said, "Farzana helped, and there wasn't much to do."

Mustafa wasn't impressed by Farah's quick responses or her entitled attitude, and he wished Maiheen would address her misbehaviour with greater concern and consequence. No more lectures about delicacy, diplomacy, and ladylike manners. Instead, he wanted Maiheen to cut off Farah financially until she changed her appearance and attitude from that of a roughneck — someone he was too embarrassed to introduce to their friends — to a properly attired young woman preparing for a professional career. No more brush cuts, army boots, or clothes that draped about her like curtains. He was even willing to pay for a new wardrobe, a collection of Farzana's choosing. Anything to bring about positive change in Farah. *But not today. Today is about Maiheen, not Farah.*

"So, Baba, I heard you met your match last night at Yasmeen

Khanome's," Farzana said, smiling good-naturedly and offering him the dish of salad.

Mustafa's frown faded as he gazed at Farzana's soft features and took in her gentle spirit. He accepted the serving dish she offered, as well as the opportunity to change the tone of the conversation.

"You mean Jaleh Khanome?" Mustafa asked with a wink.

"Yes," Farzana said. "I heard she sang you into silence."

"Well, she does have a decade on me," Mustafa explained with a chuckle. "She knows songs older than I am."

Maiheen and Farah served themselves silently, and while Maiheen smiled at the small talk, Farah didn't bother to look up from her plate. Mustafa could feel his temper rising at his daughter's rudeness. *Why does she have to be so difficult? Why can't she follow her sister's lead?*

"I didn't realize she was that much older," Farzana said, looking from one parent to the other. "Mama said she has her own business. Catering?"

Mustafa didn't pause to read the room or finishing chewing his mouthful before he replied, "Ridiculous! A woman her age! She's wasting the best years of her life."

Farah jumped at the chance to lambaste him. "Why?! Because she wants to do something with her life. You know, Baba, women do more than have babies and get manicures. In fact, if more women participated in the labour force, our gross domestic product could increase by billions. Billions."

Mustafa rolled his eyes and scoffed at Farah's tirade. *She's never earned a paycheque or paid a bill. What's she know about gross domestic product?* He had no use for loudmouths, especially a young one who lacked real-world experience. *Farah doesn't understand what it means to sacrifice your last decades working instead of spending time with your children and grandchildren.*

He glanced at Farzana, who returned a sympathetic smile, and then at Maiheen, whose eyes refused to meet his. Instead of debating Farah, he distracted himself with another mouthful.

"Mama, everything is delicious. *Dast-e shoma daard nakoneh,* my deepest gratitude," Farzana broke the tension with praise.

"*Khahesh mikonam,* you're most welcome," Maiheen replied with a brief smile. "How is work? Do you have any new leads? For other positions."

"Leads?" Farzana asked. "Um, I think this job, at the call centre, is working out well. They've got me helping the supervisors."

"Of course, sweetheart. You're a smart girl. They're lucky to have you, but your mother and I want to see you working at the job you studied for," Mustafa said. "All that time studying how to run a big company, and you're not even a manager."

Every day since she was born, he had considered Farzana's future prospects, reconsidering his estimations often with the political and economic winds of change. She would become a person of integrity and prestige, a woman of the world who was as successful professionally as she was personally. His expectations of Farzana were detailed and well-known. From the first day of grade school, he had conveyed to her his plans and enumerated every accomplishment expected of her.

It was with a broken heart that he witnessed her plateau following her university graduation. A year had passed since she received her business degree, and Farzana was working as a telemarketer, a job that didn't require a high school diploma. Worst of all, she didn't seem concerned about her lack of progress. Mustafa worried that she might have given up hope of establishing herself as a businessperson, a formidable force among elites.

"Well, see, there's a possibility I could move up," Farzana explained. "Annette, the department manager, she thinks that I have what it takes to be a supervisor."

Mustafa frowned at Farzana's naïvety, "Of course, she does.

You're a highly educated person. You could do her job, most definitely. That doesn't mean it's the right job for you."

He glanced at Maiheen, who typically shared his opinions and supported him in regards to Farzana's job prospects. Across the table, his wife occupied herself by preparing a pita wrap stuffed with crumbled feta and mint leaves. Mustafa felt injured by Maiheen's lack of involvement.

"Can't you see Farzana likes her job?" Farah interjected.

Of course, she would capitalize on her mother's silence. Mustafa snarled, "Mind your manners, Farah. This doesn't pertain to you."

"Whatever!" Farah snapped back. "No one else's opinions matter to you. Typical!"

From under hooded eyelids, he observed her rise, kiss her mother's cheek, and retreat to her bedroom with her plate half-full. Farzana chewed on her lower lip, and Maiheen prepared another feta and mint wrap. Neither woman looked directly at Mustafa, and he suspected that they judged him harshly for raising his voice at Farah. *They've babied her for so long, and see how she acts. Like a ruffian, like those white kids with their torn clothes and big mouths.*

"There might be an entry level position I could apply to," Farzana offered after some time had passed. "It's customer service, at a bank."

"Great!" Mustafa rejoiced, relieved by the good news. "Now you're talking. That's a good start, get your foot in the door, and before you know it, you'll be running the place."

Still, Maiheen didn't look his way. She smiled encouragingly at Farzana and returned to staring at her plate like a welcome distraction. Mustafa felt she was taking it too far — whatever was bothering her was ruining Mother's Day for everyone.

"Oh, and something's happened with our apartment," Farzana said in an apologetic tone, "and I have to move at the end of the month."

Maiheen's attention was captured by this news, and she asked with a concerned expression, "What's happened? You've only been there six months. Why do you have to move?"

Mustafa was glad to hear the concern and urgency in his wife's voice, and he smiled despite the upsetting nature of the conversation.

"It's the landlord. He needs the apartment for his family, some relatives who're arriving soon, from China, I think," Farzana replied, looking back and forth between her parents.

"Is that even legal?" Maiheen asked, having abandoned her wrap. "Can he just kick you out like that?"

"Well, yeah," Farzana said. "It's for his family, so he can take the apartment when he likes."

"It's how they work. You know that," Mustafa said with a knowing look directed at his wife.

Maiheen didn't respond to his inference. He knew they shared opinions about the shortcomings of various ethnic groups, and it frustrated him that she was withholding her approval.

"That doesn't leave you more than a couple of weeks. What are you going to do?" Maiheen asked.

"Well ..." Farzana began but Mustafa interrupted her with a resolute voice.

"You will return home, of course," he said to Farzana, and then turned to Maiheen. "This is perfect. She can stop wasting money on rent, and she can help you around the house. Farah doesn't lift a finger. Farzana will be a big help." *Remaking Farah is too much to hope for, but at least Farzana can lift Maiheen's spirits.*

"No, no," Maiheen said, looking at Mustafa directly for the first time since their run to the supermarket that morning. "She's not moving back. I don't need help."

Confused, Farzana looked at her mother and then at her father. She opened her mouth to respond but Mustafa interrupted again.

"Of course, she'll move back. You're always going on about the housework and how there's so much to do. This is perfect. Farzana can help, and she'll save her rent money for a down payment," Mustafa insisted.

Farzana's eye widened at this last statement, and Mustafa wondered whether she had forgotten about their plans for her to buy a house before she turned thirty. *Poor girl's probably given up on everything, no career, no house, no family. This is ruinous.*

"What are you talking about?" His wife glared at him. "I don't need Farzana to cook and clean for me. She has her own life."

Again, Mustafa watched his daughter look back and forth between her parents, her gaping mouth and bulging eyes giving the impression that she was stunned by the conversation.

"She can have her own life from here. She'll be good company and a good influence on Farah," Mustafa declared.

"What?! Farah is moving out in a couple of months," Maiheen said bewildered.

"She can take a page from Farzana's book and stay home too," Mustafa retorted, proud of his reasoning.

"Wait, I ..." Farzana started but couldn't compose her sentence fast enough before she was interrupted again.

"No, no," Maiheen said wildly shaking her head. "We're not going back in time, Mustafa. No one is coming back home."

"No one's talking about going back in time," Mustafa argued. "This is just common sense. You want her to move into a shelter? Live on the streets?"

"Don't be ridiculous. Of course, I don't," Maiheen said brusquely, and turned to Farzana. "What's Soreyah doing? Can you find another place together?"

"Oh, uh, Soreyah ..." Farzana stammered, reluctant to finish her sentence. "Uh, she's staying with her parents for a while."

"There you go!" Mustafa said with due emphasis.

"But they live downtown, really close to her work," Farzana

explained with a hint of apology in her tone. "It would take me more than an hour to get from here to my job."

Mustafa tried not to glare at his daughter despite his disappointment, so he pinched the bridge of his nose to shield his eyes. Maiheen had stopped looking his way and leaned towards Farzana attentively.

"So what are you planning to do?" Maiheen asked.

"Well, I was looking at some bachelor apartments near work," Farzana said, plaintively glancing at Mustafa.

"And how much is that going to cost?" Mustafa grumbled, pushing away his plate.

"It's a bit more for rent but I think I can get a second job to cover it," Farzana answered.

"Another dead-end job to pay for an apartment she can't afford," Mustafa announced grimly to the room. "This is useless."

As he pushed away from the table and left the dining room, he heard his wife whisper to his daughter, "Don't worry about him."

That's exactly how he felt, overlooked and unwanted.

Charles caught sight of Farah when she was a few metres from the end of the path that began at her building's front entrance. Night was falling, and the dial of his luminous watch displayed nine. Farah was dressed in a hoodie and jeans, no backpack. He wondered whether she was heading downtown. He sat lower in the driver's seat. His car was at the side of the building, in the visitor's lot, inconspicuously parked among other cars. His position allowed him to survey the foot traffic leading to and from her building. *Where are you going, Farah?*

Where the footpath split, one way leading to the sidewalk and street, and the other winding towards an identical apartment building, he watched her choose the latter. She was practically skipping, she moved so quickly along the paved stones. If he didn't get out of the car, he would lose sight of her. *Where are you going, girl?*

Charles walked on the grassy side of the same footpath, using the shoulder-high shrubbery as cover. Dusk, with its fine balance of light and dark, allowed him to see Farah in the distance whilst he remained unseen among the shadows. She entered the vestibule of the other building, and Charles waited a couple of minutes before approaching. He imagined she was visiting someone, but he didn't have a clue how long she might be, or how long he would remain. There was no reason to leave. She was the most pressing matter at hand, Farah.

The vestibule was identical to the one at her building, an eight-by-eight-foot room with glass walls, a secured door, an intercom system, and not a single CCTV camera. It was vacant but Charles didn't enter. He couldn't be sure where she was, possibly standing a few feet around the corner, waiting for an elevator.

Anxious about being exposed, he walked around to the dark side of a massive concrete pillar, a few metres from the front entrance. From his vantage point, he could hear the footsteps of passersby while remaining hidden by the structure and its shadow.

Charles leaned against the cold, jagged concrete but he noticed only his bodily sensations. He felt no physical discomfort, and he couldn't remember the last time he had experienced physical pain. In fact, he had freed himself of pain, illusions of pain, really. No longer was his mind governed by his body or the senses that had once triggered panic and encumbered his intellect. Charles was master of his experience and nothing could touch him if he didn't allow it to.

Minutes passed but time and its duration were statements of fact, useful as markers but insignificant to his objectives. He had been there all evening, and he felt confident that he was serving his purpose. Charles straightened his posture and slowed his breathing, a technique he'd learned to settle his thoughts. When he heard her voice, he opened his eyes.

"Cool. So, where?" Farah asked from the direction of the front entrance. "Like, just out of curiosity."

Charles listened closely, not daring to lean around the pillar to get a view of her and her companion.

"Joey's Bar, on the Danforth," a young man said. "But I still have time."

The sound of a lighter failing to ignite was followed by the smell of cigarette smoke. Charles thought about the addiction to cigarettes and the pathetic sorts who claimed that they couldn't help themselves. *Feeble of mind and body.*

"Cool ... uh," Farah said, "so, the usual people?"

"Yeah, the guys. You wanna go around back?" the young man asked.

"Yeah, sure," Farah said.

The sounds of feet shuffling gave Charles confidence to peer around the pillar. He saw Farah and a young man in a dark trench coat walking down the footpath. Near the corner of the building, they veered right and onto the grass, heading around the back of the building. *Where are you going, Farah?*

Charles waited another couple of minutes, allowing his breathing to slow and his mind to settle. Excitement and ambition were a hazardous blend of emotions, and he refused to be influenced, distracted from his mission. He could wait a little while longer before he trailed her to find out what was happening around the corner. The answer seemed obvious but Charles wasn't interested in speculation. Speculation didn't require hours of patience and surveillance. He wanted to know the facts of her existence, exactly who she was and what she was doing. He needed to see for himself what was happening around the back of the building.

With a heightened sense of awareness, Charles stepped out from the shadow of the pillar and proceeded down the footpath. When he reached the corner of the building, he didn't turn right onto the grass. He continued farther along the path and crossed the worn dirt path that led to the visitor's parking lot.

At his car, he climbed into the back seat of the blue sedan and procured his binoculars. From his vantage point, he could see the shadows of two people amongst the overgrown shrubbery in a darkened corner. It was no longer speculation. Charles could see that they were having sex. *Oh, Farah.*

He lingered a few moments longer, peering through his binoculars at the brief rendezvous. His mind raced with suspicions and judgements, and the sensations that had festered skin deep threatened to penetrate deeper. Charles climbed into the driver's seat to regain composure. Several deep breaths followed, and he assumed the equanimity that allowed him to return home, unhinged and unnoticed.

4

Monday, May 10, 1993

Farzana arrived at work on Monday morning an hour earlier than necessary and for no other reason than to avoid a run-in with Soreyah, who rose at eight to get to her retail job. It had been three days since she broke up with Amir, and Farzana was certain that he had informed his sister by now. *More than likely Soreyah is avoiding me, too.*

Except for the caretaker who was cleaning out the refrigerator, the office was empty. Farzana slipped off her short suede jacket and hung it from the back of the swivel chair at her cubicle. Call centre representatives weren't assigned to specific cubicles, but everyone had their preferences. Of the seventy-five spaces, the sixteen seats in the last aisle were prized for their remoteness. Reps clamoured for a spot there, like teenagers rushing for the back seats on a bus, and they spent the shift chuckling at off-colour jokes and sexual innuendos.

Farzana preferred the cubicle at the end of the first aisle, directly in front of the glass wall of the supervisors' office, which was jammed with eight cluttered desks. Since her escape from Khanome Parsa's shop and the relentless harassment by the sales duo who cornered her when she was alone, she wanted to remain in plain sight to eliminate any opportunity of being targeted again. In the first aisle, in full view of the supervisors, she was lonely but safe. *Doesn't matter. Just focus on the numbers. I'm not here to make friends.*

From her mini knapsack, she removed a paperback novel,

Virginia Woolf's *Mrs. Dalloway*, and tried to pass the time, to ignore the physical discomfort of losing her two closest friends, Amir and Soreyah. Her appetite was replaced by a tight knot, sleep had become elusive, and the bouts of crying left her head aching and her throat sore. She had no one to blame but herself, and she had no one to turn to.

She sipped her coffee and absentmindedly reread the same lines, a story about a woman who chose a pliable husband to avoid a lifetime of brokering with a spirited one. Farzana empathized since she had ended her relationship with Amir to avoid family complications — romance being no match for her filial obligations. *It's not fair to mess up their lives just 'cause I fell in love with the wrong person. I made a mistake and now it's fixed.*

Farzana gave up on the book and sighed. From between the pages, she removed a folded sheet with the telephone numbers for the advertised apartments she had passed on her way to work that morning. If she wanted to find a place for next month, she needed to overcome her sadness and make the calls.

Yesterday's conversation with her parents returned to mind, and she puzzled at the turn of events. Her mother had surprised her by supporting her decision to live downtown, in contrast to her father, who had played the expected hand and capitalized on her circumstances to force his agenda. The lie she had fabricated about her landlord needing the apartment for his family, an excuse which she had considered dubious because of its cramped timeline, had been accepted readily, but Farzana was dissatisfied despite achieving her aims.

She looked at the clock and then at the list of numbers, and with a lonely heart, she set to work calling landlords.

☽

Farah's three-hour macroeconomics exam started at noon in the Athletics Building. Gymnasium A was partitioned into sections for different exams, filled with four hundred desks spaced a metre apart and bordered by multiple proctors. She tried not to be intimidated by the grand scale of the event or distracted by every cough and scraping chair. Instead, Farah focused her attention on the numerous equations, principles, and theories she had memorized. Her performance on her four exams that week would dictate whether she achieved an excellent grade point average or an exceptional one.

Mr. Rothschild, the department head, had highlighted the necessity to demonstrate outstanding academic and extracurricular performance to receive his endorsement for the sizeable scholarship. Farah planned to astound the old man, secure his endorsement, and receive the largest scholarship the university had to offer an undergraduate, twelve thousand dollars. With that money, she could live independently for a year, without financing from her parents or student loans. All she needed to do was ace four exams in four days. *I can do it. I did it last semester and this one's much the same.*

The proctor announced the commencement, and Farah set to work reviewing the questions and scribbling equations in the margins for later use. After writing non-stop for nearly three hours, her fingers were cramped and her faculties were depleted. Twice, she had reviewed her twelve pages of answers, and when the proctor called an end to the session, Farah was grateful to hand over the exam. There was no time left for doubt, to rewrite responses or fret over wording and calculations. Exhausted, she dragged her feet to the gymnasium doors and joined the herd of fatigued students shuffling out into the hall, the stench of anxiety-induced perspiration causing her to stand apart.

In the main hall, a cacophonous cement tunnel that circled the perimeter of the Athletics Building, foot traffic was nearly at a standstill and she had no room to manoeuvre. More students poured out of Gymnasiums B, C, and D, and everyone stood shoulder to shoulder, taking small steps toward the open double doors, the sunny campus green in view. Farah groaned inwardly and tried to accept the futility of pressing forward.

"Hey, you," Taari called from a few metres away.

"Hey," Farah said with a wave.

Taari signalled that she would meet her outside and Farah nodded her agreement.

On the campus green, some students splayed out on the grass in groups or huddled to compare notes, but most dispersed to study for other exams. Farah spotted Taari sitting on a low wall, dressed in her typical bohemian skirt and delicate frilly top.

"How'd it go?" Taari asked, offering Farah a lit cigarette halfway finished.

Farah took the smoke and joined her on the low wall, her back to the floor-to-ceiling windows of the Student Life Centre and the cafeteria tables packed with students scarfing fast food and cramming for finals. Sunshine greeted her with warmth, so she unzipped her hoodie and wrapped it around her waist.

"Good, I think," she answered humbly though she was confident that she had aced the exam. "You?"

"Yeah, it was okay," Taari said, looking out onto the green, where a group had started playing ultimate Frisbee nearly on top of a couple making out. "I think I got all the main ones, but a couple of the permutation problems just lost me."

Farah understood that Taari was referring to math problems, but she was at a loss as to which humanities course involved permutations. *Stats, maybe?*

Statistics was a course required by anyone thinking of graduate school. They had both attended Introduction to Women's Studies, so Farah had assumed that Taari was also pursuing a liberal arts degree, possibly psychology or political science. She had even worried about their being in competition for the humanities scholarship for undergraduates.

"Cool," Farah replied. "What course is that?"

"Discreet Math," Taari finished the smoke and crushed it against the wall, placing the butt next to her thigh.

Confused but relieved, Farah nodded. "So, is math your major?"

"God no, majoring in math is for ultra-geeks," Taari joked and nudged Farah softly. "I'm doing a computer science degree. We have to take math courses but they're not pure math or anything."

"Oh, cool," Farah said.

She was amazed and even more intimidated than before. Her impression of Taari as a human rights advocate, a radical feminist on the world stage denouncing the IMF, was flattened by this new information. Suddenly, Farah's lack of knowledge about computers, other than for writing essays and playing solitaire, felt devastating. If Taari realized how little Farah knew about computers, what would she think? Already, Farah had perceived Taari as a renaissance woman, a creative type who excelled in practical projects, grasped world affairs, and engaged others emotionally. Now, she was a tech wizard, too. What did Farah have to offer her in a friendship? Beset by her bruised ego, Farah became silent.

"Most people don't think it's cool," Taari said, lighting another cigarette and handing it to Farah.

Farah accepted the smoke, "Yeah, people are stupid. It's cool. I mean, you'll be rich, right? That's cool."

This comment caused Taari to burst out laughing. She slapped Farah's thigh and spit at the base of the wall.

"That's what my parents hope, anyway," Taari said, accepting the smoke back from Farah.

"Is that why you're doing it?" Farah asked, thinking this might explain Taari's career choice and the seeming mismatch between her disposition and her degree.

"No," Taari said. "I like it, and I'm good at it. Or at least, I was good at it in high school. The assignments are harder now. There are some really smart people here, and I'm just regular."

Upon detecting agitation in her friend's voice, Farah doubled down on her supportiveness, "I bet you're great."

Taari laughed at her sudden enthusiasm. "Thanks, Farah. How about you?"

"Me?" Farah asked, pausing to buy time. "Uh, I suck at computers, now and in high school. Probably forever."

Taari laughed again and nudged her to answer the question, "*Your* degree."

"Oh, well, I'm supposed to be doing econ, not hard like computers," Farah said.

She chewed her lower lip and glanced at Taari to see a non-judgemental expression, then she continued, "I like numbers, and models, and predicting the future. A witch, really. Or, a sorcerer of scalability."

To Farah's delight, Taari laughed aloud and nudged her again.

"That's cool," Taari said, nodding her approval. "Witches are cool, and math witches are the coolest."

"Right!" Farah said, feeling less anxious. "Thanks."

"And your exam went well?" Taari asked.

"Yeah, I think so. One down, three to go," Farah said, handing back the smoke.

Taari waved it off and took out a pack of gum, offering a stick to Farah. "I have another one in an hour, combinatorics."

Farah accepted the gum and pocketed it. "Is that some kind of disease? Polio, tuberculosis, combinatorics."

Taari jumped off the low wall, chuckling and shaking her head. "I like you, Farah. You're funny."

"Thank you. Thank you very much," Farah said, doing her Elvis impersonation. "I'm done being tortured today. My next exam's tomorrow."

"Lucky you," Taari said as she hoisted her carpet bag over her shoulder and turned to cross the green. "Catch ya later."

"Yeah, for sure. Good luck on your exam," Farah called out, and then remembering that they hadn't spoken since the party, she added, "And thanks again for inviting me to your party. It was really fun."

"Good, I'm glad," Taari called back, sidestepping the couple rolling about and glancing back at Farah with an amused expression.

Farah laughed and shrugged in exaggerated dismay. When Taari was out of sight, Farah looked at her wristwatch. It was half-past three and she didn't have anywhere to be. She considered calling Michael for another rendezvous, preferably on his bed. The possibility of spending an hour or two with him motivated her to head home. She donned her headphones and began a speedy trek northwards, where an entrance to the subway station was located within a block of campus.

On Sunday evening, she had called Michael on a whim, mainly to get out of her own apartment, where tensions were running high between her parents. Over the phone he had sounded pleased, almost enthusiastic about seeing her, but it turned out that he was excited about meeting up with his friends later on.

She feigned nonchalance because it was important that Michael associated her with happy feelings and good times, or else he might not want to spend time with her at all. Once she was safely in her room, she allowed sorrow and heartache to consume her. *He wouldn't care if I disappeared. He already told me he doesn't want to date me.*

Those piercing messages, along with any truth they contained, had lost their power by the time Farah awoke on Monday. Instead, she revelled in her precious new memories of holding, tasting, and kissing Michael. She wasn't ready to give up on him, not after two years of trying to win his affection. Memories of their intimate moments could sustain her for some time.

Farah walked along the narrow asphalt path that veered left around Camden Library, a monolithic structure that resembled an abandoned honeycomb, and ended at Lot 7C, a vast parking lot that buttressed a quiet residential street and led to the subway station. On the right side of the path stood the rear entrance of the Humanities Building, occupied by green dumpsters and a loading ramp. For a few metres, Farah walked in the shadow of the two buildings as she approached the nearly vacant lot. She shivered from the shade and tunnelling wind and stopped to pull on her hoodie for warmth.

Farah spotted the familiar metallic blue sedan first, parked in the far-right corner of the lot, a few metres away and tucked in the darkest shadow of the Humanities Building. Charles leaned against the trunk, his back to her. He was dressed in a beige suit, appropriately attired for a management meeting. *What the fuck?! Why is he here?*

Farah pretended not to see him and continued to walk across the parking lot, increasing the distance between them by angling unnecessarily to the left.

"Farah!" Charles called to her.

She didn't turn around to his greeting, and though she heard him clearly, she feigned ignorance and touched her headphones as a subtle signal of her selective impairment.

"Farah!" He called again and from the same distance.

Worried that he may pursue her if she continued to ignore him, she looked over her shoulder in his direction, not stopping her steady stride. Charles remained leaning against the trunk of his car, waving casually and looking unperturbed by her unsocial behaviour. Farah waved to acknowledge his greeting, and then turned away, eager to be out of his view.

"Bye," she heard him call. "See you later."

Get lost! Fucking creep! Farah's heart was racing and her t-shirt was damp with sweat, though she felt foolish for having run away from a friendly man who seemed in no rush. She was two blocks away from the lot, in sight of the subway station and on a street crowded with foot traffic when hot tears rolled down her cheeks. Farah bit her lip to remain composed as she entered the station and paid her fare. *I'm fine. Nothing happened. I'm fine.*

Physically, she was unharmed, but while she waited for the eastbound train, frightening questions leapt at her from a menacing realm, a place occupied by malice and misdeed, and she felt disturbed. She wondered about Charles's bizarre arrival, his self-assured attitude, and his assertion that they would see each other again. With every new question, she felt more distraught. To soothe her frayed nerves and calm her jittery limbs, she assured herself that the experience was unpleasant rather than frightening. *He's just a confident jerk, a guy who can't take a hint. Fucking annoying but harmless.*

☽

Mustafa had never been happier to be at work as on that Monday following the disastrous Mother's Day. He was still reeling from Maiheen's ungrateful and unrelentingly miserable attitude. This was not his wife, and he had no idea how to remedy this situation. He didn't even know what was wrong or what was happening, other than that he could do nothing right. *Is this part of menopause? I thought we were finished with that. God help me.*

While at work, his day improved considerably. The tips were generous and the workload was reasonable. Alongside Hossein and Afewerk, two longtime car-wash attendants Mustafa respected for their work ethic, it was easy to be in a good mood.

The morning rush consisted of enterprise vehicles, mostly taxis, as well as limousines and luxury cars brought by chauffeurs, followed by the midday mania of minibuses, which were unimaginably disgusting. Mustafa's back hurt from stooping and his right shoulder ached from the repetitive motions, but he didn't complain. He didn't want the guys to think he was too old or too slow for the job.

When the opportunity came, Mustafa headed to the alleyway

behind the building to stretch his muscles without an audience. The rear entrance of the building was designed to receive customers, so it was uncluttered, newly painted, and outfitted with signs advertising services and directing customers.

After Mustafa performed the calisthenics he had learned as a youth, the same ones he had disliked performing before a football match or track meet, he felt more limber as well as more sentimental about his many years playing sports. He lit a cigarette and walked back into the car wash via the open garage door at the rear.

"Mustafa, remember this guy?" Afewerk asked, his Eritrean accent trilling his pronunciation.

In the car-wash tunnel, underneath the window of the cashier's booth, Afewerk and Hossein sat on milk crates and leaned against the brick wall. Years earlier, the men had requested chairs but the owner had refused, citing issues with insurance. Candice, the elderly cashier and the owner's wife, sat on the one chair that could fit in the small booth. Typically, she faced the empty seating area, a cigarette in hand, and a pile of paperback novels kept her occupied.

"This guy," Afewerk said, folding the newspaper to a display a picture and handing it to Mustafa.

Mustafa sat to Afewerk's right and examined the photo. He recognized the picture of Javeed Bahmeeni, the man whose daughter had jumped to her death. By Javeed's hairline, Mustafa recognized that the picture was dated, by at least a decade.

"You remember him? He was here in '88, no '86. Remember?" Afewerk asked. Without waiting for a reply, he turned to Hossein on his left, "This guy worked here, not long. You weren't here, then."

"I started in 1985," Hossein said, leaning across Afewerk to accept the newspaper from Mustafa and examine the photo.

"No! You didn't start in '85," Afewerk argued mischievously. "That's not right. Mustafa, when did you start?"

"1984," Mustafa said, pulling on his smoke. "The year of three prime ministers, Trudeau, Turner, and Mulroney, and a pack of smokes cost a dollar twenty-five."

"Remember this guy?" Afewerk returned to his original question.

Mustafa didn't want to talk about Javeed Bahmeeni, a man he disliked because of his malcontent disposition. Mustafa preferred to look on the bright side even if it was artificial light of his own making. Javeed used coarse language and complained incessantly about his private affairs as well as matters that didn't involve him. Mustafa suspected he was from a family of lowly, uncultured types, people who hadn't been educated to speak or behave properly. His own parents revered the propriety and rectitude of the upper classes, especially the Pahlavis, the last royal family of Iran, and they instilled the same ideals in their six children. He didn't want to discuss the man for fear of speaking ill of someone who was mourning the loss of his child.

"I remember him," Hossein said and handed back the newspaper to Afewerk.

"No, you don't," Afewerk insisted, teasing Hossein. "You hadn't got off the boat yet."

"Whatever you say," Hossein replied in his easygoing manner.

Mustafa lit a second cigarette and offered the pack to the other men, who declined affably.

"Well, this guy, Javeed, he killed his daughter," Afewerk announced.

"What?" Mustafa nearly spit out his cigarette. "What are you talking about?"

"See here," Afewerk placed the newspaper in Mustafa's hands. "He threw her off the balcony."

"Why the hell would he do that?" Mustafa asked, disturbed by the news.

"I don't know. He's probably crazy," Afewerk offered. "It says the girl was covered in bruises."

"What?" Mustafa scanned the article looking for keywords. "Well, of course, she was. She jumped from the balcony. It's bound to leave bruises."

"No. Old bruises," Afewerk said, pointing to a paragraph about the medical examiner's findings.

Mustafa was nauseated as he read about the autopsy, the internal bleeding and broken bones that predated her fall. He handed the newspaper back to Afewerk and smoked silently.

"Maggot!" Hossein hissed, staring off into the distance.

"Yeah, I never liked him," Afewerk repeated the sentiment.

Moments passed and Mustafa didn't voice his agreement. Like his friends, he was disgusted by the report and its implications about Javeed Bahmeeni. The man was accused of violently beating his daughter and then throwing her to her death. It was a crime perpetrated by a father against his own child. Mustafa was aware of child abuse, of white people neglecting the basic needs of their children, but this was different, this was close to home.

In his community, among Iranians, there was no prevalence of child abuse or discussion of any such phenomenon. Parents were venerated by their offspring, and children were reared and safeguarded by their devoted parents. Some parents used corporal punishment to discipline their children but that wasn't a crime or an act of brutality. It was intended to teach valuable lessons that would serve the child into adulthood. People who harmed children were deranged, social pariahs, not parents.

Javeed Bahmeeni had transgressed every principle of parenting that Mustafa had acquired from his own parents, grandparents, and Iranian upbringing. More than anything else, Mustafa was ashamed of his cultural and linguistic association with Javeed, an accused murderer. He had to invalidate the connection between himself and a killer, and the simplest tactic was to refute the evidence. An Iranian father, irrespective of his crass or disgruntled personality, could not intentionally harm his daughter. It was unthinkable. *Something else is at play. What could she have done to deserve such a fate?*

☽

Maiheen washed the grime from her skin and the odour of smoke from her hair, lingering under the hot water of the shower and allowing her muscles to unclench. Her work day at Coffee Express was over, and she was starting her second shift at home. There were two loads of clothes to press, fold and put away, dinner to prepare, and a stack of mail that needed her attention. She reminded herself that she could watch her favourite daytime drama while ironing and folding clothes but this didn't console her. Past remedies, like soap operas, talk shows, and sweets, no longer offered respite from her restlessness.

She towelled off and dressed in casual clothes, ready to start another marathon of tidying, cleaning, and cooking. When she finished putting on a fresh pair of socks, she stretched out on the bed, arms spread and unmotivated to begin her chores. Instead, she considered the day's conversations that flitted about her head. Top of mind was her chat with Yasmeen early that morning.

Yasmeen was talking at length about her recent foray into commercial real estate, having earned a contract for a Class B building situated on Finch Avenue, which had been targeted for restoration. Maiheen was dismayed to hear that Yasmeen's manager was reluctant to assign her the contract because he worried that commercial clients would not have confidence in a female agent. How could anyone not have confidence in Yasmeen after she had grossed over sixty thousand dollars the previous year? Had Maiheen been naïve to assume that her ethnicity was the greatest obstacle to her career when an intelligent and ambitious Iranian woman was treated so miserably by her Iranian manager? *Good for Yasmeen for twisting his arm. May I have the same courage and resolve.*

Aloud, Yasmeen brainstormed plans to attract investors. Her

enthusiasm was contagious and soon Maiheen joined in, suggesting potential buyers and business opportunities. Between preparing food, cleaning sticky tables and emptying ashtrays, Maiheen helped Yasmeen compose a rough marketing plan, including the value proposition of owning a twenty-year-old building. Maiheen had flashbacks to business school when she and her classmates composed detailed such plans based on fictitious companies.

In her bedroom, gazing at the ceiling, Maiheen caught herself smiling, happy. That half hour in the morning with Yasmeen had carried her through the monotonous day. The property, the investors, the marketing plan, all of it filled her head with so many calculations and considerations, so many ideas that were complex and intriguing. Long after Yasmeen left the coffee shop, Maiheen thought about one aspect after another, delving deeper into the details of the project, until it was too much to remember for the next time she saw Yasmeen, so she began to write down her ideas.

Presently, Maiheen leaped to her sore feet and grabbed her handbag. She found the stack of notes and returned to the bed, spreading them out and reviewing the viability of her ideas. Questions continued to present themselves, some about the legal relationship between owners and renters, others about commercial property leases, and Maiheen grew frustrated by her lack of knowledge.

It occurred to her that she might find some answers in the mortgage brokering textbooks she'd inherited from Ahmed. Soon, she'd retrieved the plastic bag of books from the back of the closet and begun researching her questions. The technical language was difficult to follow but she was determined to understand the concepts and legal terms. From a dresser drawer, she fetched her English-Farsi dictionary, which she hadn't used in years, and looked up unfamiliar words, like collateral and escrow.

"Hello? Mama, I'm home," Farah called from the front hall.

Maiheen startled. She checked her wristwatch to find that she had spent an hour reading textbooks and jotting notes. Discomfited by having neglected her chores, Maiheen's voice fluttered in response. "*Salaam*, Farah," she said while she swept the books and papers into the plastic bag, which she pushed under the bed.

Maiheen composed herself to meet her daughter. Peeking down the hall, there was no sign of Farah. Maiheen picked up the first basket of laundry and carried it past the closed door of Farah's room and into the open area of the living room. On her way back to her bedroom to collect the second basket, Maiheen knocked on Farah's door. There was no answer.

She knocked again and called out, "Farah, are you hungry?"

As she spoke the words, Maiheen regretted asking the question. She was tired of tending to her daughters as if they were little children, anticipating their needs and facilitating their self-care.

Maiheen considered the hours of contemplation and labour she had invested in Farzana and Farah, whether she was buying thrifty brands to discourage their expensive tastes or networking to expand their employment options, and the predictable responses from both daughters. It stung when Farah spurned her mother's efforts outright and accused Maiheen of meddling, but at least that was easier to process than Farzana's false enthusiasm and evasive measures.

She had resolved to change her tactics, to be available but not indispensable, to await their requests and check in with herself before tending to their needs. This new approach was an affront to everything she had learned about parenting from her own parents.

Every time she visited Maiheen, Maman-*jaan* had arrived with a basket of prepared dishes and a discrete gift, typically a personal item, such as a package of cotton underwear, a tube of face cream, or a box of hair dye. "This is proper mothering," Maman-*jaan* would have explained.

Maiheen bit her lip when she thought about her own response

to her mother's presents: always a variation on the same sentiment, feigned gratitude, the same sentiment Farzana offered Maiheen. The result being a closet filled with unwanted toiletries and undergarments, and an otherwise meaningful mother-daughter relationship tarnished by white lies and misrepresentation.

"No, I'm good," Farah answered from behind the closed door. "I'm about to go out."

"Can you open the door to say hello to your mother?" Maiheen prodded.

A moment later, Farah opened her bedroom door and pointed to the phone that was pressed to her ear, its cord stretched to its full length from across the room. Maiheen began to ask whom she was calling but Farah shushed her with a finger to her lips. With a loud sigh, Maiheen trudged back to her bedroom to collect the second basket of laundry and the ironing board. When she heard Farah shut her bedroom door, it sparked anger in her. *A child! She acts like a child! Doesn't even ask if I need help? Child!*

In the living room, Maiheen propped up the ironing board and set to work. A few minutes later, Farah crossed the hall to the kitchen. Maiheen heard the fridge door open and a pop can hiss, and then Farah crossed back to her room.

"Farah," Maiheen called, hearing the irritation in her voice. "Farah, can you come here, please?"

Dragging her feet, Farah appeared in the living room, frowning and unimpressed.

"Do you see any of your clothes in these baskets?" Maiheen asked sardonically, pointing to the knee-high piles.

Farah shrugged, "I guess so."

"So, you are aware that I fold *your* clothes?" Maiheen asked as she carefully positioned the hot iron.

"Yeah," Farah frowned, momentarily confused by the question. When Farah thought she'd figured it out, she added earnestly, "But you don't have to. You can just dump mine on my bed. I don't care if they're folded."

Maiheen nearly spat out her response, "I care, and so should you."

Farah shrugged again, despondent, "Sure, okay. Whatever you want." Then she turned to leave.

"Farah!" Maiheen called, exasperated. "I'm asking you to iron and fold these clothes."

"All of them?" Farah asked, annoyed and then recovered at the expression on Maiheen's face. "Yeah, okay. Right now?"

"Yes, right now," Maiheen asserted. "You can go out afterwards."

"Fine. My plans got cancelled anyway," Farah mumbled as she placed her pop can on the coffee table and grabbed the remote control to find background entertainment.

Maiheen was drained from the interaction, but she managed to give Farah a few reminders about how to iron her father's slacks and the setting to use for her nylon shirts. Farah assumed her position behind the ironing board and in front of the television, slouching in a defeated stance.

"Sorry about your plans," Maiheen said gently, stopping on her way to the kitchen.

"No big deal," Farah said, her voice trailing off, drowned out by the din of the talk show audience.

Maiheen intuited that Farah was more disappointed that she let on. From the short phone calls that enlivened her daughter and caused her to depart suddenly, she suspected that Farah was enamoured with a boy. On a couple of occasions, Maiheen had tried to coax Farah into talking about her friend, using conviviality and shared womanhood to set the mood, but Farah pretended to misunderstand her questions about romance and relationships.

With Farzana, Maiheen hadn't realized her eldest was in love for the first time at age seventeen until the relationship was finished and her daughter was sobbing into her pillow and listening to the same sad love song over and over. Somehow, it was easier to console a daughter who had lost love than it was to gain the confidence of a daughter who had found love.

During her adolescent years, Maiheen had been infatuated with an older neighbour boy, a boy who became a man while she was still in her girlhood. Guarded about her unrequited affection, Maiheen had been too sheepish to admit her crush to anyone, including her mother. *Why was I so shy? She was so caring, so loving, and I didn't trust her reaction. Do all mothers and daughters struggle to find a safe occasion to share their experiences of love and longing?*

"Can I make you something special for dinner?" Maiheen asked of Farah.

Without turning away from the television, Farah shrugged and said, "Nah, whatever."

"Oh," Maiheen said, slightly disappointed.

"Uh ..." Farah said distractedly, then added, "How about those mini pizzas and fries?"

"Pizza and fries?!" Maiheen reproved, regretting her offer. "I don't think so."

"Fine, whatever," Farah turned back to the television and the ironing. "You asked."

"I'm making *khoresh-e bahmee-e*," Maiheen called over her shoulder as she headed to the kitchen. "That's real food. Not like pizza and fries."

"Ok, fine," Farah mumbled.

An hour passed as Maiheen worked in the kitchen and Farah completed her chore slowly in front of the television. When dinner was prepared and sitting on the stove, Maiheen returned to the living room with two pita rolls, each stuffed with walnut crumbs and feta cheese. She offered one to Farah, patting the seat beside her on the couch to suggest she join her mother. Maiheen clicked through the TV programs and settled on a favourite soap opera of theirs, one they had first watched together when Farah was in grade school.

With her mouth full, Farah exclaimed at the television, "Wait! He tried to rape Cricket and then pleaded insanity? That's not ... that's just ... so crazy."

"Michael blames her for losing his lawyer's licence, after he was sued for sex harassment," Maiheen explained.

"Sexual harassment," Farah corrected her without thought and continued in an agitated manner. "They use rape in, like, every story. Didn't Victor just save some lady from being raped? Like, by a weirdo on the side of the road. And, there was that another woman, and she didn't know if she'd gotten pregnant from being raped? Or, if it was her boyfriend's baby."

"Well, bad things happen," Maiheen said in an attempt to assuage her daughter.

"Not like this, though," Farah asserted. She spun in her seat to add, "Did you know that one in four women is sexually assaulted? And, it's usually someone they know. Someone they already know, not a weirdo on the side of the road."

Maiheen grew concerned by the fervour in her daughter's voice, and she asked sincerely, "Farah, are you worried? Has something happened?"

With dramatic eye-rolling and a frustrated sigh, Farah said, "No, Mama! I'm trying to tell you something about rape, not about me."

"Oh, good," Maiheen said with relief, taking hold of her daughter's hand in both of her own. She continued, "Because you can always talk to me, about anything, Farah-*jaan*. Anything."

Farah turned back to face the screen, looking disappointed in their exchange, "Yeah, I know."

For a few minutes, they watched television in silence, each woman in her own thoughts.

Is Farah angry about the crimes perpetrated by some men and generalizing her feelings towards all men? Is this the reason she dresses in loose clothing and cuts her hair instead of wearing outfits that show off her nice figure? Is she avoiding men's attention? It would explain her antagonistic attitude towards Mustafa and her disinterest in using her charm to appeal to others.

"How was your exam?" Maiheen changed the subject, not wanting to end their time together on a sour note.

"It was good," Farah said, still staring at the screen.

"That's great, Farah. I'm happy for you," Maiheen said. "You have another one tomorrow, yes?"

"Yeah," Farah said. "Tomorrow, Wednesday, and Thursday."

"I'm sure you're doing great on all of them. You're a smart girl," Maiheen affirmed.

"Woman," Farah corrected her, "not a girl. That's just a sexist way of talking about women. Infantilizing them."

"Okay, a smart woman," Maiheen conceded, and then changed the subject again. "Do you know if Farzana's had any luck finding a new place? I haven't talked to her today."

At this comment, Farah spun again to face her mother with a bewildered look. "She's moving? How come?"

Maiheen was surprised that Farah didn't know. She recalled that Farah had left the lunch table before Farzana announced that she had to move by the end of the month, but Farah had visited Farzana's apartment overnight only three nights earlier, and it seemed odd that she wasn't aware of the impending move. Maiheen was aware that her daughters hid personal information from her, but she presumed that they shared their lives with each other.

"Her landlord needs the apartment for his family," Maiheen explained. "She's looking for a place for next month."

"Next month? That's impossible," Farah commented.

"She didn't tell you when you visited?" Maiheen probed.

"Uh, I think I would have remembered that," Farah said in an acerbic tone. "Is she finding a place with Soreyah?"

"No, Soreyah is moving in with her family," Maiheen said, taking time to compose her next question. "Did everything seem alright with Soreyah?"

"Uh, yeah, I mean everything was really nice," Farah answered, sounding very nearly wistful.

"And the two of them weren't fighting or anything?" Maiheen pressed for more information.

Farah paused and blinked several times before she answered, "No. No one was fighting. It was all really nice."

Maiheen didn't ask any more questions. She turned back to the TV program, as did her daughter.

From the confusion in her younger daughter's response, Maiheen realized that Farzana hadn't confided in her younger sister. Maiheen pretended to watch television for another few minutes while she considered how to approach Farzana without precipitating more secrecy and lies.

☽

Farzana arrived at her apartment late afternoon, expecting to have the place to herself while Soreyah finished the last couple of hours of her shift. She was tired and hungry, but mostly in need of a quiet place and some time without interruptions. The unmet need for space from others, from their chatter and presence, had caused her grief since childhood. It wasn't until she moved out of her parents' apartment that she enjoyed long hours of uninterrupted time alone, glorious hours spent reading, writing, and pondering philosophically. *At least I'll have that when I live on my own again.*

After leaving phone messages at rental offices that morning, Farzana grew depressed about moving away from Soreyah. So, she started a mental list of reasons why she would enjoy living alone. Having more time to herself now topped the list. The only other reason on the list was that she wouldn't have to clean as often because no one would be keeping track.

As soon as she cracked open the front door, she realized Soreyah was home. Farzana considered letting the door shut, walking downstairs, and hiding at the diner around the corner.

"Hey, you! Get in here, I've made nachos," Soreyah called out.

Too late. Think fast. "Uh, I think I forgot something at work. I'll be back," Farzana said, leaning into the apartment just enough to be heard.

"What?" Soreyah exclaimed. "Did you not hear me say nachos? Nachos, woman! Get in here."

On top of being tired and hungry, Farzana was very confused. It seemed peculiar that Soreyah was in such a playful mood, and with her, the woman who had broken her brother's heart. Uncertain and unable to think clearly, she followed her natural inclination to take orders until her will reasserted itself.

Once she removed her shoes and washed up in the bathroom sink, prolonging each task as much as possible, Farzana joined Soreyah in the kitchen at the two-person table occupied by a cookie sheet covered in cheesy tortilla chips.

"*Bokhor, bache-e.* Eat, child," Soreyah mimicked the order heard from so many Iranian parents.

The two sat knee to knee and picked at the cheese-encrusted chips. Soreyah rose to grab a couple of bottles of beer from the fridge. She smiled at Farzana, and Farzana tried to smile back but tears welled up in her eyes.

"*Chi shode?* What happened?" Soreyah asked, rubbing Farzana's thigh.

The individual tears became rivulets, and before long Farzana was sobbing and gasping for breath, unable to say anything. Soreyah jumped up and returned with a dish towel, offering it to Farzana with tears in her own eyes.

"Huh?" Farzana asked, perplexed, looking at the dish towel and then at Soreyah.

"To wipe your face," Soreyah explained with a quivering lower lip.

The unusual choice caused Farzana to chuckle and snort, which brought a small smile to Soreyah's face. Farzana accepted the towel and patted her wet cheeks and wiped her running nose.

"*Beya*, here," Soreyah said, offering Farah the opened bottle of beer.

"*Merci*, thanks," Farzana said. She sipped a little and placed it on the table, where her gaze remained.

"You wanna talk?" Soreyah asked, craning her neck to catch Farzana's eye.

A shudder rippled through Farzana's chest when she took a breath to speak. She exhaled and slumped in her chair. Buying time, she bit her lower lip and picked at flecks of nothing on her skirt.

"Is it about these?" Soreyah asked.

From the ledge that housed the phone, she grabbed a notepad which she handed to Farzana. On it, Soreyah had the recorded the names and numbers of three superintendents who had called back in response to Farzana's inquiries from that morning.

"Oh, Soreyah, I'm so sorry," Farzana said, biting her lip harder to avoid a flood of tears. "I didn't mean for this to happen."

Calmly, Soreyah asked, "Can you tell me what's going on?"

Farzana shuddered again and a moan escaped from her pursed lips. "I just ... I want you to ... I want to ... I don't want you to feel ... This is your place, and I don't want to intrude."

She stopped to wipe her nose again and took a moment to breathe and collect her thoughts. A deep exhale followed by a deep inhale, and she slumped back in her seat.

"Is this about Amir?" Soreyah asked softly.

Another moan escaped from Farzana, and it seemed that she would imminently lose her capacity to hold in her overwhelming sadness. She held the dish towel to her face and wiped indiscriminately, anything to shield herself from Soreyah's distressed expression.

"You're moving out because of Amir?" Soreyah asked, this time less softly.

"Uh-huh," Farzana said from behind the dish towel.

"Why?" Soreyah demanded.

"Huh?" Farzana replied, lowering the dish towel in case she'd misheard.

"Why? Why move? Why do you need to move?" Soreyah asked, her hands gesticulating her bewilderment.

"What do you mean? I can't stay here. I can't see him all the time," Farzana explained, a little perturbed that Soreyah didn't understand.

"You don't have to see him all the time, or at all. I mean, it's our place, not his," Soreyah retorted.

Shaking her head in disagreement and disbelief, Farzana said flatly, "He's your brother, Soreyah. He's here every weekend."

"But he doesn't have to be," Soreyah replied. "Besides, do you really think it's over with Amir?"

This question threw Farzana off course, casting her out into turbulent waters that she had veered away from for the past three days. Every article of his clothing, every journal that bore his name, every album they had bought together, all of these reminders were stored away, out of sight, out of mind, unable to reach her battered heart. All that remained was tucked in her knapsack, an envelope addressed to her by Amir, still unopened.

"It's over," Farzana said with enough force to cause Soreyah to put up her hands in surrender.

"Okay, it's over," Soreyah conceded. "But why does that mean I lose my best friend? Whatever Amir did, that's his burden, not mine."

"Soreyah, I don't want to move. Trust me. I love living with you. So much," Farzana said as she clutched Soreyah's hands in her own. "But if I stay, it'll be a nightmare. We can't hang out with everyone and pretend nothing happened."

"We don't have to hang out with everyone. This is our place. We can invite anyone we want. Right?" Soreyah pleaded. "You wouldn't invite Raiman over, right?"

At the mention of Soreyah's much-detested ex-boyfriend, Farzana reflexively mimed spitting on the floor. The two women burst out laughing and paused from the difficult conversation to drink beer and nibble at the edges of the nachos.

"Please, stay," Soreyah begged, peering intently at her bottle. "Just for a bit. Just to see how it goes."

Farzana stared at her own bottle, peeling the label slowly from the damp corners. She wanted to agree and to promise that she would never again consider moving away from her dearest friend. Yet, it was inconceivable that the siblings could continue their intertwined lives without Amir visiting Soreyah's apartment, and Farzana didn't want to come between them.

"Do it for me, Farzana," Soreyah beseeched. "I need time to find another roommate, and you know I can't afford the rent on my own. Please."

She knows I wouldn't leave her in the lurch. She knows me so well. "Okay, one more month," Farzana said to her beer bottle.

"*Bismillah!* In the name of God!" Soreyah rejoiced, leaping to embrace Farzana.

"For one month, Soreyah. You have to find someone else, okay?" Farzana spoke over Soreyah's singing and dancing in the small kitchen.

"*Hatman!* Of course!" Soreyah said, pulling Farzana to her feet to embrace and dance.

After three days of heartache and disorientation, Farzana felt herself brush against the peace and joy she had once known.

5

Tuesday, May 11, 1993

Early Tuesday morning, Mustafa awoke from a terrifying nightmare. His nightclothes were damp with perspiration, his heart raced, and the taste of bile coated his mouth. The bedroom was lit by the first rays of the sun and he heard Maiheen breathing rhythmically, asleep and hidden amongst the tangled blankets. Too agitated to return to sleep, he crept out to the bathroom in the hall.

As he performed his morning ablutions, scenes of the nightmare returned to him, jarring his experience of the present. His chest tightened with every memory, making it difficult to breathe deeply or release the tension gripping his neck and shoulders. In the mirror, he saw himself, and then he glimpsed the face of another man, someone who resembled him, but this man existed in a sinister shadow, his features blurred and dark circles in place of his eyes and mouth.

Mustafa splashed more water on his face to clear his mind, to escape the haunting emotions that refused to release their grasp. This man who lived in the darkness, Mustafa had seen him lumbering from one horrifying scene to another, dragging a heavy load, a bundle of tangled ... something, something complicated and inexplicable, something Mustafa couldn't perceive and didn't want to examine. The taste of bile returned, and without daring to revisit his reflection, he left for the kitchen to find a cure.

A glass of cold water was followed by a cup of strong coffee, which Mustafa drank while staring absentmindedly at the skyline.

To cast away the darkness inside, he turned on every light in the living room, but it had the unsettling effect of producing his disturbing reflection in the window. The image of the menacing figure, cloaked in shadows and hampered by a burden, gazed back at Mustafa. Then, one scene after another, his nightmare replayed from start to finish.

The narrative began in that same apartment, yet in a different time, in the recent past. He was himself, the persona he brandished with pride, the man he had chosen to become. He stood in the centre of the living room, the centre of his world. Maiheen was nearby, and she was worried, pacing, and unresponsive. From where he stood, he called to her several times, and each time she glanced at him briefly but turned away, never coming closer, never answering his calls. Farzana stood in the periphery, and she was weeping, quietly and steadily, wringing her hands. Mustafa called to her reassuringly, told her that everything would be alright, that he would take care of her but she refused to acknowledge him. She continued crying, whimpering softly.

When he demanded answers, first of Maiheen and then of Farzana, neither woman spoke. They stared at him blankly, and only for a moment. Mystified and infuriated, he screamed. Tremors shook the apartment and caused Farzana to cry loudly. He made to cross the room, to comfort her, but he was encumbered by a heavy load, something he had been holding all along. Farzana's cries grew louder and Mustafa laboured in vain. Frustrated by his slow progress, he resigned to unburden himself.

He lifted the load to his chest and hauled it towards the balcony, to rid himself forever of the weight. As he approached the glass door, he saw his frightful reflection. He looked gaunt and ghoulish, like a monster, ill and depraved. His appearance consumed all of his attention and he never gazed lower at the bundle in his arms, though he sensed that it was warm and wet.

On the balcony, Mustafa had felt light, overcome with feelings of relief and certainty in his duty to rid his family of this burden. He scolded himself for not having discarded the weight years earlier. It was at that point in the dream when Mustafa realized he was carrying the mangled body of Farah, gathered like so much refuse. Anticipating triumph, he lifted his arms over the railing and released her to the ground.

The nightmare ended there, on the balcony, his arms empty, and his heart content. Mustafa awoke to the knowledge that he had dreamed of killing his daughter, willfully and righteously, of ending the life of the little girl whose tiny hand had held his index finger as they walked side by side. Who was this man, this father who had dreamed of destroying his own child? What seed of darkness had rooted itself in his psyche and sprouted a poisonous desire that threatened to destroy him from within?

Now, Mustafa tried to look past his reflection in the window pane but there was no escape. Knowing eyes stared back at him, at the man who had learned something about himself, something he had never imagined to be true, a truth he had never wanted to perceive. The nightmare, with its perverse juxtaposition of brutality and bliss, was a hyperbole, that much was true. Yet, the underlying themes of resentment and hostility resonated with Mustafa at a depth that shamed him to admit.

Years of animosity had layered, calcified, and formed a barrier between him and Farah. The sweet girl he'd adored as a child, the one who'd listened attentively and sought his approval, had developed into a young woman he scorned, a loud and contemptuous personality destined to aggravate humankind. From sun-up to sundown, she was difficult in every aspect of daily life, whether she was challenging authority, deflecting responsibility, or disturbing social norms. There was no end to her antagonism.

Sometime during the later years of Farah's adolescence, when back talk and confrontation had become the norm, along with her dressing like a transient, Mustafa had lost heart and had ceased all efforts to remould her in the image of her mother and sister. All hope for her transformation into a bright and beautiful woman had faded, and Mustafa had mourned his loss privately. He had also changed tactics and treated her like the mutineer she had become, visibly abhorrent of her opinions and intolerant of her mannerisms. *I might be her worst critic but that's because I'm the voice of reason. It doesn't matter that she doesn't like me. When she's a mother, she'll understand my sacrifice. She'll understand what it means to be responsible for someone else's upbringing. My job is to prepare her for life, not to pander to her delusions.*

Mustafa's ghostly reflection had vanished. Through the window pane, he watched the sun sparkle on the glassy surfaces of the cityscape. The appalling emotions had released their hold. He felt his sure footing, his solid reasoning, there beneath him, supporting him. *I'm not that man. I would never hurt her. I love Farah.*

At nine o'clock, Maiheen refilled the coffee machine for the fourth time that morning and brewed another carafe of the house blend. The steady stream of customers at Coffee Express helped to offset the boredom of repeating tasks hour after hour, but that morning she was particularly restless. Under the counter, in her handbag, were the sales and marketing notes she had composed for Yasmeen, about the office complex on Finch Avenue which her friend had been tasked to sell. Maiheen had been tempted to rewrite her notes in English, thinking it might seem more professional to a business person like Yasmeen, but then she reconsidered the endeavour, worried that her grammar might fail her or her script might appear childlike.

"Another cup, eh?" asked Frank, one of the regulars.

He placed his ceramic mug and a few coins on the counter and then turned to start a conversation with a customer sitting nearby.

Maiheen smiled, accepted the mug and coins and performed the task mechanically.

"Thanks, sweetheart," he said, taking the mug and dropping a coin in the tip cup.

"Thank you," Maiheen replied distractedly, thinking about her notes.

In Farsi, Maiheen composed articulate messages that rivalled the prose of authors and journalists. Even her handwriting was performative, as she expertly stretched lines and shaped curves, creating images of words. During Farzana's grade-school days, Maiheen had invested hours in training Farzana's hand to write fluidly, gracefully. Farah, who attended only the first grade in Iran, never learned to read or write her native tongue, and Maiheen hadn't the time or energy to instruct her on the weekends. *No matter, Farah's strengths lie elsewhere.*

"Two coffees, one black, one cream and sugar," ordered a familiar woman in a pantsuit. "Oh, and a box of those little ones, yes, there." She pointed to the smallest donuts. "And, I need the receipt."

Maiheen prepared the order, and the woman counted out change.

"Thanks," she said brusquely as she left with an armload of cups and donuts.

"Have a nice day," Maiheen replied automatically, still thinking about her youngest daughter's voracity.

Farah conquered every realm she entered, except the interpersonal. Maiheen continued to agonize about Farah's bullish disposition, her tactlessness, and her attitude of entitlement, but she didn't worry about her daughter's skill or determination in achieving her goals. With each passing year, Maiheen grew more confident that Farah would etch out her niche in the world, even if she was secluded on a deserted island.

Her daughters were hard at work building a future suited to them, and it was time for Maiheen to do the same. There were decades ahead and she could achieve so much, if she started now. She needed to begin immediately, to avoid slipping further into a dark, defeated place where she felt powerless and worthless, a mindless cog in the machine of someone else's ambition.

"*Salaam*, Maiheen," Yasmeen said, walking through the front doors with her head held high, looking every bit the part of a successful businesswoman.

"*Salaam, Khanome!* I was wondering when you'd get in," Maiheen replied cheerily, taking a moment to exchange kisses before setting about preparing Yasmeen's usual order.

"It was a crazy morning. The plumber came by, and he needed access to the utility room, and the super was ... Oh, *merci,* thank you." Yasmeen interrupted herself to accept the cup of coffee.

She continued, "*Dast-et daard nakoneh*, my deepest gratitude. Anyhow, I don't know where he was. He was supposed to be on call but ... Oh," she interrupted herself again, "*babakhsheed*, forgive me, this is so mundane. How are you?"

"Oh, I am doing well," Maiheen said, trying not to appear juvenile though she felt as giddy as a child with an ice cream cone.

"Uh-huh, go on," Yasmeen said as she settled into her seat and eyed her friend's unusual expression.

"I've made a decision," Maiheen continued, trying hard to avoid grinning.

"You're going to do the course! *Elah-e shokr!* Thank god!" Yasmeen exclaimed as she hopped to her feet and began a dance with her shoulders to music only she could hear.

Stunned by Yasmeen's correct guess, Maiheen stared, motionless.

"Come on, Maiheen," Yasmeen teased, still dancing on the spot. "You were made for this."

"Brokering mortgages?" asked Maiheen, sounding doubtful.

"Not exactly," Yasmeen said, slowing down her movements until she reached her stool and reseated. "You were made to make money, to do business. You're a natural at it."

Maiheen's shoulders sagged. The elation she had felt a few moments earlier was replaced by the sadness and gratitude that comes with being seen after a long period of being overlooked. For years, no one had seen her. Not her employers, coworkers, or customers, not her daughters or their teachers, and not even Mustafa, who knew her better than anyone else. No one saw the steadfast businesswoman who guided her team of tellers as they faced the most drastic change Iran's banking system had ever experienced. No one saw the intelligent thinker whose opinion piece about customer-oriented service appeared in Isfahan's daily newspaper. For years, no one had acknowledged her intellect, and while she was grateful for Yasmeen's recognition, she was also depressed by her realization.

"*Chi?* What?" Yasmeen asked, leaning over the counter to hold the hand of her friend.

"Just the past," Maiheen replied, and with a sigh her shoulders drooped further.

"I know," Yasmeen said. "Luckily, it's in the past. Hm?"

A customer walked in the door and Maiheen recognized the friendly regular who bought coffee for her office mates. Maiheen greeted the woman, who had her payment in hand, and quickly prepared the four cups of coffee and two cups of tea, each with a unique combination of cream and sugar that she had recorded on a sticky note, posted by the coffeemaker. With speed, precision, and a smile, she served the customer and bid farewell until tomorrow. Before she returned to her conversation, Maiheen put on a new pot of coffee.

"Do you want another one?" Maiheen asked Yasmeen and lifted a carafe.

"Oh, no. I've had enough, and there's always more at the office," Yasmeen said, checking her watch.

"Yasmeen, listen," Maiheen said solemnly and leaned over the counter. "I ... Is it okay ... Can this be ... Can we keep my decision private? I mean, just for a while? I still haven't ... Mustafa isn't ... He doesn't know."

"What doesn't he know?" Yasmeen asked pointedly.

Maiheen set her lips to maintain composure. She didn't want to become emotional at work, not in front of her customers. Already, the male customers intruded into her private space and pressed her for personal information. She didn't want to encourage their entitled attitudes and probing by giving them a glimpse of her emotional state.

"He doesn't know how I've been feeling. I need to ease him into this," Maiheen explained.

"You know best, *azziz-am*, my dear," Yasmeen said respectfully. "Shall we talk again soon?"

"Yes, of course. You know where to find me," Maiheen said with a smile.

Yasmeen walked around the counter and embraced her friend, planting kisses on each cheek.

"Take care, and I'll see you tomorrow morning," she said as she walked out of Coffee Express.

Maiheen watched her cross the street, attaché case under her arm, and envisioned the day she too would walk away.

Farzana waited until the midday break to approach the department manager, Annette, about her possible promotion to the ranks of call centre supervisor. When the floor had mostly cleared of callers and supervisors, out for a smoke or running across the road for a bite, Farzana walked down the hall to the closet-sized, windowless room where Annette worked.

Despite Annette's attempts to enliven the room with framed portraits of her young sons and a group shot at the beach with their glistening umber skin, her office remained demoralizing. The narrow space was jammed with filing cabinets and file boxes, and Annette was confined in one corner by a wide metal desk and two unmatched chairs. The fluorescent bulb overhead hummed and flickered, and the stagnant air was ineffectively masked with an unpleasant floral scent. Under the unnatural light, Annette's profile appeared sallow and sapped as she hunched at her keyboard and squinted at the screen.

Farzana didn't want to interrupt her concentration but she worried that her career was falling off the radar with each passing day.

"Good morning, Annette," Farzana said, stepping into the doorway.

"Hm?" Annette answered and glanced briefly to examine the speaker. "Hello."

"Hi. I don't want to interrupt you," Farzana paused to give Annette the opportunity to insist that she didn't mind the interruption.

When Annette didn't respond, Farzana plodded on self-consciously, "I wondered if you have time to talk about my, um ... The conversation we had last week, about opportunities to, um ... possibly there being a supervisor position."

Annette blinked at her, and Farzana was ready to run back down the hall. She was utterly disappointed in herself. All morning, she had practised her lines, using a confident tone and a clear speaking voice. Now she had bungled her introduction and couldn't remember what to say next. *Tell her about your degree, your work terms at Clark & Summerset, how good you'd be as a supervisor. Say something!*

Still, with all her ambition and intellect raring for release, Farzana struggled to proceed, and silence persisted.

"Come in," Annette said, pointing to the chair directly in front of Farzana. "Just gimme a sec."

While Annette typed for another minute, Farzana sat upright and went over her speech inwardly.

"Alright, there," Annette said with one last keystroke, and turned to Farzana, leaned back and sighed. "Needed to send that off this morning."

"I understand," Farzana said in a professional tone.

"Hm, so what can I do for you, Farzana?" Annette asked.

She remembers my name. That's good.

"Thanks for making time for me, Annette," Farzana began, remembering to lift her chin and smile.

"No problem," Annette replied. "How's the job going?"

"Really well, I think. I mean, I am very happy to be part of the team. This is a really great company," Farzana spoke confidently.

"Yes, it is," Annette said less assuredly.

Farzana expected her to say more, possibly praise for the personnel or the corporate culture, but a moment of silence turned into an awkward pause.

Farzana started, speaking quickly, before she lost her nerve, "I think, I mean, I want to contribute in a more substantial role. I've worked in this field before, fundraising and corporate development. I did three work terms at Clark & Summerset, and I'm a very hardworking person, and I think I would be a good supervisor."

"Hm, I see," Annette said, not unkindly. "You've been here, how long?"

Excited about the exchange, Farzana answered cheerfully, "Five and a half months, full-time. It's been a real learning experience."

"Hm, yes. So, you want to work as a supervisor?" Annette asked, turning away to browse through an open file box.

"Oh, yes. Very much so. I think I can make a positive contribution to the team," Farzana said, slightly distracted by Annette's search. *What is she looking for?*

"Okay," Annette said, turning back to Farzana, empty handed. "Well, right now ..."

"What up, girl!" said a man from the hall.

Startled, Farzana spun in her chair to see who had addressed her boss so casually. Leaning in the doorframe stood an athletic young white man in a business suit, a person from head office on the upper floors, someone Farzana recognized from elevator trips. She had also seen him with Annette, walking to an eatery during the midday break, along with a group of other young white men in suits.

As on every other occasion, he didn't acknowledge her presence. Farzana repositioned herself and looked into her lap. She felt like an obstruction to a more pressing conversation, so she preoccupied herself with her hands to give them an excuse to exclude her.

"Hi, Steve," Annette replied warmly.

"You coming?" Steve asked, drumming his hands on the doorjamb.

With her back to Steve, it was difficult for Farzana to distinguish his speech from that of a randy frat boy.

He stage-whispered, "Nick said the server's wearing somethin' even crazier, like you can see everything."

His comment shocked Farzana and her eyes flitted up at Annette for a moment. She reminded herself that the higher-ups at the company didn't speak to each other as formally as they did to the supervisors and callers, but something about the slight change in Annette's expression communicated her shared discomfort with the nature of Steve's comment.

"Great, thanks, Steve," Annette said amicably. "Just a couple of things to sort out, you know. I'll catch up."

"Cool. Peace out," Steve said in a false lower octave.

Annette turned her gaze to Farzana, and her friendly smile drained away, replaced by the tired expression of an overworked manager.

"So, you want me to hire you as a supervisor?" Annette asked plainly, interlacing her fingers on her desk and tilting her head to the left.

The matter-of-fact tone of the question unsettled Farzana. The truth was that she did want Annette to hire her as a supervisor but to state her opinion outright seemed like a brazen act, possibly an affront to Annette's own judgement and authority. After all, who was Farzana to judge herself as worthy of the position?

"I think I would make a positive contribution to the team," Farzana compromised.

"I'm glad you recognize the importance of the team," Annette began, re-lacing her fingers. "Teamwork is at the core of this department. We count on each other to meet individual and collective goals."

"Yes, of course. Teamwork is essential. I agree," Farzana replied.

Annette waited for her to say more, then tilted her head to the right and continued, "Tell me about the contributions you've made to the team?"

"Uh, I've been ... I've set daily records for pledges, and I've signed up the most number of monthly donations, and ..." Farzana stumbled.

She couldn't think of one example of teamwork she had participated in. Quantitatively, she had grossed thousands of dollars in donations but she had performed all of her work independently. On the occasions when teamwork was possible, such as coaching new callers, Farzana had remained distant and inaccessible. The two smoke breaks during each shift were the only instances when Farzana spent time with the other callers, and even then she was mute. After five months, most of them didn't know her name, and she only knew a few of theirs.

"I noticed that you sit apart from the other callers," Annette said.

"Hm, yes, I work better in a quieter environment," Farzana explained.

"I'm sure that's true, but it also means that you're not in contact with the other callers," Annette said, tilting her head to the left.

"I know what's going on in the office. I'm aware of the initiatives and I follow the progress boards," Farzana excused herself.

"Yes, I am sure," Annette replied, and with a sigh, she leaned back in her seat. "Supervisors aren't chosen because of their grossing numbers. They know how to generate top numbers but their greatest strength is their people skills. They can relate to the callers. They can motivate others to do their best."

"I can do that. I assure you. When I worked at Clark & Summerset, I ..."

"I need to see that in action here," Annette said, tapping her desk with a stiff forefinger. "Show me how you can relate to the other callers, people from all walks of life. Show me how you can motivate others to do as well as you."

"Uh, how? I mean, how should I ... What should I do for them?" Farzana asked, flabbergasted.

"Start by sitting with them," Annette offered, looking at her watch. "If you exclude yourself, you'll never be part of the team. Step one of forwarding your career."

Farzana was out of her depth and felt deflated. This wasn't where she imagined the conversation would lead. Teamwork wasn't her forte, or even something she liked. She didn't do well with people, unless they were potential donors, clients. Relating to coworkers was a necessary evil, not her aspiration.

"All set, then?" Annette asked, moving files about her desk and glancing over her shoulder at the screen.

"Yes, thank you," Farzana said politely. She rose, remembered to smile, and added, "Thank you, Annette. I appreciate your help very much."

As Farzana walked down the hall to her desk, she grew overwhelmed with despair. *I'm never going to get ahead. I'm not made for this.*

☽

Taari was thoroughly pleased with the day, especially the gorgeous afternoon sunshine that had warmed the campus green, where she was splayed out with an iced coffee, a lit cigarette, and her latest issue of *Computer Gaming World*. She wore a fetching summer dress that exposed her chocolate skin to the sun, and it felt like liquid warmth was pouring in, loosening muscles that had tightened over the long harsh winter.

An hour earlier, she had completed an exhausting calculus exam, and she planned to pass the next hour sunbathing, until her four o'clock exam on functional program design. Someone else might have used the break to review study notes, but Taari was seduced by the sun to lie on her stomach and lazily turn the pages of the robust magazine. Reading gaming articles reduced her anxiety about school and reminded her of her real future, life after assignments and exams, when she would be designing and creating programs of her own choosing.

"Hey, girl," said a young man who stepped into her light. "Whatcha reading?"

He crouched down and leaned over her to look at the magazine.

Taari glared at him and hissed, "Do I know you?"

"I'm Rich. What's your name?" He asked, still kneeling by her shoulder, unfazed by her frown.

"Do you need something?" Taari asked.

"Yeah," Rich replied, nodding and flashing a wide smile. "You seem nice. I thought I'd introduce myself."

He lay down perpendicular to Taari and gazed into her eyes. Taari was frustrated by his audacity and obliviousness but she wasn't surprised. Summer attire signalled the start of catcalls, unreciprocated flirting, and men intruding in her personal space. She had experienced this phenomenon since her teen years, and it was most prevalent among white men, who asked her about her birth place, complimented her dark skin, and informed her that they liked brown women better than white ones.

"We have class together," Rich said, smirking. "Program design."

Taari wouldn't have been able to recognize this man, or any other, from her computer science courses because she sat in the front row and focused exclusively on the lecturer. This allowed her to ignore the fact that she was one of two women in a two-hundred-person course.

"Okay," Taari said. "Did you need something?"

"No, just wanted to talk," Rich shrugged and smiled. "Whatcha reading?"

Taari considered brushing him off, but she reconsidered and decided to give him the benefit of the doubt, as she might if a woman were to approach her. She sat up cross-legged and flashed him the cover of the magazine.

"You a gamer?" Taari asked.

"Yeah, of course," said Rich, and with a look of dawning realization, he asked, "You game?"

"No, I found this in the bathroom," Taari joked. "Yeah, I game. I design them, too."

"Oh yeah, I did that in high school," Rich said casually. "Everyone did, but that's cool that you do it, too."

"Whatever," Taari brushed off his attitude. "My work is prize winning. I won youth category of the Golden Joystick. In '91. In London. England."

Taari realized she was bragging, but she wanted it to be clear that their conversation was about computer science and not her sexual availability. Besides, she didn't know him and she didn't owe him anything.

"Cool, I guess," Rich said with a shrug. "Someone's got to win it, right?"

"What?!" Taari exclaimed. "Is that what you'd say to Sega designers for Sonic winning game of the year?"

"Sonic, that's a good game," Rich said, pleased with his response. "I like Wolfenstein, and Metal Gear, and of course, Night Trap."

"Yeah, that shit's trash," Taari sneered, butting out her cigarette.

"What do you mean? They're hard core," Rich said, sounding personally offended.

"Yeah, if you're a dick with thumbs," Taari retorted. "Those games are all about murdering and screwing. I design games for entertainment, not to fulfill the misogynist fantasies of psychopaths."

"People like playing those games 'cause they're fun," Rich opined like a sage, "and a lot of people buy them. They make, like, millions."

The conversation had become heated, and Taari had grown furious with her counterpart. She wanted to convey her opinions in a calm manner, relate to him at his level, and ideally, win him over with her clever arguments. Instead, she had forfeited those goals in exchange for the visceral satisfaction of chiding him for his preferences.

"Just 'cause a lot of idiots do something doesn't make it right," snapped Taari, shoving her magazine into her carpetbag and grabbing her drink.

"And you would know because you won one award?" Rich asked, his eyes darting about angrily.

The nearby clusters of people on the campus green had noticed the heated conversation, and they openly eyed the duo, eager to see how the argument would play out. Taari rose to her feet, and Rich matched her stance. The two stood arm's length apart and glowered at each other.

"No, I know because I read," Taari said with one forefinger tapping out her message on the other palm. "I follow industry projections and I study marketing trends. That's why my game designs win awards."

"Hm, are you sure?" Rich asked cynically, smirking with arms crossed at his chest.

Unsettled by the odd tone of his question, Taari frowned deeply and answered, "Yeah, I'm fucking sure."

"So, it had nothing to do with your ... other attributes," Rich paused, giving her a knowing look.

"What?" Taari snarled.

"Well, not all prizes are given for merit. Just like not everyone gets into university because of their grades," Rich explained his meaning.

"You think they gave me the award because I'm a woman?" Taari asked in a low growl.

"I'm just saying that it's not always about merit. Minorities, affirmative action and all," said Rich with a shrug to express his sincerity.

"Fuck you!" Taari flared up, jabbing her finger in his direction and proceeding slowly towards him. "You don't know shit! You jealous son of a bitch!"

Rich moved back a step and then several more as Taari continued towards him. Among the onlookers, a couple of men taunted her, calling her a ballbuster, and provoked laughter in other groups. Heartened by the presence of the spectators, Rich tugged comically at his collar for their amusement.

"Chill out, lady!" Rich ordered, extending his arms in front of him and his palms up. "I'm just telling it like it is. Not my fault if you live in a fantasy world."

"You're a fucking dick. Don't ever fucking talk to me again," Taari said as she turned to walk off the campus green.

"Don't worry, bitch," she heard him say, followed by more laughter.

Taari was enraged with herself for giving that man the time of day. Less than ten minutes ago, she was enjoying the day, her cold drink, and her magazine. Now she was breathing hard and stomping away from her place in the sun. She told herself to calm down, that she was in charge of her reaction, and she needed to slow her breathing and temper her anger.

As she passed the Athletics Building, the main doors opened and students began to pour out every which way. Another set of midday exams had ended, and everyone was eager to distance themselves from the place. They flooded the paths leading to the Student Life Centre and adjacent buildings.

Taari used the opportunity to slow her gait and reconnect with the warmth of the sun and the sweet flavour of her iced coffee. There was more than a half-hour of break time remaining before her next exam, and she decided that a leisurely walk about campus would help towards putting the confrontation behind her.

She started along a quieter path, one flanked by newly blossomed cherry trees, which led around the rear of the Athletics Building and towards Camden Library. The path was something of a dead end since it coursed between the inaccessible sides of two monstrous buildings and led to a parking lot, which was mostly vacant during exam time. Yet, the path was peaceful for the same reason, being deserted, and she appreciated a chance to stroll and sip her drink whilst looking at the blue sky.

Rounding the bend to the back of the Athletics Building, she spied Farah coming out the rear exit, her back to Taari. *Smart woman, avoiding the crowds.*

Taari considered calling out to Farah but her friend was wearing headphones and walking at a fast clip. There wasn't anything to talk about in particular, but Taari would have liked some conversation to distract her from the exchange earlier. Still, Farah was walking so quickly that she was already quite far ahead, entering the narrow, darkened gap between the rear of the library and the Humanities Building. *She must need to be somewhere quick.*

Taari lingered under a tree with low branches covered in fragrant blossoms, and she watched Farah proceed to the end of the path, nearing the parking lot. The vicinity was deserted, and for this reason, Taari quickly spotted the man, who was dressed head to toe in black, as he emerged from the shadows at the rear of the library and began walking in Farah's steps. Taari waited a moment, holding her breath, apprehensive to assume foul play at hand. *What's he doing? Is he running at her?*

Time stood still as Taari watched the hooded man walk to within a few metres of Farah. His arms lay flat by his side and his footsteps matched hers. The surreal quality of seeing one person stalk another seized Taari. It seemed that the wind had stopped blowing and the ambient sounds of the outdoors had silenced. There was only the horrifying scene unfolding before her widened eyes and the nausea rising in her curdling stomach. *Oh my god! Oh my god!*

She opened her mouth to scream but inhaled sharply at seeing the man grab Farah from behind and drag her off the path, to the right and into deep shadows.

"Farah! Help! Farah!" Taari screamed as she ran in their direction, casting aside her load without thought, sprinting the two hundred metres to her friend.

What had happened to her friend? What would she find around the corner? Did she really see a man attack Farah?

She was running towards an unspecified danger, not towards a burning building, a car crash, or into the path of a hurricane, but towards an unscrupulous person, someone compelled to act irrespective of moral or criminal law, and it terrified her. Who was this man? What was he capable of? Was she in danger herself? What would she do when she reached Farah?

Taari continued to scream for help as loudly as her burning lungs permitted. She rushed around the corner, uncertain of which way to run next, and ready to combat the monster. When she arrived, she found Farah alone, lying on her right side in the shadow of the Humanities Building, trembling and crying. Taari rushed to her and knelt by her side, panting too hard to speak but placing her hands on Farah to make her presence known.

The right side of Farah's face was covered with abrasions, her lower lip was split and bleeding, and her eyes darted about wildly, filled with tears and terror. When their eyes met, Farah moaned loudly, her opened mouth revealing two rows of bloodied teeth.

"Farah, Farah!" Taari said, coughing because of her parched throat. "Are you okay? I saw everything. Are you okay?"

Taari realized that she was crying as well, partly for Farah's sake and partly out of fear for her own well-being. She scanned the area and saw no one. The rear of both buildings and the parking lot were vacant. It had taken her at least a couple of minutes to run the distance, and in that time, the attacker had taken off.

"Farah, where did he go?" Taari asked softly. "Which way did he go?"

Farah curled up, sobbing and shaking her head so that her mangled headphones, disconnected and dangling from her neck, tangled further with the motion.

"It's okay. Don't worry. It's okay," Taari said gently, rubbing her friend's back as her own mother would have comforted her. "Come on, let's go inside. We can't stay here."

Taari helped Farah get to her feet and wrapped an arm around her shoulders to balance her gait. Farah tucked herself into her friend's shoulder and hobbled along silently. At a laborious pace, they returned to the path and headed towards the front entrance of the Humanities Building. Along the way, they collected Farah's left shoe, her cracked cassette player and backpack. Taari spotted her carpetbag in the distance where she had begun her sprint.

"Why don't you sit here and put on your shoe?" Taari suggested, pointing to spot in the grass. "I'll run back for my bag. That way you don't have to walk so far."

Farah's face contorted with fear and she beseeched, "No, no, don't go, please don't go. Please, don't leave me."

Taari felt awful for having suggested as much, and she promised that she would remain with Farah. Together, they proceed slowly, stopping for Farah to put on her shoe, and then hobbling along to pick up Taari's bag.

They plodded on, Taari directing them to the nearest door into the Humanities Building. The administrative offices on the first floor were closed for the day but the doors to the dean's office were open. The receptionist jumped to her feet at the sight of the blood covering Farah's face and Taari's dress, and ran around the desk to direct the women to a pair of seats against the office wall.

Taari guided Farah into a seat before sitting adjacent. Farah curled into the nook of her friend's body, and Taari wrapped her arm around Farah, enveloping her protectively.

Kneeling before the seated women, the receptionist asked, "What happened?"

Farah, who remained tucked into Taari's body, wept and shook her head in response. Taari rubbed her back and nodded in understanding. She swallowed the lump in her throat and tried to answer on their behalf.

"There was a ..." Taari said quietly, and then she dissolved into tears.

☽

Farzana held her skirt above her knees as she took the flight of stairs two at a time to reach the dean's office. She was still in her work clothes, having jumped into a cab as soon as she answered Taari's call, shortly after arriving home. From the brief conversation with Farah's friend, she grasped that Farah needed her immediately. Without question, Farzana headed to campus, preparing herself along the way for the worst-case scenarios, most of which involved altercations between her younger sister and authority figures. *Ugh, Farah. When will you learn?*

She rushed down the hall, reading floor maps as she passed them, and found the dean's office just as she thought she was lost. The plush waiting room was fully occupied by one male and one female police officer, a wizened man in a tweed sports jacket, and a middle-aged woman wringing her hands. Farzana stood at the doorway and looked around for Farah while the four inside stared back at her.

"You must be her sister," the woman said pityingly, biting her lip.

"Yes," Farzana replied, frustrated by the room of staring eyes. "Where is Farah?"

"Her friend took her to the washroom, to clean up. They'll be back any second," the woman explained. "Come in. You can wait in here."

"Which way is the washroom?" Farzana asked without budging.

"They'll be back any minute," the woman said, looking to the old man and the police officers for support.

"Which way?" Farah insisted with a forced smile as she stepped back into the hall and looked in both directions for a marker.

"It's three doors down that way," the woman conceded, pointing right.

Farzana was at the washroom in a flash. There was a jog in the entrance, which led into a small mirrored seating area, and then a sharp turn to reach the handwashing area and the toilet stalls. Farzana could hear running water but not much else.

"Farah? It's Farzana," she said, moving slowly around the corner towards the sound of running water.

"We're here," a young woman called out, and Farzana presumed this was Taari.

The scene that met Farzana gripped her with such force that her body froze in motion, in breathing, and in all conscious thought. Her little sister's face was scratched and bruised, blood stained the front of her shirt, and there was a gash on her lower lip that made Farzana's heart ache. She rushed forward to Farah and grabbed her gently by the shoulders, leaning in to examine the damage close up.

"What happened?" Farzana asked, chasing Farah's gaze to meet her own.

Farah's eyes, puffy and bloodshot, welled with tears, and she shook her head in response.

Growing frustrated, Farzana commanded, "Tell me what happened."

Farah's tears turned to sobs and her body shook with the heaving motion. Farzana released her shoulders and enveloped her in a long embrace. It was at this point that she noticed Taari standing steps away, at a sink, with wet paper towels in hand, tears running down her cheeks, and her own dress stained with blood.

Farzana continued to hold Farah's quivering body, but she needed to know what had transpired. Did they need to go to the hospital? Was anyone else hurt? Was there an accident? Why had the police been notified?

"Taari, can you please tell me what's happened?"

Taari nodded, wiping her cheeks, and composing herself.

"A man attacked Farah. He did that to her," Taari said, pointing to her own face to indicate the cuts and bruises on her friend's.

"Who? What man? Where?" Farzana asked in quick succession, her head spinning with more questions.

"I don't know who. He ran away," Taari answered, sounding disappointed in herself. "It was just behind the Humanities Building."

"Fuck," Farzana said in a long exhale. Then more questions arose, "And you? Did he attack you, too?"

"No, no. I wasn't with her. I saw him but I ..." Taari choked up for moment and then stammered, "I'm so sorry, I should have yelled sooner but I didn't know what he was doing, and then he was dragging her, and I yelled but no one came and I ran, I ran as fast as I could ..."

The explanation revived Farah's sobbing, and rivulets of tears ran down Taari's cheeks. Farzana consoled them both with a shushing sound her mother used during her childhood.

"It's alright now. You're both fine now," Farzana said, though it didn't feel like the truth.

Neither of the young women seemed fine. They were physically safe from harm, but they were obviously traumatized by the experience. They couldn't speak about the event without reliving the fear. Suddenly, Farzana wanted her mother and father to be present, to care for all three of them. They needed parents, not an older sister with good intentions.

She pulled Farah away, at arm's length, to face her and explain, "We have to call Mama and Baba, and you too, Taari. You must call your parents."

Taari nodded quietly, in agreement that she wanted the comfort of her family, but Farah shook her head and refused to meet Farzana's gaze.

"Farah, this isn't your fault," Farzana assured her. "They will help."

Farah continued to shake her head, and Farzana allowed her to return to their embrace.

"The police want a report," Taari said, almost childlike. "We're supposed to go back to the office."

It relieved Farzana to hear that their next step had been determined, giving her a chance to collect her thoughts. *The police will know what to do. They'll help.*

"Okay, let's do that," she said. "You can call your parents from there. Can they pick you up?"

"Uh-huh," Taari said, obviously reassured by Farzana's assuming responsibility for Farah.

Farzana helped them clean their faces, and soon they returned to the others in the waiting room. The dean led them into his private office, a spacious room with an oversized mahogany desk on one end and a set of dark leather couches around a glass coffee table at the other. The young women clustered in the centre of the large room, uncertain of how to proceed, while the dean and the officers stood near the entrance. The officers' aloof demeanour surprised Farzana, and she grasped at reasons for their coldness. *Is Farah in trouble? Did she break the law? Is that why they're being standoffish?*

"Shall I go?" The dean inquired of the officers.

"Yes, please," Farzana interceded, repulsed by the thought of a spectator. "And, thank you for your help."

To counteract her directness, Farzana offered the dean a saintly countenance which she reserved for men who excluded her from discussions, a look to express her regret for having spoken out of turn while underscoring her resolve to be heard. This was another tactic she had learned from her mother, to play demure while upholding her dignity.

The dean looked to the officers, who nodded their assent.

"I'll be right outside, if you need me," he said to the officers as he closed the door behind himself.

Farzana turned back to Farah and Taari. They looked miserable in their dishevelled and stained clothes, their hands tucked under arms, and their eyes downcast. How could she comfort them? What did she have to offer?

"Sit," instructed the female officer gruffly, nodding in the direction of the leather couches around the square coffee table.

Taari and Farah silently took seats next to each other on a couch, and Farzana occupied an armchair to their left, within reach of her sister's hand. Obtrusive in navy uniforms and Kevlar suits, the officers strode to the couch across from Farah and Taari. Each constable perched on the edge of their seat in a wide-legged posture that gave the impression they were eager to proceed, ready to get on with the formalities. Meanwhile, a two-way radio clipped to the male officer's shoulder emitted a jarring stream of garbled voices, static, and distressing beeps. Farzana considered asking them to turn off the radio, to create a calmer atmosphere for the young women, who were clearly upset, but she second-guessed herself. *They must need to have it on. It doesn't make sense to keep it on if they don't need it.*

Sitting directly across from Farah was the pale female officer, whose expression caused Farzana's stomach to churn. The officer brandished her pen and notebook with extraneous effort, causing hostile creases to form around her mouth. When the radio crackled again, clipped speech that was indiscernible to Farzana, the officer elbowed her partner and they snickered, sharing an inside joke.

Still smiling to himself, the ruddy-faced male officer removed his peaked cap, revealing matted hair and a band of reddened skin along his forehead. He flipped through his notebook unhurriedly, stopping to massage the back of his neck and crack his knuckles.

After a long and uncomfortable silence, during which neither officer acknowledged the three women, the female officer leaned forward and addressed Farah offhandedly, "So, what happened?"

Farah continued to look down into her lap, and Farzana saw tears trickling off her nose and onto her dirt-streaked pants. While the police radio crackled with garbled voices and piercing beeps, Farzana took hold of Farah's hand and squeezed it for reassurance.

In Farsi, she said, "Farah, it's important that you tell them what happened."

Farzana felt the officers' gaze upon her as she spoke in Farsi. She realized that her speaking a language which they didn't understand would incite their animosity. Like her friends and relations, she grasped that multiculturalism was a fashionable concept with limited practical application. Canadians who spoke a language other than English and French were suspect, especially by shopkeepers and government employees, whose eyes narrowed with distrust. Still, Farzana refused to deny her sister the support and privacy she deserved. She would endure the officers' accusing glares.

In a quivering voice, Farah responded, "*Nametoon-am.* I can't."

Farzana urged, "*Toh bayade.* You must."

The female officer shifted in her seat and began a side conversation with her partner about a weekend barbeque. Farzana was losing patience with the two constables, and when the radio crackled and beeped again, she snapped at them, "Can you please turn off the radio?"

The officers exchanged amused glances before the male officer shook his head unapologetically, "We have to keep in on, in case of an emergency, you understand.

Farzana didn't have a chance to question or dispute his statement. The female officer leaned in to bridge the distance between her and Farah, and said, "If you want our help, then you have to talk. Otherwise, there're other people who need us."

She leaned back with an air of satisfaction, having delivered her ultimatum, and she flipped her notebook closed, content to leave without Farah's report. Farzana stared at the police officer incredulously, unable to fathom the insensitivity toward her sister, the victim of a crime. Under other circumstances, Farzana could rationalize such contempt. Had Farah been behaving recklessly, ignoring the years of parental and sisterly advice to avoid dangerous situations, then Farzana might understand their attitude, their lack of sympathy. *She wasn't asking for it! It's not like she was wearing a miniskirt and walking a dark alley.*

While Farzana chewed her inner cheek to avoid an angry outburst, Farah ignored the officer and pleaded to Taari, "Tell them, please."

Taari nodded in agreement. She sat upright and prepared herself, looking first to Farzana and then to the female officer.

"Can I?" Taari asked of the officer.

"Sure," answered the officer with a shrug, and then to Farah, "but you'll have to give your statement next."

For the next few minutes, Taari described the scene she had witnessed an hour earlier, pausing whenever the radio chatter drowned out her voice and dutifully answering the officers' pointed questions about time and place. Her account of a man attacking Farah and dragging her off into the shadows horrified Farzana to such an extent that she lost awareness of the disinterested police officers and her distressed sister. It could have been the script for a run-of-the-mill thriller, a film in which the audience expects the worst fate for the woman because that's what happens in movies to lone women. Instead, Taari had saved her sister, prevented greater harm, and possibly her disappearance and death.

Farzana's eyes darted between Taari, Farah, and the officers, who were recording the testimony. She wanted acknowledgement of the young woman's bravery, her courage to run into harm's way to save another person's life. It was obvious that the incident had traumatized both young women but they were alive and present, and Farzana was dearly grateful for Taari's altruism.

Without acknowledging the terrifying nature of the account, the female officer shifted her cold gaze to Farah, "Your turn."

"Hm ... um, alright," said Farah in a weak voice.

"What happened when he took you ..." The female officer stopped to listen to the radio chatter, and then exchanged entertained glances with her partner before she finished her sentence, "took you to the side of the building?"

Farah's eyes were downcast and her lips disappeared into her mouth in a gesture Farzana recognized as shame. With one hand, she squeezed Farah's knee, and with the other, she rubbed her shoulder. For fear of talking over her sister, Farzana didn't dare utter any words of encouragement, knowing that Farah wouldn't be able to repeat herself with all the shame that weighed on her.

"Hm ... um, he pressed me against the ground. Um ... he was on my back, with his knees, I think," whispered Farah, her eyes darting about the floor, avoiding everyone's gaze.

Tears rolled down her cheeks but her expression grew severe, her brows pulled in and her lips pursed. Farzana wondered if she was in physical pain from the attack, whether they should visit the hospital.

"What'd he do next?" asked the female officer, not bothering to look up from her notebook.

"Uh, he pushed my face down ... and, um, then he was gone," Farah said, wiping her eyes with her scuffed shirt sleeve.

Farzana wanted to demand an end to the torturous questioning, but her inner guide, her mother's voice, a woman whom Farzana knew to trust law enforcement implicitly, insisted that Farah provide as much detail as possible in order to assist the police in their investigation, even if it was hard to recall or it hurt to remember. *What am I going to tell Mama and Baba? This is going to kill them.*

"Did you see which direction he went?" the female officer asked in an accusing tone.

"Uh ... no. I didn't see. I didn't have my eyes open," Farah said, her voice increasingly agitated.

"Huh," remarked the male officer, shaking his head while he noted the detail.

Farzana recognized that Farah was reaching her limit for answering questions. The shadow of brooding in Farah's eyes and the hint of irritation in her speech signalled an imminent change in her disposition, and she would soon erupt in anger or dissolve into indifference.

The female officer leaned back and asked flatly, "Do you know this guy?"

"No, of course not," Farzana snapped. "She doesn't know this monster."

Briefly, both officers glared at Farzana, and then they returned to staring at the top of Farah's head. To Farzana's surprise, her sister answered, "I think, maybe."

For the next few minutes, Farzana watched in dismay as Farah answered a series of questions about the man, provoked by her admission that he might be an acquaintance of hers, someone she met at Taari's house. Farah named and described the man, Charles, as well as his metallic blue car. She recounted his driving her home on Saturday night, then seeing him the previous day in the parking lot near the scene of the attack, as well as possibly spotting him at the end of the driveway of her apartment building on Sunday. Farzana listened, completely absorbed by the retelling, and she attempted to integrate this information into the day's events. *There's a psychopath after Farah. He's after Farah.*

When she had first imagined that this was a random attack on a lone woman walking through a deserted area, it was less frightening than the possibility that it was a targeted attack on her sister by a man who had been stalking her for days.

"Do you have any contact information for this man?" the male officer asked plainly, flipping another page in his notebook.

Farah shook her head.

"Do you know him?" Farzana interjected, directing her question at Taari. "He was at your house, right?"

Taari shook her head, opening her mouth to speak but saying nothing.

"He was at your house," Farzana said forcefully, "and you don't know him?"

"There were a lot of people there," Taari explained. "I'd never met him before."

Farah snapped at Farzana, "She doesn't know him. He was just some guy at the party."

Desperate for information, Farzana insisted, "Someone must have invited him to the party. Someone must know who he is."

Seemingly bored by the conversation, the male officer rolled back his shoulders and concluded, "Well, it's not much to go on. Sounds like the guy got carried away. Thought you were interested in him and took it too far. You're okay now. Just be smart about how you get around."

He placed his cap back on his head and motioned to his partner to head out.

Farzana's eyes were bulging out of her head as she watched the officers prepare to leave. Nothing made sense: not the fact that Farah knew the attacker and Taari didn't, not the officers' disinterest in the attack, and not their conclusion that nothing would come of the police report.

"What're you gonna do next? You're gonna find him, right?" Farzana demanded, standing up to face the officers.

"Not much to do. I mean, the guy is gone," the male officer answered, adjusting his Kevlar vest. With a nod in Farah's direction, he added, "She didn't see where he went, and all we have is a first name. It'll blow over in a few days."

Farzana followed the officers as they walked away from the sitting area, "What does that mean? How is this going to blow over? This psychopath is obviously after her."

"Look, she's fine now," the female officer said loudly over the radio chatter. "If anything happens, or if you get more information, call us." She thrust her business card at Farzana.

Without another word, the officers walked out of the dean's office, leaving Farzana befuddled in the centre of the room, grasping the card. Through the open door, she heard their small talk with the dean and his receptionist, a polite conversation undisturbed by the police radio, which they had courteously turned off for their chat. Then, they were gone, and only the radio could be heard as the beeps echoed through the empty hallways of the Humanities Building.

Farzana looked back at Farah and Taari, who remained sitting dejectedly. She thought to run after the officers and demand more of them, but she couldn't imagine what she might say. They didn't seem concerned or compelled to do more, and Farzana suspected that her personage didn't hold sway with them. What might her mother do? How might she manage the obstinacy which kept the officers from seeing Farah as a person in peril? What tactics had she forgotten to teach Farzana about handling bigotry? Because she was sure that's what it was. The only lessons that came to mind informed her to be realistic in her pursuits, conserve her energy for viable aims, and remain aware of invisible boundaries.

The open door of the dean's office might as well have been bricked up because she didn't intend to waste her efforts running down the hall after those officers. They didn't see Farah as a person in need of help, and Farzana wasn't interested in trying to change their opinions. Instead, she would attend to Farah and provide the necessary care and compassion.

Without asking for permission from the dean, Farzana strode to the mahogany desk and lifted the receiver. She called the car wash and waited on hold for her father to take the line.

"Farzana? *Khoob-e?* Are you okay?" Her father asked over the din of the water jets.

"*Bale*, yes. Um, I need a ride. Right now," Farzana said, twisting the phone cord nervously.

Without missing a beat, he replied, "*Hatman*, of course. Where are you?"

"Campus, the Humanities Building," Farzana answered, her eyes squeezed shut, praying that her father wouldn't probe further.

"Campus," he repeated to himself. "I'm leaving now."

"*Merci*, thank you. We'll be in the parking lot."

"Yes," he paused. "Is Farah okay?"

"Yes," she replied assuredly.

After Farzana replaced the receiver, she slumped in the dean's leather office chair, exhausted by the effort of being bold and brave.

Maiheen arrived home from work at the usual time, and she set about completing her chores at breakneck speed. They were minor tasks, like vacuuming, scrubbing the bathrooms, and cooking dinner, which Maiheen planned to finish before anyone else arrived home. She wanted to dedicate an hour to focus on more pressing matters, namely preparing a convincing argument about her decision to become a mortgage broker, to present to Mustafa.

Once her second shift was complete, she settled in at the dining table with a pot of tea, a legal pad, and a reliable pen. In Farsi, she titled the page *Benefits to Mustafa* and inked her first bullet point in the right margin. Her plan was to list every potential improvement to Mustafa's quality of life as a result of her pursing a new career. Maiheen herself wasn't convinced that there were any payoffs that would appeal to Mustafa, any outcomes that he would consider improvements, but she pressed on, if only to convince herself that a positive change in her life was of benefit to her family.

Okay, so first, what's most important to Mustafa? This question was easy to answer. Being a good father to Farzana and Farah was the most important part of Mustafa's life and central to his identity. He had high expectations of himself in this respect, wanting to protect and provide for his daughters even when they discouraged his pampering or parenting.

Since their move to Canada and their subsequent loss of income, his anxiety about the girls had flared up, and it had become customary for Mustafa to fret about the cost of living and school expenses, keeping Maiheen awake late into the night. He described his worst nightmare, losing his ability to earn an income, and the tragic fallout, Maiheen forced to work long hours to pay for household expenses and being absent from home, and Farzana setting aside her career to work the same long hours to pay for Farah's tuition.

Maiheen wrote her first point: a professional career as a mortgage broker and the increased earning power could provide the safety net that would cushion them financially in the event of a tragedy. Its strength and relevance energized her, and for another half-hour, she wrote about the necessity to save money to purchase a permanent home for the girls, one they would inherit, and to save for retirement so the girls didn't spend their earnings on their parents. There was a point about her need to perform less physically grueling work, but she reconsidered mentioning her ailments for fear that it might cause Mustafa to feel guilty about his wife working in pain.

It also occurred to her that she could mention her mental health, the potential for her to feel happier, more satisfied by her work and less depressed by the lack of stimulation. She wrote a few lines but then became self-conscious about her psychological and intellectual needs, which she hadn't discussed with anyone. What would Mustafa think about her despondency over the lack of challenge in her daily work? Would he consider her spoiled or ungrateful for their easy life, unable to appreciate its worth? *Mustafa has no interest in complicating life with more challenges. He's happy with things as they are.*

With that in mind, she scratched out the last item on her list, the note about the positive impact of a fulfilling career on her mood and her relationship with him and their daughters. Just then the apartment door opened, and she scrambled to tuck away her notepad into a nearby newspaper basket.

She heard Mustafa say, "Take her to bed."

Immediately, Maiheen bristled with apprehension at his unexpected arrival and the severity of his tone. The thoughts that had occupied her up to that point fell to the wayside, and she rushed through the kitchen and intercepted him in the front hall. There she encountered a tableau she would never forget. Standing shoulder to shoulder, her husband and daughters wore downcast expressions, looking defeated and at a loss. Confused by their sudden appearance and eerie silence, it took Maiheen another moment to notice Farah's muddied sweater, the abrasions on her cheek, and the bandage on her lower lip.

"Dear god! What's happened?" she exclaimed and hastened to her daughter to examine her wounds.

Gently, Maiheen lifted Farah's chin with her forefinger and their eyes met. Tears welled in Farah's eyes, and soon she was wrapped in her mother's embrace and sobbing into her blouse. Maiheen grasped her youngest with all her strength and stroked her back, soothing her with shushing sounds.

Over Farah's shoulder, she looked at Mustafa and Farzana with a demanding gaze. She wanted answers, immediately, and she willed them to speak with her glare.

In response, Mustafa laid down Farah's backpack, which he had held under his arm, and then quietly excused himself to wash up. Farzana slumped on the bench in the front hall and held her head in her hands. Maiheen stared about her, trying to find her bearings, and decided to guide Farah to bed herself.

Mother and daughter walked together slowly to Farah's bedroom. With Farah seated on the bed, Maiheen removed her shoes and socks, noting that one sock was muddy and grass-stained. She asked Farah to lift her arms so as to remove the muddied sweater, and Maiheen suppressed a gasp when she caught sight of a hand-shaped bruise on her daughter's bicep.

As an excuse to examine Farah's body more closely, Maiheen procured pajamas and asked for permission to change her into sleep clothes. Farah conceded with a subdued nod, her eyelids drooping and her jaw slack. Maiheen's cursory examination of her daughter's body caused her to choke up with tears as she found one bruise after another along her torso.

She wanted to ask questions, a dozen occurring to her with each passing minute, but it was obvious that Farah was in no condition to answer. Instead, Maiheen tucked Farah into bed and curled up beside her, stroking her hair and kissing her forehead until her daughter's weeping subsided and she was asleep.

Shortly thereafter, Maiheen rejoined Mustafa and Farzana. Her husband sat at the head of the dining room table staring into a low-ball glass of amber liquid, and her daughter was tucked into a corner of the couch, a throw blanket covering her folded legs, and though her eyes were closed, it was evident that she was awake.

Maiheen didn't know where to sit, whether at the table facing Mustafa or on the couch next to Farzana. Both of them seemed reluctant, or unable, to discuss the matter, retreating as they were into their inner worlds. So, Maiheen stood in the centre of the living room, made herself visible to both of them, and requested an explanation.

"What happened? Was she in an accident? Does she need to go to the hospital?" she asked with the authority of a concerned mother.

First, there was silence. Mustafa didn't even raise his eyes to meet hers. Then, Farzana stirred in place and gazed up at her, a plaintive look that Maiheen had never before observed.

"We took her to the campus health centre. A nurse examined her. No concussion. Nothing's broken, only bruises and the cut on her lip," Farzana explained, glancing in vain at her father for corroboration.

"She's covered in bruises. Her back is purple. What happened? Was there an accident?" Maiheen insisted, though she realized from the hand-shaped bruise on Farah's arm that it was unlikely that this was an accident.

Farzana offered the same pitiful look and again glanced at her father, who shielded his eyes with one hand. When her husband didn't acknowledge the question, her daughter answered.

"She was attacked at school," Farzana said with a sharp intake of breath, as if she were mustering the effort to continue.

Suddenly, Maiheen found herself sitting on the coffee table, consumed by this bizarre information.

"Who attacked her? Why? When?" Maiheen asked with rapid-fire delivery, and then turned to her husband. "Mustafa, what is this about?"

Mustafa lowered his arm, and Maiheen beheld his anguished

face. He raised his eyes to meet hers but he only shook his head in response to her question. A moment passed, and then his hand returned to grip the bridge of his nose, and his eyes closed again, unable to take in the present moment.

Maiheen leaned forward, locking eyes with Farzana, and instructed her, "Start from the beginning."

Without interrupting her eldest, Maiheen listened to Farzana's description of the attack on campus, the heroism of Farah's friend, the assistance of the dean's office, the meeting with the police, and the possibility that the attacker is known to Farah, someone who had been following her for days.

After Farzana concluded, Maiheen asked one question, "*Azzi-atesh kaard?* Did he abuse her?"

Farzana shook her head, answering the euphemistic question about whether Farah had been raped.

Then, Maiheen joined her family in quiet contemplation as more questions piled up in her mind, question which neither Farzana nor Mustafa could answer.

☽

Mustafa was no longer gripped by the shock and fear that had initially overwhelmed him when he met his daughters at the dean's office. Sitting at the head of the table, he was nursing the same drink he had poured two hours earlier upon their arrival home. Maiheen flitted in and out of the rooms, checking on Farah, who continued to sleep, then on Farzana, who stared absent-mindedly, and briefly resting a hand on his shoulder before busying herself in the kitchen again.

The distress he had felt hours earlier regarding Farah's physical well-being had dissipated after the nurse's examination at the campus health centre. The half-hour during the examination, while he paced the hallway, Mustafa had been completely absorbed by his care and concern for Farah's physical well-being. When the nurse informed him that his daughter had suffered minor cuts and bruises, and Farzana confirmed that Farah had not been raped, Mustafa cried with relief.

At the same time, his emotions and thoughts changed course, switching tracks from the initial fear and anxiety centred on Farah's well-being to the subsequent indignation and incredulity of how such an event could have transpired. It was anger and disillusionment that pinned him to his seat at the dining table, causing his jaw to clench and keeping him from answering Maiheen's questions or Farzana's pleading looks. He feared that were he to open his mouth, he might release the howling wrath within him. *Stupid girl. Stupid, stupid girl.*

Mustafa's questions piled on top of one another like a heap of rotting trash, the stench of which penetrated every corner of his mind. How had his twenty-year-old daughter become involved with a middle-aged man? When had she started drinking this much? When had she begun to take rides from strangers, men whose last names she didn't know? *Does she have a death wish? Stupid girl.*

Out of fear of whipping the glass of scotch across the room, he released his hold and flexed his fingers. It seemed that he would remain seated in his chair eternally. His mind and body were charged; surely any action or speech on his part would produce bolts of rage, and he refused to be that man. He was not the man from his nightmare, the brutal savage who inflicted pain on his loved ones to lessen his own suffering. No, Mustafa planned to remain still and silent until he could think clearly, objectively.

Through the slits between his fingers, he watched Maiheen set the dinner table places for Farzana and him. Then she headed to the kitchen where she filled two plates of food, roasted chicken and rice, and returned to place them on the table.

When she finished setting the table, Maiheen arrived by his side. She put a hand on his shoulder, as she had several times during the previous two hours, and squeezed the taunt muscles. This time, she remained at his side, and her right hand travelled down his back and firmly rubbed the body she knew so well.

"*Azziz-am, lotfan bokhor.* My dear, please eat," she urged, nudging the plate towards him.

Then, she kissed the top of his head and walked over to Farzana, taking their daughter's hand and leading her to the table.

Standing in the kitchen doorway, Maiheen insisted, "*Lotfan, bokhoreed.* Please, eat."

Then, she returned to the counter, and Mustafa observed her preparing chicken soup, for Farah he presumed. Her own plate of chicken and rice sat alongside the cutting board and spices, and in between cooking tasks, Maiheen fed herself spoonfuls.

Was he hungry? He couldn't distinguish emotions from sensations. His psyche was inflamed and he was preoccupied with controlling his body, not tending to its needs. When Mustafa noticed that Farzana was sitting with her hands in her lap, looking devastated, he collected himself, sat upright, pulled in his chair, and nodded in her direction, indicating that she should begin her meal. She nodded in response and averted her gaze to the plate of food before her, indifferently consuming a spoonful.

For the sake of pretence, to lessen the anxiety that weighed on his eldest, he fed himself. At first, he was surprised at his ability to swallow past the rock that had wedged itself in his throat. From then, Mustafa chewed mechanically and focused on Farzana, his smart and beautiful daughter. A young woman who possessed every quality he had hoped for her. Farzana, the daughter who persevered through the difficult formative years after settling in a foreign country, who excelled academically despite the language barrier, and who did it all without complaint or quarrel. She was the ideal role model for her younger sister, a reliable helping hand to her mother, and a point of pride for her father. *What happened to Farah? Is her belligerence an attempt to distinguish herself from her sister? Is she jealous of Farzana's success? Why is she sabotaging her own future, putting herself in danger? Doesn't she realize that just one bad choice has the power to destroy her chance at a happy life?*

Mustafa's contempt turned inward, and he questioned his own part in Farah's failings. He shouldn't have distanced himself from her when she became difficult to manage. He should have doubled down on his efforts to moderate her behaviour. They should have constrained her financially, refused to pay for the offensive clothes and music, and limited her participation to the types of activities that promote good manners and a strong work ethic. They should never have allowed her to date, to attend rock concerts, or to hang out with the kids at the mall all weekend. *She doesn't respect anyone, and she doesn't realize how the world works. She nearly died because she didn't know to call home when she needed a ride. Stupid girl.*

There was more regret in his heart than he could have imagined possible. He was certain that he had failed as a father. After all, she was the child and he was her parent. It was his responsibility to prepare Farah for life's challenges, and he had neglected her by yielding to the girl's will and complaining about her choices from the sidelines. She needed a strong parental figure to shape her, to mould her into a competent woman, someone who understood risk and perceived threats. Someone who didn't become a target.

Unwittingly, Mustafa had finished his meal. He wiped the corners of his lips, drank the scotch in one mouthful, and excused himself for the night.

☽

Farah awoke to a crippling headache that originated in the burning muscles of her upper back and up through her neck, stiff and sore. The movement of turning in bed, to check the alarm clock on the night stand, caused her to wince in pain. In seconds, her mother was at her side, rubbing her head and whispering soothingly, "It's okay. I'm here. What do you need?"

"My head, it hurts," Farah said, her eyes squeezed tight and tears streaming from the corners into her hairline.

"I'll get a pain reliever. Just a second," her mother said, and Farah heard her leave the bedroom.

Moments later, she returned and assisted Farah into an upright position. The blinds were drawn, the room was dimly lit, and Farah saw a makeshift bed on her floor. Her mother handed her a tablet and a cup of water, and Farah accepted both with a nod.

"I have some cream to help with the pain," her mother offered, holding a familiar tube of topical analgesic from the medicine cabinet. "Can I put some on your back?"

"Hm," Farah managed, along with a slight nod, finding it difficult to receive kindness in spite of her obvious need for care and affection.

Her mother sat in bed directly behind her, lifted her pajama shirt, and applied the cool ointment to Farah's skin with the slightest pressure. Farah caught sight of the time, nearly midnight, and she wondered what had happened since they arrived home. Evidently, her mother had been sleeping on the floor of her bedroom, but where was her father? Had Farzana returned to her apartment? Was there any more information about Charles? What did her mother know?

"Would you like some soup?" Her mother asked quietly, lowering Farah's shirt and kissing the nape of her neck. "You must be hungry."

Hungry? Just as the question occurred to her, Farah's stomach rumbled, and she realized that she was famished. The last time she ate was thirteen hours earlier, a chocolate bar and a bag of potato chips she had inhaled on her way into her noontime labour economics exam.

Without Farah answering the question, her mother perceived

her need. She rose and held out a hand for Farah to join her. Farah pivoted with less pain than before and slipped her legs over the side of the bed. One hand in her mother's, they walked out into the unlit hallway. Farah glanced leftwards into the darkened living room and noticed Farzana sleeping on the full length couch.

She allowed her mother to lead her rightwards, farther along the hall. At the end of the hallway, the door to her parents' bedroom was ajar and Farah could hear her father snoring rhythmically. Having arrived at the bathroom, her mother turned on the nightlight above the sink, which was gentler and more forgiving than the fixture overhead.

Whispering in Farah's ear, her mother said, "Go on. Meet me in the kitchen afterwards."

Her mother stepped aside to allow Farah to enter the bathroom but the young woman hesitated. Farah feared seeing her reflection and the physical reminders of the attack. Already, she had seen too much of her face in the bathroom mirror on campus, having caught a glance as Taari washed the dirt and debris from her wounds.

The nurse at the health centre, who had informed her that the half-inch cut on her lip didn't need stitches, had applied an adhesive bandage to her lip and antibiotic ointment to the abrasions on the right side of her face. Having explored her lower lip with the tip of tongue and touched the abrasions with her fingertips, Farah felt uncomfortably aware of her appearance.

"Okay," her mother replied to Farah's inner thoughts.

She leaned back into the bathroom and shut off the nightlight, creating a dark space. Farah peered into the darkness, and then nodded in agreement to the adjustment.

"You're doing great, sweetheart," her mother whispered before she disappeared down the hall.

A few minutes later, Farah joined her mother in the kitchen. The space was lit by the warm light above the stove, and her mother was quietly warming soup in a small saucepan. On the counter, there was a plate she had prepared with apple slices and small clusters of red grapes, as well as colourful Italian cookies from Farzana's Mother's Day present. Pulled up to the counter was the bar stool that her mother kept in the corner and used for breaks from standing.

Her mother patted the bar stool and said, "Come sit. Eat this first while I heat the soup."

Farah considered her usual reply, to insist that her mother simply use the microwave and finish the task, instead of making a production out of an uncomplicated process. However Farah had felt in the past about her mother's habits, presently she was filled with gratitude for the warm atmosphere and the thoughtful presentation.

While Farah nibbled at the fruit and cookies, her mother served two mugs of chicken soup, the smaller one for herself. They drank silently in the glow of the light, her mother leaning against the counter with one hand resting on Farah's thigh. She ate everything that her mother offered, including a final course of warmed pita smothered in butter, drizzled with honey, and rolled into edible scrolls.

The sensation of being satiated, combined with medicated relief from the pain of her aching muscles, helped to reduce the anxiety and obsessiveness that had clouded Farah's perceptions since the attack. Her mother's tending and nurturing discouraged Farah from regurgitating the disturbing images and conversations from the day. She was safe at home, and her mother would care for her. It was possible to exist in the present, even if only for a moment.

"Mama," Farah started, speaking for the first time since she awoke. "I ... uh, there's something ..."

Her mother turned to Farah and waited patiently, her hand rubbing Farah's thigh.

"I want to tell you ... um, I want you to know that I ... um, I didn't say I liked him, the guy," Farah choked on her words, hot tears streaking her cheeks.

"Of course not, I know," her mother said assuredly. "Of course, not."

Farah swallowed, wiped her cheeks, and continued, "Really, Mama, I didn't. I told him I didn't want to date anyone ... and, and ..." Farah's voice quivered but she persisted, "and, when he was at school, I, I walked away from him, Mama. I, I didn't act interested at all."

"Of course not, I know, darling," her mother repeated, brushing away Farah's tears before wiping away her own. "Farah-*jaan*, everything is going to be okay. See, you're home now. You're going to be fine."

Farah shook her head in frustration, and insisted, "No, no, no. Mama, you have to believe me. Mama, I, I didn't act like, like, like ... I wasn't, like, doing anything with him. I don't know him. I swear, Mama."

Her mother took Farah's face in both her hands and looked directly into her eyes as she said, "Okay, I believe you, Farah. I believe you."

Farah trembled with emotion and her mother embraced her tightly. She sobbed heavily into her mother's shoulder until her tears stopped and her tremors quelled. Farah imagined that she would feel relieved upon hearing her mother's words, her testament of belief, but anxiety and doubt reigned in her psyche, denying her the privilege of accepting others at their word.

"Let's go back to your room," her mother suggested, offering her hand.

With downcast eyes, Farah nodded and returned to her bedroom with her mother. She lay in bed and allowed her mother to tuck her in. When it seemed that her mother was about to leave, Farah made a pitiful sound.

"I'll be right back," her mother assured her.

Farah heard her mother walk to her parents' bedroom. The baritone voice of her father travelled the length of the hall, and Farah heard him ask about her. Her mother's voice was too soft to hear, and a few moments later, her mother appeared at her side. They cuddled and Farah cried silently, eventually falling asleep to her mother's touch.

6

Wednesday, May 12, 1993

On Wednesday morning, Farzana stirred at six, tangled among bedsheets on her parents' couch. It was the sound of her father rustling in the kitchen that woke her. She could hear him putting together his takeaway lunch, a task typically performed by her mother.

She sat up and straightened the long cotton nightgown she had borrowed from her mother. Her back was cramped from the plush cushions which offered little support, so she stretched her limbs to regain dexterity.

Aside from the sound of kitchen cupboards and drawers closing, the apartment was quiet. The sunrise lent its light to the living room but the other spaces remained in shadow. She tidied the bedsheets and tucked them neatly under the pillow, and then joined her father in the unlit kitchen.

"*Sobe-bekhair*, good morning, Baba," Farzana whispered from the doorway.

"Oh, *bebakhsheed, azziz-am.* My apologies, my dear," her father whispered too. He walked over and kissed her forehead. "I didn't mean to wake you. I was just ..."

Her father shrugged and nodded at the odd assortment of partially filled plastic containers and a stack of mismatched lids.

Farzana had never known her father to feel embarrassed about his shortcomings. In fact, he readily admitted to his weaknesses and requested help from someone more proficient. It wasn't that her father was unselfconscious or especially humble. Instead, her father treated his inability to perform a task as evidence that the task wasn't suited to him, that it was work intended for someone else, usually a woman. Her father was willing to perform what he considered women's work as long as he wasn't expected to perform it well or regularly.

"Would you like me to finish that?" Farzana asked.

"Oh, no, that's fine. I'm almost done," her father answered as he pushed a roasted chicken thigh into a container that was too small.

"I'd like to," insisted Farzana, in the doting tone she had adopted from her mother.

Her father smiled and accepted her help. While Farzana repackaged the chicken in a larger container with rice, he washed his hands in the sink. From underneath the sink, he procured a plastic shopping bag and offered it to Farzana. She placed the container, along with several pieces of fruit, in the plastic bag and put the bag by the front door, so he wouldn't forget it on the way out.

Back in the kitchen, her father asked, "Can I make you some breakfast? Maybe some eggs?"

Farzana smiled and thanked him, but refused his offer, "No, thank you. I was thinking of catching a ride with you downtown. Would that be okay?"

"*Hatman*, of course," he said, replacing the dish towel on the handle of the oven door. "I thought you might stay, though."

"I will come back later," Farzana assured him, "but I should go home and change, and I'm supposed to be at work today."

The truth was that she needed to be away from her family, for even a short period of time. She wanted to be present for Farah and to help her parents as they sorted out the next steps, but she felt at a loss while she was at their apartment. There wasn't anything for her to do other than watch television and perform housekeeping, and she was desperate for a cigarette and some time to journal her thoughts. She needed space to herself to be herself, not the reliable older sister or the dutiful daughter.

"*Hatman*, sure. We can go as soon as you're ready," her father said.

"Go? Where?" Farzana's mother asked softly as she stepped into the doorway, wearing an identical cotton nightgown.

"*Sobe-bekhair*, good morning," her father said, gathering her mother in his arms and gently kissing her.

In a matter-of-fact tone, he continued, "I am driving Farzana to work, and I'll pick her up on my way back home later in the afternoon. I'll call you around lunchtime. Alright?"

First, her mother looked back and forth between the two of them, and then she examined the empty containers on the counter, and the pristine dining table.

"What about breakfast? You can't go to work without breakfast," her mother objected. "Let me put together some scrambled egg sandwiches you can eat on your way."

Her mother was already at the fridge, filling her arms with the butter dish, a carton of eggs, and a bag of pita bread. When her father looked at Farzana, she shrugged her approval. There was no point arguing with her mother when it concerned food.

While her mother prepared the egg sandwiches, as well as an oversized takeaway lunch for Farzana, her father gathered his belongings, and Farzana dressed in the bathroom. She heard her parents discuss their agenda for the day, her mother taking time off and her father leaving work early. *It's crazy how well they're handling this. I'm so glad they're not freaking out.*

By seven o'clock, father and daughter were in the family car, waiting for the automatic doors of the underground parking garage to rise.

Farzana recalled Farah's description of Charles's car, a metallic blue sedan, and she readied herself to write down the licence plate number of every blue car they passed. *Is it possible that Charles will return to the apartment? Is he still stalking Farah? How long will this continue? To what end?*

The questions that occurred to her were as frightening as the events of the previous day. It was possible that what had already happened, the attack on Farah, was easier to address and digest than the uncharted future. Previously, Farzana had walked the world in a stupor of sorts, taking for granted her ability to ignore strangers and dismiss peculiar behaviour. Now, people seemed sinister and nothing was a coincidence. Farzana was gripped by the knowledge that one of those people had attacked her sister, failed in his attempt, and might return to complete his objectives, whatever they may be.

"What's that?" Her father asked, glancing at the notebook on Farzana's lap.

Farzana scribbled the plate number of another blue car, a total of five within one block of their apartment.

"The blue cars, that's what he drives. I'm taking down their plates," Farzana said quietly, feeling self-conscious but continuing to scan the neighbourhood.

Her father didn't respond right away, but soon asked, "Did you get that one?"

Farzana turned to the direction he was looking, over his left shoulder. A vacant blue car was parked on the street, and Farzana squinted to better read the plate. She added the information to her list.

"*Merci*, thanks, Baba," Farzana said.

She appreciated his support because it seemed like a longshot that her jotting down plate numbers would be helpful to the investigation. Yet, it felt good to keep her mind and her hands busy, and she suspected that her father felt similarly.

They sat in silence for the rest of the trip, and following a half-hour drive through morning traffic, he double parked in front of her apartment. They arranged to meet later for the ride back to Farah and her mother.

"Farzana, be safe," he said with a final embrace.

A few minutes later, Farzana entered her apartment and heard Soreyah in the shower. She sighed with relief at the knowledge that for a few hours she would exist in her own world, according to her own terms.

She decided to call in sick and stay home to recuperate. The decision brought even more relief, and Farzana considered how best to spend the following hours before her return to Farah and her parents. Possibly finish reading *Mrs. Dalloway*, tidy the apartment, or watch a movie. *Too bad Soreyah is going to work.*

By the front closet, she took off her shoes and untucked her shirt from her skirt. When she stepped on a letter-sized white envelope, she thought it was a piece of mail that their landlord had slid under the door. Sometimes, their mail ended up delivered to the restaurant on the ground floor. She turned it over to read the sender's information, and found that it was addressed to her, in Amir's handwriting. *A second letter, when I haven't read the first.*

Whether to take her mind off of Farah's attack or to satisfy her curiosity, Farzana conceded to reading Amir's first letter. She shut herself in her room, lit a cigarette, and procured the letter she had been carrying around for two days.

☽

In his usual spot, the alleyway behind the car wash, Mustafa parked his car and popped open the trunk. He sat on the ledge of the trunk to slip on his clean coveralls and sneakers, and then grabbed his bagged lunch from the back seat.

Mustafa buzzed for Candice to come open the locked rear entrance. It was another quarter-hour before the start of business hours, when the back doors were opened. A minute later, Candice arrived at the door, peeking through the plexiglass window before opening it to Mustafa. They greeted each other cordially, with respect but not overly friendly.

Candice and Mustafa had been working together for years. They were aware of each other's pet peeves and idiosyncrasies, and they shared a similar work ethic and attentiveness to service, but they didn't involve themselves in the other's home life.

Mustafa assumed Candice didn't discuss her family life because she was embarrassed by her surly adult children. He didn't discuss his private affairs with Candice because years earlier he had decided that Candice didn't know how to be a good mother. He had met her children on several occasions, when they dropped in at the car wash to borrow money, leave a grandchild for babysitting, or continue a prior argument. So he didn't value her judgement or her opinions, but more than anything, he pitied her.

On the other hand, he also didn't discuss his family life with Afewerk and Hossein. Both of them were younger men with much younger children, and Mustafa didn't trust their ability to put his parenting challenges in perspective. They were men who had control over their children, simply on account of their children being so young and dependent. That was a phase of parenting that Mustafa remembered and lamented. He too had felt powerful and commanding, and he had judged other parents as incompetent and undisciplined because of the inherent challenges they faced in rearing older children.

It occurred to Mustafa that besides Maiheen there was no one to speak to about his anguish over the attack on Farah. Details about the attack and the attacker churned in his mind, evoking anger, frustration, fear, and anxiety. No matter how many times he tried to distract himself from thinking about the attack, he had returned to mulling over a phrase or a scene.

He had hoped to discuss the matter with Maiheen the previous evening but she had remained with Farah all night, a choice that Mustafa supported. The churning continued within, and Mustafa chastised himself for his weak mind.

Not long after Mustafa greeted Candice, Afewerk and Hossein arrived at work. The three men settled on the milk crates to enjoy a customary smoke before the car wash opened its doors. Afewerk had bought coffee from the deli across the street. He passed around the cardboard tray with the four distinctly marked takeout cups, and Hossein took the last cup, an extra sweet and milky coffee, in to Candice.

When Hossein returned, he stood before Mustafa and teased him, "Who peed in your Cheerios?"

"Huh?" Mustafa asked, distracted and rolling his lit cigarette between his fingers.

"It's an idiom," Hossein explained proudly, taking a seat on his milk crate. "I learned it last week in night class. From the movie, *Wall Street*?"

"I never watched it," Mustafa shrugged. To discourage conversation, he stared at the ground between his feet.

Hossein, who sat on the other side of Afewerk and didn't notice Mustafa's retreat, continued, "It means, what's bothering you?"

"Hm," Mustafa replied, sipping his coffee and pulling on the cigarette, his gaze still downcast.

"So, what's bothering you?" Hossein asked pointedly.

Mustafa manoeuvred out of answering the question and asked, "So, night class is good?"

"No pain, no gain!" Hossein joked, elbowing Afewerk. "Get it? That's another idiom. It means ..."

Afewerk interrupted him, "We know what that means. Man, you've been in Canada for five years and ..."

Hossein interjected, "Ten, ten years."

"Okay, ten," Afewerk conceded, exhaling a plume upwards.

"That's even worse. You've been here for ten years and you're still going to English classes? What for? Are you going to write a book?"

They heard Candice chuckle inside the booth, and Hossein teased her through the open door, "Why is that funny?"

Candice looked up from her book innocently and replied, "Sorry, are you talking to me? I was just reading something amusing."

"Uh-huh," Hossein ribbed her before turning back to the other men to say, "Some people believe that learning is a lifelong process."

Afewerk pivoted on his crate to give Hossein the side-eye.

"Man, then, shouldn't you be learning something new? Not the language you already know?" Afewerk retorted.

"This is the plan," Hossein explained patiently. "First, I get my language proficiency certificate, then I get my millwright certificate, and four years later, boom, I get my certificate of qualification."

Afewerk shook his head sorrowfully, and said, "You've been at this forever. It's all talk. Come on, man."

Unfazed, Hossein sipped from his cup and said, "Yes, but this time it's going to happen. Safie is working full-time now that the kids are older, and we can manage on one paycheque."

"You're going to make your wife work so you can play school like the kids," Afewerk accused with a grin.

"Mustafa, help me here. This man doesn't understand," Hossein begged with hands pressed together in prayer. "My wife likes her work. She couldn't wait to go back."

Mustafa wasn't following the thread of the conversation as he was preoccupied by the idea of surveilling his neighbourhood for blue cars. He fantasized about finding the man sitting in his car, possibly parked in the shadows, and pulling him through the open window and ramming his head against the pavement until his face was unrecognizable.

"Whoa! Buddy!" Afewerk exclaimed and jumped to his feet.

The sudden movement startled Mustafa, and he looked up at

Afewerk, who stared back at him. Preoccupied by his violent fantasy, he had clenched his hand and crushed the paper cup, causing coffee to spurt in all directions. A light brown puddle formed around his shoes, and Mustafa cursed his foolishness.

Afewerk knelt before Mustafa, and in a mannerly tone, he asked, "So, who peed in your Cheerios?"

Hossein burst out laughing, but upon seeing the severe expression on Mustafa's face, he stopped abruptly and rose to fetch paper towels from a nearby shelf. He offered a stack to Mustafa and extended a hand to take the broken cup for disposal.

"*Merci*, thank you," Mustafa said, not looking at either man.

"Gentlemen, you're on!" Candice announced the start of the business day.

Mustafa took the opportunity to busy himself. He unlocked the back entrance and the garage doors at both ends of the tunnel, while Afewerk turned on the conveyor system and Hossein tended to the detergents.

A bell sounded, indicating the presence of a customer at the back entrance. Mustafa pressed the wall-mounted button to open the rear garage door, and as he walked to the back to greet the customer, he grabbed the clipboard with the tearaway price sheets. The windowless tunnel of the car wash was flooded with light, and Mustafa's vision was dazzled momentarily. When he stepped outside, within an arm's reach of the glimmering vehicle, he perceived its blue sheen. Mustafa dropped the clipboard as he felt his chest constrict with sudden rage.

☽

Maiheen prepared a vast spread for breakfast, including eggs over-easy, a toasted sesame seed bagel with cream cheese, warmed pita, freshly shelled walnuts, chunks of feta cheese, sour cherry jam, a mug of hot chocolate, and a fruit salad, freshly made. These were Farah's favourite foods for breakfast, though the hot chocolate was a drink she hadn't requested in many years, and truth be told, Maiheen included the fruit salad for its nutritional benefits. Still, Maiheen was pleased with the assortment laid out on the dining table.

Mustafa and Farzana had departed an hour earlier, when Farah was still asleep, and Maiheen had used the time to shower, dress, and prepare the meal. When Farah awoke, Maiheen suggested that she take a warm shower to loosen her tight muscles, and surprisingly, her daughter didn't argue. Briefly, Maiheen wondered whether her subdued disposition was related to the attack and whether it was a temporary or permanent change.

She returned to the kitchen, and pulled her stool to the counter. From a drawer, she collected a pen and notebook, and she made a list of tasks for the day. An unexpected day off work was unusual for Maiheen, and Yasmeen would be surprised, and possibly concerned, to find Maiheen missing from Coffee Express at nine o'clock. So, she made her first task of the day a call to Yasmeen's office. Within a few minutes, the list was ten tasks long, and most of them involved household chores.

Then, Maiheen reconsidered her list. It seemed unfair to leave Farah to entertain herself while Maiheen did chores. Possibly, her daughter might appreciate some pampering, like a manicure or a facial. Maiheen loved to dote on Farzana with such treatments, and they would talk endlessly while she massaged her daughter's calves or applied polish to her buffed nails. But then reality set in, and Maiheen dismissed her plans for a mother-daughter spa day. *Farah is not going to want a pedicure or a head massage. She doesn't even moisturize.*

"Hi," Farah said, entering the kitchen and heading to the fridge.

"Wait, I've made breakfast. It's on the table," Maiheen intervened, gently closing the fridge door and ushering Farah to the dining room.

"I just want some cereal," Farah whined, rising to her tiptoes to examine the cereal boxes above the fridge. "Do we have the crunchy corn ones?"

"I have your favourites," Maiheen insisted, smiling diplomatically.

The expression on Farah's face was as bitter and familiar as the taste of lemon rind. Maiheen realized that no matter the effects of the attack on Farah, it had not extinguished her recalcitrant attitude.

Pursing her lips with resentment and dragging her feet in defiance, Farah followed her mother into the dining room. Maiheen smiled brightly to prompt her youngest to change her disposition and perform the niceties she had been taught. Farah responded with an eye roll and mumbled words of gratitude before slumping in her seat. Maiheen accepted the minor display of resistance as par for the course, though she had hoped for a greater show of appreciation.

Maiheen took her seat at the table, and asked, "*Azziz-am*, my dear, what would you like for lunch? I can make your favourite. Or, something Canadian, maybe? Pizza? Hamburger?"

Farah finished chewing her mouthful, and then replied, "I'll probably get something on campus. Like a hot dog, or something."

Maiheen's face fell as she grasped Farah's meaning. Was her daughter planning on returning to the place where she was attacked just yesterday? Was this a joke? The statement confounded Maiheen, and she considered how to pose her next question without provoking Farah. From experience, she knew that Farah reacted dramatically to criticism and questioning, and she was prone to walking off, possibly out of the apartment, when she became upset.

"Can you tell me more, please?" Maiheen asked sweetly, serving herself a bowl of fruit salad to feign indifference.

"I have an exam at noon, so I can get something from the Student Life Centre right before," Farah answered, forcing a large parcel of pita and egg into her mouth.

Maiheen tried to control her breathing to ease the tension in her chest. Her daughter wanted to attend her exam, and that was understandable. In a way, Maiheen appreciated Farah's studiousness. It was admirable that Farah wanted to follow through with her goals, however ill-conceived was her approach. It was Maiheen's challenge to use subtle reasoning to dissuade Farah from leaving the apartment.

She pierced a grape with her fork and placed it daintily in her mouth. With a smile, she chewed and swallowed, allowing a minute to pass. Then, she offered a plate of feta cheese and walnuts to Farah, who declined. Maiheen understood that any sudden comment or question could spook Farah, precipitating a rock slide of defiance that would halt Maiheen in her tracks.

"What exam is it?" Maiheen asked, continuing to gaze at her plate.

"Principles of microeconomics," Farah said as she slathered a torn piece of pita with sour cherry jam.

"Oh, sounds important," Maiheen commented earnestly. "One of your ... what did you call it? The other ones are ... electives, right? What are the ones you have to take?"

"Requisites. It's a requisite course," Farah said around a mouthful. Then pointing to the steaming mug nearest her place setting, she asked, "Is this hot chocolate?"

"Uh-huh," Maiheen smiled. "I thought you might like it."

Farah rolled her eyes, but only slightly. Then, she picked up the mug, took a sip, and said, "Thanks. It's good."

"So, this is an exam for a required course," Maiheen started. "I see, that is important."

"Yeah," Farah agreed, mumbling through the emptier side of her mouth.

"And, is it taught often? Or, infrequently?" Maiheen asked, intently piercing a chunk of strawberry.

"I know what you're doing," Farah said, glaring at her mother across the table.

Placing the strawberry in her mouth just in time to keep from talking, Maiheen replied, "Hm?"

"You don't want me to go. You want me to miss my exam," Farah stated plainly, no longer chewing or attending to her meal.

"Oh, no. I think it's important that you follow through. I'm proud of you for being so serious about your studies," Maiheen adlibbed, uncertain of where her statements were leading but appreciating their subduing effect on Farah.

Farah frowned but she returned to eating. Speaking through another mouthful, she said, "Okay, 'cause I'm leaving in an hour."

"Alright," Maiheen heard herself say, piercing another grape and chewing it methodically.

There had to be another way to dissuade Farah from leaving the apartment, another option that met her need to perform well academically.

"So, your friend yesterday, what is her name?" Maiheen asked pleasantly.

Farah looked sternly at Maiheen, blinked and swallowed. It broke Maiheen's heart to see the effect on Farah when she mentioned the previous day.

Farah opened her mouth to speak very slowly, "Her name is Taari." Then, she simply stared at Maiheen, waiting for the follow-up.

Maiheen was caught off guard by the intensity of Farah's gaze. She had planned to remind Farah that, according to the conversation overhead by her sister, Taari had missed her exam and the dean had made arrangements for her to complete the exam in the future. Yet, with Farah staring at her in anticipation, Maiheen found it impossible to proceed. Given Taari's bravery and altruism, Farah might feel protective about her and sensitive to any possibility of criticism directed toward her.

"Taari is a wonderful person," Maiheen said, and she felt this was true, even if her comment was intended to de-escalate the tension. "I would like to meet her. I want to thank her myself."

Farah nodded and dropped her gaze, looking assuaged.

"Maybe you can invite her for lunch?" Maiheen asked, recalibrating her tactics upon seeing Farah's softening expression.

Farah nodded again, this time smiling a little. She wiped the corners of her lips, and rose with her plate.

"I can help you clean up," Farah offered. "I have time before I go."

"Yes. *Merci, azziz-am*. Thank you, my dear," Maiheen rose and gathered several plates together.

As mother and daughter worked to clear the dining table, Maiheen took a moment to hug and kiss Farah. Her daughter accepted the gesture warmly and returned a kiss to her mother's cheek.

"Farah-*jaan*," Maiheen began as filled the sink with warm soapy water.

At the counter, Farah was placing the remaining fruit salad, cheese, and bread in plastic containers to store in the fridge. She didn't look up but made a small sound to acknowledge having heard her mother.

"I would like to see campus," Maiheen said, focusing on the dirty dishes.

"Sure," Farah said with a shrug. "It's not going anywhere."

"Okay, well, that's good," Maiheen replied and continued in an easy manner. "I don't usually get time off work, and we usually don't spend time together downtown."

Again, Farah uttered a sound to acknowledge the comment. She was working efficiently to store the containers, but it was difficult to find room among the many other foods in the packed fridge.

"If it's okay with you, I have the day off," Maiheen said, taking a deep breath to control her emotions and assume her desired casual tone, "and I'd rather see campus than do chores."

Behind her, the sounds of Farah packing containers in the

unaccommodating fridge had stopped. Maiheen waited another moment before she turned slightly to smile over her shoulder at her daughter. Farah was standing in front of the opened fridge, holding a jam jar and a bag of pita bread and avoiding her mother's gaze.

"Hm, 'kay" Farah said, and then she stooped to shove both items into the crisper, crushing the bag of grapes.

Maiheen was unhappy about the grapes, but she was overjoyed by Farah's reaction. The eye rolls, the shrugs, the grunts, and the silence were all better than Farah storming out of the apartment. The compromise, to accompany her downtown to her exam, was unexpected and less than ideal, but it was the safest course of action. Maiheen knew that Mustafa wouldn't approve, and most likely, he would consider this compromise to be a failed attempt at controlling Farah and forcing her to submit to her parents' will. Still, it was manageable, and Maiheen could accept the consequences of disappointing Mustafa.

"I'm leaving in a half-hour," Farah stated flatly as she walked out of the kitchen.

"Great! I'll call the cab," Maiheen replied, sucking in her lips to keep from grinning at her own deviousness.

Farah reappeared in the doorway and asked, "A cab?"

Maiheen, who bore an innocent expression and subdued smile, explained, "It's my day off. I'd just rather treat myself."

Farah frowned and replied with a slow nod, "Hm."

When she was alone in the kitchen, Maiheen sighed with relief.

Then, she slipped into the dining room, where her oversized handbag rested on a chair, and she inspected its contents. Between the stash of hard candies and her cosmetics bag was the kitchen knife she carried for protection. Its six-inch blade offered her a modicum of courage, and she would gather more along the way.

Farah's back and neck muscles ached with every movement but they hurt equally when she leaned back in her seat. To ease her pain during the half-hour cab ride to campus, she shifted at various angles as she reviewed her exam notes. While she was confident about her understanding of microeconomics and untroubled about the exam, submersing herself in lecture notes offered several benefits. First, it meant that she didn't have to talk to her mother, who glanced at Farah with a doting smile every couple of minutes. Also, it provided an escape from the recurring thoughts about Charles and the anxiety that began mounting when they left the apartment.

She was determined to ace the last two exams, receive the endorsement of the department head, and secure the scholarship money for next year. The attack wasn't going to keep her from making her dreams come true, even if her dreams panicked her. Every time she thought about her upcoming moving date, in another three months, and living on her own downtown, Farah's heart raced, her breaths shortened, and her stomach knotted.

Moving out was her dream, as was living downtown within walking distance of campus, spending Saturdays at dive cafés, and watching foreign films at revue theaters. Farah had imagined a new life for herself, a vision that had once exhilarated her and caused her to beam upon waking, and she would realize her new life, even if being alone in the world was currently terrifying.

"I'm very proud of you, Farah-*jaan*," whispered her mother, leaning closer.

"Thanks, Mama," Farah said, not taking her eyes off her notes.

Farah was certain that if she looked her mother in the eyes, the woman would recognize the anxiety she felt about being in public. She resented herself for feeling vulnerable and afraid of a second attack. That morning's posturing about attending her exam had produced shooting pains in her stomach. She wouldn't have been able to step onto the sidewalk alone, she realized. How had she imagined boarding a bus, transferring onto a subway, and walking the two blocks to campus?

When her mother requested to come along, Farah nearly cried with gratitude. It was a convenient story on her mother's part, and Farah was glad to accept the pretence without question. Mentally, the attack was affecting her perceptions and reaction, making it difficult to think clearly or respond reasonably, and the last thing Farah wanted was for the attack to diminish her independence and credibility.

If she allowed her parents to set the agenda or influence her decisions, Farah would never regain her independence. She needed to complete her exams this week to have a chance at the scholarship. With the scholarship, she would be able to afford a place without their help. She wouldn't have to worry about her parents deciding that she wasn't safe living alone, and she wouldn't risk the chance to fulfill her dream.

"It's going to be okay," her mother cooed. "I promise. It's going to be okay."

Farah realized she was crying when her tears fell onto the lecture notes. Her mother offered her a tissue, and Farah declined it, preferring to dry her wet cheeks with her sweater sleeve. She needed to shake off her anxiety and focus on the future. *Deep breaths, you!*

Following Farah's directions, the cab driver pulled up to the parking lot of the Athletics Building. There was a quarter-hour left before the exam. Her mother paid the driver and thanked him graciously, in a manner that embarrassed Farah.

"I will come inside," her mother insisted as they approached the opened doors of main entrance.

"Okay," said Farah with a shrug, though she couldn't imagine walking in alone.

From all directions on campus, students were filing in to the building and filling the circular concrete hallway that led to the four gymnasiums at its centre. Farah directed her mother to follow her to one of the posted exam schedules. She learned that her exam was being conducted in Gymnasium C, towards the back of the Athletics Building. This was the same route she had taken yesterday, after completing her exam in Gymnasium A and before exiting through the rear entrance of the building, walking two hundred metres, and being attacked.

"I am here," her mother squeezed her hand.

Farah realized she had stopped in the middle of the hallway and students were flooding past her. Her mother squeezed her hand again, and Farah nodded in acknowledgement. *Deep breaths! Come on!*

They proceeded towards Gymnasium C, following the tide of students, and at its open doors, Farah turned back to her mother.

"I'll be right here," her mother said assuredly. She pointed to an empty bench along the hallway, and added, "I'll be right here the whole time. You're going to do great. Everything is going to be okay."

"Hm," Farah managed and nodded.

She was already crying silently. If she spoke to express her heartfelt thanks, it would probably end in sobs, and she didn't want to attract any attention. Instead, she turned and entered the examination hall.

Farzana lit another cigarette and reclined on her bed after rereading Amir's first letter for the third time. The pages rested on his side of her bed, and she caressed his script with one finger and recalled treasured passages.

What had she expected from him? Had she imagined angry demands, insults, or accusations? Why had she carried his letter about like a martyr burdened with the weight of a boulder? Who did she think he was? Farzana was ashamed of herself for assuming that Amir's intentions were malicious, that he had wanted to hurt her with his words. Obviously, he was a better man than she gave him credit for.

She heard Soreyah emphatically singing U2's "Mysterious Ways," and she smiled at the jumbled lyrics. It felt good to be home, in her own place, even if she was nonplussed by the messages in the letter.

Amir's prose was simple and direct, even while his expressions of love and acceptance were nuanced. He apologized for chiding her sense of filial duty, and he empathized with Farzana's dedication to her parents, admitting that he felt equally devoted to his family. As a testament to his earnestness, Amir described junctures when he had sacrificed his personal goals for the benefit of his loved ones.

In the past, Amir had been tightlipped about his affection for his immediate and extended family. When Farah had touched on his habit of accommodating and prioritizing their sudden needs, especially those of his young nephews, Amir had downplayed her observations. Farzana had assumed that he was being humble or felt self-conscious since his actions revealed his love and dedication.

The sound of a blow dryer started. It would be another hour before Soreyah knocked on her door. Her boss at the clothing store demanded that she appear with a blowout, a full face of makeup, and smooth, visible legs. It was an expensive and time-intensive process that Soreyah performed five days a week.

Farzana pulled on the cigarette and rolled onto her side. She touched the pages and scanned the letter for endearing phrases.

It was gratifying to read Amir's acknowledgement of his family's centrality in his life and his remorse for having dismissed her sense of obligation to her parents. More than ever before, Farzana was proud of the solidity of her relationship with her parents and sister. The events of the previous day had underscored the importance of their bonds to each other, their reliance on one another's strengths, and the care and comfort they reciprocated and provided unconditionally. It had hurt deeply to hear Amir cast aside the people she cared for most in the world, but his letter went a long way to mending the tear in her heart.

The cigarette had neared its end and Farzana promised herself to not light another. Her next paycheque wasn't due for three days, and there was only enough money in the bank for the necessities, not extra packs of smokes.

To distract herself from the desire to smoke incessantly, she changed out of her work clothes from the previous day, donning a pair of comfortable, if overly skimpy, denim shorts and a cotton tank top. While looking at her reflection in the full-length mirror affixed to her closet door, she pondered Amir's words.

After begging for her forgiveness for his insensitivity, the letter had continued on another topic altogether: his plans to attend college and secure work as a professional hotelier. Farzana had reread that paragraph several times to make certain that she hadn't mistranslated the Farsi script. Amir described his research into a local two-year hospitality diploma and the possibility of securing an overnight concierge position at the Radisson by the airport.

Farzana realized that this was a declaration of Amir's commitment to her. If her parents wanted their daughter to marry a man of consequence, then he respected their wishes and he was determined to become that man. In case there was any doubt about his intentions, Amir described the day they would sit across from her parents and ask for their permission to marry. *Marry? He wants to marry. I hadn't imagined it all these months. We were in love. We are in love?*

Farzana frowned at her reflection. What was she going on about? She had ended their relationship. Why was she torturing herself by thinking of the past or about future plans that would never transpire?

Amir had ended the letter with a promise to continue writing to her regularly about his progress. He assured her that he would not try to contact her in any way and that if she wanted to speak to him, he was at her beck and call.

Farzana returned to her bed, kneeling before the letter. She touched his signature and a shiver rushed up her arm. Waves of feelings crashed upon one another as, in turns, she felt elated and enamoured, then distraught and despondent.

Amir's intentions were heartwarming, that much was certain, but her parents held lofty ideals about her future. Farzana tried to guess at her parents' impression of a hotel manager. Was it possible that they might consider it acceptable for a son-in-law? How had Amir come up with this plan? She tried to recall his having expressed an interest in hoteling before. Of course, he liked working with people and he had savvy customer service skills but that could translate into any number of jobs. *Besides, he hates school, and he likes his job. How did he come up with this plan? He can't force himself into a job he doesn't really want. This is crazy!*

Still, Farzana caught herself smiling, a great big optimistic smile that spread from ear to ear. He had declared his love for her, his desire to marry her, and he was determined to make it happen. Of all the possible outcomes Farzana had imagined, this reaction had not occurred to her. They had never discussed marriage or expressed their love for one another explicitly, even though they both knew they were in love.

There were too many competing demands at play. Farzana struggled to connect with her own desires as she considered her parents' ideals and Amir's aspirations. As elusive as grasping a speck of dust that catches the light for a moment before disappearing, Farzana strained to pinpoint her needs, even to see the distinction between others and herself. Where did the ambitions of others end and her intentions begin? What distinguished her personhood from her parents, or Amir? *What do I want? What if it doesn't work out with Amir? Am I jeopardizing my future?*

Despite her earlier resolution, Farzana lit another smoke and assured herself that she could manage. Sitting at the edge of the bed, with her back to the letter, she examined her reflection in the mirror. *This is not the time. I need to focus on Farah.*

She grabbed her bag and notebook, and then headed to the

kitchen. Soreyah was still blow-drying her hair behind a closed bathroom door. Seated at the breakfast table, Farzana dialed the number on the business card of the female police constable.

"Hello, this is Farzana Ghasemi," she said when the officer picked up. "We met yesterday. My sister, Farah, was ... um, was attacked on campus."

"Yes," the female officer replied.

In the background, Farzana heard the din of tenor voices, calling and laughing, and the shrill tones of multiple phones ringing asynchronously.

"I ... uh, I have some information. I thought, maybe, uh ... it might be useful," Farzana stammered, feeling unfamiliar with the protocol and fearful of being dismissed.

"Like what?" the officer prompted her.

"It's some licence plate numbers ... of cars that matched the description, in Farah's neighbourhood ..." Farzana stalled, imagining that the officer just rolled her eyes in response.

"Okay, shoot," she replied.

Trying not to be discouraged, Farzana continued, "Uh, okay, well these were from this morning, within a block or so of the apartment. Okay, so the first one is ..."

Farzana read aloud the numbers deliberately and waited for a sign of acknowledgement.

"Got it," the officer started, ready to end the call.

"Wait, I ..." Farzana stalled, desperate for a more meaningful interaction. "Are there any leads from Taari's housemates?"

"It's early days. I'll let you know," she answered and hung up abruptly.

"Bye, Officer," Farzana said to the dial tone, holding the receiver to her chest.

"Officer?" asked Soreyah as she walked into the kitchen, looking gorgeous. "What was that about?"

Farzana sighed and pulled out her pack of smokes. She knew that she was blowing her budget, but chain smoking on such a day seemed justified.

"You won't believe what happened yesterday," she started.

Soreyah leaned against the counter, crossed her arms, and asked in a concerned voice, "It's not Amir, is it? Did he do something stupid? He can be so dumb sometimes."

Farzana chuckled a little at Soreyah's sisterly criticism but shook her head in response. They spent the next half-hour talking about Farah and the attack, drinking strong coffee, and smoking the last of Farzana's cigarettes. Then, Soreyah left for work, and Farzana took her last smoke out to the balcony.

The sidewalks were crowded with vendors opening shops and people commuting on foot. The streets were equally busy with cars and busses, and a parade of cyclists passed in the narrow gap between the parked cars and the jammed traffic. Farzana sighed with relief at the privilege of staying home from work.

She reflected on her conversation with Soreyah, which had alleviated a great deal of her anxiety. Soreyah had offered the sympathetic ear that Farzana needed, the understanding of a likeminded friend. Farzana realized that her friendship with Soreyah was one of the most fulfilling and healthy relationships in her life. In Soreyah's company, Farzana could feel the contours of her own identity and the shape of her desires. Their friendship never required Farzana to choose between investing in her own ambitions or supporting Soreyah in hers. They cared for each other, depended on each other, but they remained distinct and independent. In their friendship, Farzana never lost her sense of self. *Why can't I always feel like this?*

Into the coffee tin of murky water she threw her last cigarette butt and then returned inside to fetch her wallet and run out for another pack.

☽

Mustafa stood before the hood of the metallic blue sedan that had arrived at the car wash entrance. The clipboard with its tearaway price sheets lay on the asphalt by his shoes. Typically, he would greet the customer, determine the type of service they wanted, mark up the price sheet, and send them to Candice with the tearaway portion while he drove the car onto the conveyor. Typically, he wouldn't stand in front of a car, squinting at its blinding windshield and debating how much to say when he pulled the driver out by his shirt collar. Of course, nothing had felt typical since the attack on Farah.

"Should I leave the keys in?" asked a woman leaning out of the driver's side window.

The revelation jarred Mustafa and he stammered, "Uh, yes ... keys in." *This is not the attacker's car. This is just another blue car. There are a million blue cars.*

He processed the woman's order, directed her inside to the cashier's booth, and positioned the car onto the conveyor. All the while, his hands trembled as though he had nearly escaped a serious accident.

The morning passed with the usual rush of taxis and limousines. Mustafa was grateful for the steady work because it offered a distraction from his frustrating ruminations and his inability to solve any of the problems that occurred to him. He smiled at customers, advertised specials, sprayed tires, vacuumed interiors, dried vehicles, bagged rags, and refilled detergents, anything and everything to avoid being still.

When a lull occurred near noontime, the inner stream of questions bombarded him again, and he retreated to the alleyway to avoid conversation. How could the police find a man without a surname in a city of two million people? Given that the attacker knew where Farah lived, was it more prudent to move across town or out of town? What had been the man's plan when he attacked Farah?

Mustafa smoked and paced, disturbed by his sense of a looming catastrophe and his inability to produce answers.

"Everything okay, Mustafa?" Afewerk asked, startling him.

Mustafa stopped pacing and nodded in response. Nothing was okay, everything was in disarray, and after a day of mulling over his options, Mustafa hadn't any next steps other than to keep Farah at home and out of harm's way. How could he explain his situation to Afewerk without seeming like an incompetent father? Mustafa held himself accountable for Farah's actions leading up to the attack. She behaved recklessly, making herself a target, and Mustafa contributed with his negligent parenting. Surely, Afewerk would arrive at the same conclusions.

The two men leaned against the brick wall of an adjacent building, in the shade of a determined young tree that had grown out of a patch of exposed soil. Afewerk retrieved a cigarette from his pack, and asked for light. Mustafa handed him a plastic lighter and told him to keep it.

"It's alright, thanks. I have a couple in the car," Afewerk said, handing back the lighter.

Mustafa said nothing, pulling on his cigarette to excuse his silence.

"You know, we've been working together for ... how long now? Eight, nine years," Afewerk said, looking ahead into the car-wash tunnel.

"Hm," Mustafa replied, bending over to wipe imperceptible dirt from his sneakers.

In a tone that was restrained but appreciative, Afewerk continued, "You've been there for me, many times. Many times. I consider you my closest friend." He paused, and then added, "My closest non-Eritrean friend, of course."

The qualifier, and the punchline, caught Mustafa off guard, and he chortled, which caused him to cough out a lungful of smoke. Afewerk smiled proudly and patted Mustafa on the back.

They recognized that their close friendship was unlikely, though not unique. Raised continents apart, they had both learned the same lesson, to perceive a person's worth by the colour of their skin. In Canada, where people and systems covertly applied the principle, ethnic communities continued to revere and resent those with paler skin, and detest and demean those with darker skin.

Honey-toned Iranians, like Mustafa and Hossein, didn't broaden their social circles to include sienna-toned Eritreans, like Afewerk. They invested in friendships with other Iranians, those who spoke Farsi, prepared similar foods, and shared cultural knowledge, even if on an individual basis a person was less compatible as a friend, like Yasmeen's philosophical husband Ahmed. *We wouldn't be friends if we didn't work together. I mean, I don't have other Black friends. Iranians don't make friends with Blacks. But Afewerk is different, different from other Blacks and Iranians. He's smart and tough. He's a good family man. He's probably my closest friend.*

"So, friend, tell me," Afewerk said, blowing out a cloud of smoke towards the sky.

"Hm, it's good. The tips were okay today, yeah?" Mustafa avoided answering the implied question.

"Uh-huh, tips were good," Afewerk agreed. "And Maiheen? How is she?"

Mustafa had used this same gambit on Afewerk in the past. Get him talking about his wife until he revealed his hand, but Mustafa didn't want to be worked over for information. He wanted to lead with his chin and come clean about his failure to protect his daughter.

"Someone attacked Farah, my youngest," Mustafa said, and then he spit.

"Shit!" said Afewerk as he pushed off the wall, flicked away his cigarette, and stood before Mustafa. "What happened? Is she okay?"

"Yeah, she's at home with Maiheen. Some cuts and bruises but she got away," Mustafa summarized, butting out his own smoke.

"Did they get the guy? Where'd it happen?" Afewerk asked, shaking his head in disbelief.

"At her school, and he got away," Mustafa said. "Fucking asshole."

"There are some bad men out there," Afewerk said, sucking his teeth. "Mustafa, I'm real sorry about Farah."

Mustafa stared at his shoes and nodded, unable to form a response.

After a pause, Afewerk asked, "So, how're you doing?"

"How you think I'm doing?! This is killing me," Mustafa snapped. He pushed off the wall and paced the alleyway.

"Yeah, I can ..." Afewerk started, but Mustafa cut him off.

"It's all my fault. She counted on me, and I dropped the ball," Mustafa said angrily, pacing and smacking his forehead with the palm. "I mean, what kind of father am I? I'm supposed to be running interference for her."

"Mustafa, I think ..." Afewerk began.

"You don't know how it feels. I can't ... I don't even know where to start," Mustafa stepped away and spat again. He resumed pacing, and his hands flew about in anger as he continued, "This guy, what the hell am I supposed to do? He's out there ... just ... what? Just ... getting ready for another chance? I will kill him. I will fucking kill him."

"Sure, yeah," Afewerk said, nodding profusely.

"What am I supposed to do?" pleaded Mustafa, stopping in front of Afewerk but not giving him the opportunity to speak. "I would do anything for Farah, anything but I can't think of what to do. Should we move to another city? Like Hamilton? Or, farther maybe, somewhere in Vancouver? What about Farzana? How can I leave her behind?"

Mustafa was overwhelmed by his lack of agency and confounded by competing priorities. He couldn't negate the threat to Farah or determine how to proceed with their lives. He pressed the balls of his hands into his eyes and furtively wiped away the hot tears that had formed.

Afewerk held Mustafa's shoulders and said, "Just hold up, my friend. Take a breath."

Mustafa didn't debate the instruction and took a deep breath. Consternation overtook shame in the race between his emotions, and he crashed into hurdles of distress, one after another, unable to catch his footing and resume his once-confident stride. Tears streamed down his face faster than he could wipe them away, and soon he found himself in the formidable embrace of his friend.

"Everything is going to be okay," Afewerk said confidently, pulling away but continuing to grip Mustafa by the shoulders. "She got away, remember. She is a strong young woman. She's *your* daughter. Yes?"

Mustafa looked to the sky and swallowed the lump in his throat. When he exhaled, his body trembled and he clenched his jaw to regain composure. Afewerk wrapped one arm around Mustafa's shoulders and led him back to the shade of the tree. There, Afewerk lit two smokes and handed one to his friend. When Mustafa eyed the lighter that Afewerk had procured from his coverall pocket, his friend smiled back.

"Guess I did have one," Afewerk said with an innocent shrug.

They smoked in silence for a few minutes, watching the foot traffic at the end of the alleyway and the chipmunks that ran in and out of small gaps between buildings.

"This is a terrible thing. I wish it hadn't happened to Farah. Or, to you," Afewerk said, looking at the blue sky.

"Hm," Mustafa replied, too weak to express his gratitude for the sentiment.

"Salma's sister was ... back home, when we all lived in Keren," Afewerk recalled, referring to his sister-in-law. He pulled on his smoke and continued, "Jamela, her older sister, if you can believe it.

She was already a mother of four children, nearly forty at the time. A grown woman."

Mustafa had stopped smoking and pivoted to face Afewerk. He had never heard another man disclose personal information of this nature about a woman in his own family. It was common enough to hear men discuss the cases of rape and abuse reported in the news. Every man seemed to have an opinion about the women who went missing, the ones whose bodies were found in the woods or by the side of the highway. Mustafa had had his opinions, too, about their lack of foresight, their promiscuity, and the poor choices that led to their expected downfall.

Now, he was dismayed to hear Afewerk's description of the brutal attack on his sister-in-law, the physical trauma of the rape, the psychological scars, and the lifelong process of healing that reframed the relationships in their family.

"None of us was ever the same," Afewerk said, glancing at Mustafa.

Mustafa nodded and looked away. He had questions about the event, but he sensed that his questions were inappropriate or indicative of his not having appreciated the underlying message of Afewerk's disclosure. *He talks like the lead up to the attack isn't relevant. Why was she walking that road when she'd heard stories about it? Why was she walking alone? If we don't find out what went wrong, we can't teach women how to keep it from happening.*

Whereas Mustafa felt fixated on how his friend's sister-in-law could have avoided the attack, Afewerk seemed disinterested in that aspect. Instead of misspeaking or possibly offending Afewerk, Mustafa smoked in silence.

"I know you want to save her. It's natural. She needs you right now," Afewerk assured his friend. "She needs a strong family, people who'll help her recover."

Again, Mustafa nodded in silence. There was so much that had to be done. Find a new apartment, probably out of the city, transfer Farah to a new school, and get new jobs for him, Maiheen and Farzana. They had to build a new life.

"It was tempting to blame Jamela for the attack," Afewerk admitted. "I thought those things, too. Why did she go to market alone? Why didn't she scream for help? I'm ashamed to admit it but at that time, I was angry with her. Really angry."

Afewerk turned to Mustafa and placed a hand on his shoulder. He continued softly. "It felt like she had ruined our lives. Everything that was once easy had become scary. I kept thinking that if she had been more careful, then we would be living normally."

Mustafa didn't look at Afewerk, certain that his friend would recognize the same sentiment in his eyes.

"That passes. The anger, the fear. It passes, and your head clears," Afewerk said and patted Mustafa's shoulder before lowering his arm. "You learn to listen to them. You become more helpful."

Mustafa resisted the urge to shake his head, to disagree with Afewerk. *Farah was the one who had trouble listening. Hadn't she proven that much? She never stopped talking, and to what end? What more could she need to say?*

"If you need anything, my friend, anything, you can count on me," Afewerk insisted. "Okay?"

"Yes, thank you," Mustafa said, holding out a hand to shake.

Afewerk brushed away his hand and embraced him in a tight hug. Then he left Mustafa to finish his smoke under the fledgling tree.

Maiheen stood up on the low bench where she had sat for three hours, in the cold circular hallway of the Athletics Building. She steadied her breathing and inwardly repeated empowering messages to steady her nerves and fortify herself for the journey home. These techniques she had learned from a book which Yasmeen had loaned her, a book she'd heard about on the *Oprah Winfrey Show*. Maiheen didn't agree with the individualist attitudes of most self-help books, this one included, but she recognized the value of strengthening her resolve and calming her mind. *I possess the skills and abilities to handle difficulties. I am confident and competent.*

She was prepared when the rush of students funnelled through the gymnasium doors and into the hall. From her vantage point, she scanned the crowd pouring out and caught sight of Farah, a few metres away and ambling along, carried by the momentum of the others away from her mother. Farah's puffy, bloodshot eyes revealed that she had cried throughout her sitting, and her failed attempts to cross the stream of students, towards Maiheen, demonstrated her crippling fatigue.

She stepped down from the bench and in a voice that reverberated through the concrete tunnel, Maiheen called, "Excuse me! Pardon me!"

The young people who stood in close proximity to Maiheen peered at her with annoyed expressions but they parted to let her pass. She cut across the stream in Farah's direction. When she demanded room a second time, in the same matronly tone, another path opened before her, leading to Farah.

Maiheen didn't ask for permission when she took her daughter's hand and led her through the crowd and out to the campus green. Farah was too exhausted to be embarrassed or to care about anyone's opinion of her or her mother.

Once they were free of the crowd, Maiheen looped her daughter's arm in her own and clutched her handbag under her free arm, feeling the hardness of the kitchen knife through the soft leather. With Maiheen's eyes darting about for looming figures, they traversed the hundred metres to the cab. The driver who had delivered them to campus had returned, upon Maiheen's request, and waited for them in the nearby parking lot.

The journey back was a silent one but with Farah's head against her shoulder, Maiheen was content to watch the passing scenery and allow her mind to wander. She didn't ask Farah about the exam because it didn't matter. She had her daughter back in her sights, and they were on their way home.

Instead, she recalled the days and hours prior to the attack on Farah and the intense feelings that had wholly consumed her. There was her agitation about Farah's tactlessness regarding the deposit cheque, her reveries about becoming a professional again, and her private homesickness when Jaleh sang Mahasti's "Delam Tang-e" during the gathering at Yasmeen's. Then, there was her disappointment with herself for chastising Mustafa after he took her to a café on her day off and her determination in defence of Farzana's decision to rent an apartment in spite of disbelieving her reasons for moving out of her current place.

Maiheen thought it was incredible how a traumatic event reframed routines and reset one's priorities. How had these trivial encounters aroused so much emotion? If she felt passionately about caring for and protecting her daughter, how could anything as mundane as an argument have produced a similar feeling? Had she spread herself so thin that she couldn't distinguish the preeminent aspects of her life from the peripheral ones?

Farah nestled closer and sighed deeply. Maiheen placed her hand on her daughter's and kissed the top of Farah's head, the bristly black hairs tickling her nose. Outside, cars on the expressway had come to a standstill, and the driver grumbled about reckless drivers causing accidents.

Yesterday at this time, she was listing reasons to persuade Mustafa into supporting her career as a mortgage broker. Hers had been a list of remedies for every anxiety that ailed Mustafa, and it had seemed like a prudent approach to gain his approval.

Today, her reasoning seemed juvenile. Mustafa wasn't simple-minded. He valued her happiness, appreciated her need to pursue independent goals. He was the man who had supported her career at the bank and championed her return to work following maternity leave, even in the face of persistent opposition from her mother and mother-in-law.

It was true that Mustafa had changed since then, but so had Maiheen. The woman who had cleared passage through dense terrain in pursuit of her career, and the new mother who had rallied her elders to support her young family as she forged her path, that woman had changed irrevocably.

When the revolution had reconstructed her world, Maiheen had adapted and revised her career goals. The constitution had been changed, legalizing gender-based discrimination and limiting work opportunities for women, but Maiheen had maintained a sound working relationship with her superiors. Even if her career had plateaued, she was content to serve as the award-winning head teller of a successful enterprise. Maiheen had been less intrepid but still confident in her domain.

It was the move to Canada that had changed the landscape beyond recognition and caused her to lose her footing. There were no extended family or business networks to rely on, and the Ghasemis had lost their agency and their cachet as middle-class citizens. The fragments of her personage were in disarray and her identity was disjointed. Everything was in flux, everything except her duty as a parent.

So, Maiheen had doubled down on clearing paths for her daughters, and the next time she looked up from the daily grind, her eldest had graduated university and her youngest was entering her first year.

Farah's arm jerked and Maiheen realized her daughter had fallen asleep. She kissed the short hairs on the crown of Farah's head, overwhelmingly proud of her. Farah could have postponed her exams and given up on meeting the scholarship deadline. Maiheen was aware of the financial freedom that the scholarship promised Farah, her chance to live unfettered by her parents' purse strings. *It never gets easier, watching them make their own way. To think of all the stress I caused my parents while I fought my way through the ranks at Sepah.*

Maiheen kissed her daughter's head again, taking in her honeyed scent and listening to her soft snoring. The traffic inched forward as vehicles merged into the centre and right lanes to bypass the collision on the left, and Maiheen ruminated about the present.

The landscape of daily life had changed again. Her daughters no longer want her clearing brush for them. It was obvious as far as Farah was concerned but also for Farzana, whose cues were subtle. They wanted to go about forging their own way, just as Maiheen had desired and petitioned for herself during her youth.

If her experience with Farah this day was any indication of what her daughters wanted from her, Maiheen could assume that they needed her as reinforcement. Was that a part she wanted to play? It was impossible to know how she would react until they reached out for help. Would they reach out to her for help? That seemed like the main challenge of being a mother to grown women, to make it on their list of trusted helpers. *I have to be authentic. I have to take risks, to pursue my own dreams. They need to see me try. Otherwise, they'll assume I don't understand their problems.*

For the first time since she decided to take the mortgage broker course, she was excited to discuss her plans with Mustafa. After many years, he would see the return of the passionate, ambitious woman he had married. For the remainder of the cab ride, Maiheen smiled at this thought.

When they arrived at the apartment, Farah disappeared into her room, declining Maiheen's offer to prepare her a snack.

"I just need to sleep for a bit," her daughter said softly, slumped in her doorway.

"I'm here if you need anything," Maiheen replied as the bedroom door closed. "Have a good rest."

Maiheen needed a rest herself. She washed up, changed into a casual outfit, and then lay on her bed for a break. It was four o'clock, and dinner wasn't expected until seven. Mustafa had mentioned returning home for six, after picking up Farzana.

From memory, Maiheen surveyed the items in the fridge and determined that there were leftovers enough for a respectable meal for four people. She didn't need to cook but serving her family leftovers, especially with Farah recovering from the attack, seemed inadequate. *We should have something nice, something special. Something to take their mind off things.* This was Maiheen's last thought before she fell asleep and awoke two hours later to Mustafa sitting at her bedside.

☽

Farzana stored her overnight bag on a shelf in the front closet while her father headed in search of her mother. Farah's bedroom door, the room nearest to the front door, was ajar and she could be heard sleeping. Given the shocking events of the previous day, it didn't seem peculiar that the apartment was still. It was the lack of aromas that alarmed Farzana.

At this time of day, less than an hour before the dinner meal, the apartment would be bursting with the scents of onions, garlic, stewing tomatoes, sautéing vegetables, and roasting meat. Farzana expected the kitchen to be spotless, as it was, but the stovetop should have been occupied with a large pot of fluffy rice and at least one casserole dish filled to the rim with meat stew, roasted chicken, or kebab skewers. Instead, the kitchen looked abandoned, as if it hadn't been used since breakfast time.

Something was seriously askew. Farzana had expected to see her mother amidst a flurry of activity, doting on Farah, cooking everyone's favourite dishes to raise spirits, and juggling twice the number of chores to take advantage of being home from work. *Where's dinner?*

Farzana felt like a neglected child as she opened the fridge with the fleeting hope that her favourite dish, *ghormeh sabzi*, was hiding among the containers of leftovers. Her stomach grumbled and she grabbed a box of fresh dates before shutting the doors. Lunch had been her last meal, having spent her afternoon drinking tea and smoking cigarettes, and now she was disappointed and famished. Standing at the kitchen counter, she devoured a few dates and returned the box to the fridge. *What's for dinner? Are we eating leftovers? Am I supposed to be getting dinner on the table?*

She considered sneaking onto the balcony to secretly smoke a cigarette. Though both of her parents smoked, they had strongly disapproved when they learned a year ago that she had taken up the habit. Her younger sister, who had been smoking openly for two years, to her parents' dismay, accused them of hypocrisy when they lectured her. Farzana had no interest in that kind of recurring exchange, so she had promised to quit and lied about her continued habit ever since.

Looking out at the balcony and the beautiful sunset, a clandestine cigarette was tempting. Still, it wasn't worthwhile to lose their approval for one cigarette. Besides, it was hunger that was driving her need to smoke.

From her parents' bedroom, at the end of the hall, Farzana heard their voices. She decided to ask about dinner in her own roundabout way, by offering to set the table and prepare a salad. There was no reason to suspect that her parents were in the middle of an argument, so Farzana had knocked lightly and entered without waiting.

"... with her the whole time. She would have gone without me," her mother said.

"*Bebakhsheed!* Pardon me!" Farzana apologized, lowering her eyes in embarrassment for having intruded.

Both her parents were sitting on the bed, but her father was perched on the edge, facing the wall, and her mother was knelt in the centre, her knees nearly touching his back and her hands folded in her lap.

If Farzana had seen the scene depicted with oil paint, framed with gold, and hung on the walls of an art museum, she might have described it as poignant. A lovers' quarrel, in the intimate setting of their bedroom, two bodies nearly touching, separated by a sliver of space that couldn't be bridged, and the circumstances leading to that break conjured by the observer. It would have been a dramatic image, however unsettling. If they had been any other couple, Farzana might have run out of the room tittering privately about the fickleness of romance. Unfortunately, they were her parents, and it made for a different experience altogether.

"Stay," her father beseeched with anguished expression. "Maybe you can talk some sense into your mother."

"I ... um, I ..." Farzana stammered, stepping backwards towards the door.

"You're making her uncomfortable," her mother replied, offering Farzana a knowing look about her father's behaviour.

"No, I'm fine," Farzana lied in a cheery voice.

Another few steps and she'd be out of the room, but both her parents were watching her so she didn't dare move away.

Instead, she rushed her speech while staring at the carpet, "I just wanted to ask about dinner. Should I heat up leftovers, make salad? Hm?"

"Oh, I'm sorry, darling. You must be starving," her mother said regretfully. "I was going to call for takeout, maybe something Farah wanted. I fell asleep when we ..."

Her father interrupted her, "When they came back from endangering their lives! Can you believe that your mother took Farah out? And for what? An exam? Can you believe that?"

Farzana held her breath while he ranted and then reminded

herself to breathe again when he stopped. She was desperate to escape, but she was conditioned to hold her post until she was no longer needed. At that moment, they were both talking to her, and it seemed inconsiderate to walk away, even if she planned to be helpful by preparing dinner.

"Mustafa, I was with her the entire time," her mother explained, placing a hand on his shoulder.

Farzana was relieved that he hadn't brushed it away or shrugged it off. She didn't know how to react to displays of cruelty. If her younger sister had been present, Farah would have pointed out such a transgression. This habit of Farah's made others uncomfortable, including her older sister, but Farzana secretly appreciated seeing people held to account for their bad behaviour.

Her father turned towards her mother and shaking his head in disbelief, asked, "And how is that any better? You were supposed to stay home. That lunatic is out there, and you don't even know what he looks like."

Her mother was biting her lower lip and rubbing her temple. Looking in Farzana's direction, she answered, "She would have gone without me. I swear, this was the best compromise."

Farzana locked eyes with her mother and nodded emphatically to express her sympathy. She knew how difficult it was to reason with Farah, to change her mind about any course of action, and she was glad that her mother had facilitated the trip. It might be a turning point in their mother-daughter relationship. *Maybe they'll argue less. I'm tired of being their go-between.*

"Why compromise? Who needs to compromise? You're her mother!" Her father insisted, smacking his thigh with his palm.

Again, Farzana nodded, this time gravely at her father. He was concerned about his daughter and he wanted to keep her safe. It was understandable.

"She's twenty years old, Mustafa," her mother reminded him,

wrapping an arm around his shoulders and kissing his forehead twice. "I can't control her."

"We have to ..." said her father in a defeated voice as he allowed her mother to gather him in her arms.

Farzana heard them speaking softly in their huddle, too quietly for her to hear. They were absorbed in each other, and she took the opportunity to rush out of the room.

Back in the kitchen, she found Farah rooting about in the fridge.

"Hey, you," Farzana hugged her lightly from behind. "How're you feeling? Hungry?"

"Hm, uh-huh," Farah grunted in response. She pulled her head out of the fridge and her mouth was filled with slices of mortadella. In her hands, she held a pop can and a jar of peanut butter.

Furtively, Farzana assessed the condition of Farah's cuts and bruises, and she made a mental note to change the dressing that covered her sister's split lip.

"Looks good," Farzana teased, indicating Farah's bounty. "What do you say to pizza and wings?"

"Fuck, yeah!" Farah said through a mouthful, nodding enthusiastically. "Is that okay with Mama?"

"Yup, her idea," Farzana said, picking up the wall-mounted phone to dial the local pizzeria. "So, she said you two went to your exam."

Farah's face fell but she confirmed with a small nod. "Just don't lecture me on why I shouldn't have. It's not ..."

Farzana interjected, "It's awesome. Good for you."

"Huh? Why?" Farah asked suspiciously.

"I just ..." Farzana started but raised a finger to pause their conversation as she ordered their meal. "Uh, delivery, please. Yup, the number is ..."

While they waited for the pizza delivery, Farzana set the table and prepared a green salad. She could still hear her parents' voices from their bedroom, but she couldn't discern the words and the tone wasn't heated.

"Are they fighting about me? About the exam?" Farah asked, glancing away from the TV screen briefly to eye Farzana.

Farzana joined her sister on the loveseat, cuddling up to her and kissing her head.

"Yeah, badass," Farzana teased lightly. "I'm kidding. It's okay. It's not really about you."

"What does that mean?" asked Farah, not taking her eyes off the screen. "And, since when are you a psych major?"

"Watch your show," Farzana said with a nudge, resting her head against Farah's shoulder.

She didn't have the capacity to explain the scene in the bedroom, the tableau of mixed emotions, the complex body language of loving partners in quarrel. It was beyond Farah's experience, the transformation of romantic love into its unconditional form, when the whirlwind of passion was subdued and deeper emotions formed dense layers of compassion and selflessness.

Farzana thought about Amir and his words of compassion, and she sighed with longing.

☽

Farah didn't know what was going on at the dinner table but it was spooking her out. Where was the big argument she had expected, the showdown with her father about her trip to campus? Instead, the Ghasemis were eating takeout and discussing federal laws against human cloning.

"I'm not kidding. They can make people. It was in the news," her father declared, grinning and working up to a joke.

He leaned to his right to request that Farzana pass him another slice of pizza.

"I believe you," her mother insisted, also smiling easily. "I just don't think it works the way you think."

"Yeah, Baba," Farzana agreed, helping herself to wings and offering them to Farah from across the table. "You can't get a copy of yourself, like a duplicate of a grown man."

"Sure, not yet, but you wait," her father said, his forefinger raised to announce his premonition. "This week, it's a bunch of cells but next week, it's Mustafa Ghasemi Part Two. Twice the intellect, twice the manpower!"

Tears of gaiety rolled down her mother's cheeks, and she announced with equal vigour, "Twice the man, twice the problems! No, wait. Twice the man, twice the arrogance!"

"Oh, oh," Farzana joined in excitedly. "Twice the man, half the attention span."

"Hey," interjected Farah somberly, a half-eaten chicken wing in hand. "Stereotypes about men hurt everyone."

The room became still. Farah assumed that, as usual, she had ruined their fun by calling out their use of stereotypes, but barely a moment passed before her mother and Farzana were throwing back their heads, slapping palms on the table, and laughing uproariously.

Grateful for the recaptured cheeriness, Farah smiled uncertainly from one to the other. Typically, when Farah brought attention to a sexist comment or a racist euphemism, it wasn't received well by anyone in her family. This included the person on whose behalf she might have been advocating, generally her mother or Farzana.

Seeing her mother and sister respond gaily dumfounded her, and she asked, "What's so funny?"

"You! You're defending your father!" Her mother replied, wiping her mascara with the corner of a grease-stained paper napkin. "That's a first, I'm sure."

"Definitely a first," Farzana confirmed gleefully.

Farah glanced at her father, who gazed back with a flattered expression. She rolled her eyes at him and shook her head.

"Not just Baba. All men ... people. All people," Farah stammered to explain herself.

"Thank you, Farah-*jaan*," her father said, bowing slightly in his seat. "At least someone appreciates me."

The smile he bestowed on Farah captured her attention completely. How long had it been since he last looked at her affectionately? Had their animosity tainted every moment? They hadn't been on the same side or in on the same joke since she was a child.

Farah smiled back, mirroring his unguarded countenance, thinking to reach out and touch his hand, to express her affection and appreciation. How might he react? Would he echo her sentiments? Or, would he take the opportunity to lecture her, judge her?

Apprehension seized Farah, and she quickly turned her attention to the food.

"I appreciate you, Mustafa," her mother replied with a grin. "I especially appreciate that there is only one of you."

Farzana and her mother broke out into peals of laughter, and her father looked at Farah conspiratorially.

"The day your mother married me, she said ..." began her father, then he continued in a higher pitch, "Mustafa, there'll never be another man like you."

Here, her father stopped and gazed at her mother with a knowing look, and then he added, "Foolish me, I took it as a compliment! I didn't know she was updating me on government policy."

The three women laughed and the earnest adoration of her father rekindled Farah's own affection for the jovial and entertaining man of her childhood. A memory returned to her of sitting on her father's shoulders following a grade-school track-and-field meet. He had carried her home, announcing to every passerby that she was a star athlete. His proclamations were thrilling and, at that age, she wasn't embarrassed to be praised publicly. Once, she had thought the world of him, and it had been heartening to know that he felt the same way about her.

"Anyone want the last slice?" Farzana asked, holding up the pizza box.

Farah and her father responded alike, by placing one hand on the stomach and waving the other in a silent rejection. They chuckled when they noticed their shared mannerism.

"All yours," her mother replied. "But, can you pass me the extra hot wings? Are there any left?"

While her sister and mother divvied up the wings and discussed Farzana's apartment situation, her father leaned forward on his elbows, fingers interlaced, and smiled kindly at Farah. *Here it comes. I knew it. I knew it.*

Farah had spent her youth fighting with her father, first about her clothes, hairstyles, and music, and most recently, about bigotry and economic equality. Throughout, he had asserted that Farah and Farzana would never grasp the depth of his love. Farah translated his message to mean that she must concede to his directives because he is her parent. In her estimation, his love was conditional, and her not meeting the conditions meant that his love for her had lessened, diminished with each passing year.

The years of loud arguments and silent battles had trained her to expect his attacks to take many forms. His smiling sweetly was a tactic, and she was prepared to resist his challenge to her authority, even if it meant losing the remaining love he felt for her.

"How was your exam today?" he asked, softly enough to suggest that this was a private conversation.

"Good," Farah said automatically, though it hadn't gone as well as she had hoped.

"*Khosh-haalam*, I'm glad," he replied, still leaning forward and speaking quietly but sounding more somber.

"Okay," Farah said flatly.

She refused to smile, to give him any reason to believe that she had lowered her guard. Instead, she stared back, unblinking, to assert her dominance in all matters pertaining to her life. If he planned to forbid her from taking her next exam or from moving out on her own, then he was asking for trouble and she was ready to fight back.

"And, you have another one tomorrow?" he asked, returning her gaze.

Farah nodded, saving her breath for the real battle.

"Okay," he said, sighed deeply and leaned back in his chair.

Farah waited, as she had learned to do from years of experience. She would wait until she was certain that he was trespassing into her jurisdiction, wait to hear the words which would serve as proof of his infringement, statements which she would quote as evidence of his infraction.

"And, what time is your exam?" he asked, followed by another deep sigh.

Caught off guard by the specifics of his question, Farah grimaced at him and paused.

"Why?" she asked curtly.

"I want to drive you down to campus. You and your mother," he explained, his brows furrowed in an expression of concern.

For a moment, Farah stared at him trying to read between the lines. Then, her head swivelled to the left to see her mother, who had been listening in, nodding in agreement. Finally, Farah looked straight ahead at Farzana, who blinked and gave a small shrug.

Staring at her father again, Farah asked, "Why?"

"I want to help," her father answered, lifting his eyes from the table and holding her gaze.

Farah bit her lip to keep from crying. She refused to open up to him in any rush, not after all the years of being questioned and challenged for her self-expression. This could be another tactic. *Is this for real? It feels different, like he actually wants to help.*

He was offering to help her, on her own terms, for the first time.

The daughter who demanded the affection and adoration of her father, the one who repelled his attempts to mould her, the one who pushed for better from him, she insisted that Farah accept his offer. And, she did.

☽

Farzana finished removing her makeup and brushing her teeth. From the adjacent bathroom, the ensuite to the master bedroom, she heard the voices of her parents as they planned the following day and the weekend to come. The mild cadence of their conversation soothed Farzana, and she was glad to be spending the night at their place.

After tying up her hair and changing into pajamas, she packed her day clothes into her overnight bag and headed back down the hall to Farah's room. Her mother had prepared an air mattress for her by Farah's bedside.

Farzana knocked gently on her sister's bedroom door but there came no answer. She pushed the door open slightly and announced herself before walking in. The space was lit by soft lamplight, the floor was occupied by the dressed mattress, and the room was unexpectedly vacant. Fatigue was instantly replaced by fright, and Farzana's first thought was that Farah had left to visit the boy in the adjacent building. Their sordid relationship was sickly enough and now it would put her sister's life at risk. *Be calm. Don't panic Mama and Baba. Just be calm.*

Back in the front hall, she confirmed that Farah wasn't in the kitchen, dining room, or living room. Then, she checked the front closet for Farah's shoes, and she found two pairs of sneakers and one pair of army boots that belonged to her sister. *Does she have another pair of shoes? Would she go out in slippers?*

"I'm just getting a drink of water," her mother answered her father, from the master bedroom.

Immediately, Farzana crossed the hall to close Farah's door and rushed into the living room to divert attention from the missing daughter. The room was lit only by the glow of the aquarium, and Farzana peered into the murky water, feigning interest in the bubble-eye fish, a creature she hadn't acknowledged previously.

"A shame, isn't it?" Her mother asked, peeking in from the doorway.

"Hm? Oh yeah, sad fish," Farzana agreed with a solemn headshake.

"Not the fish," her mother scoffed. "Her." She jutted out her chin towards the balcony.

Discomfited, Farzana sighed as she realized Farah was on the balcony, smoking.

"Oh, what to do?!" Her mother exclaimed, leaning in to kiss Farzana good night.

When she heard her mother fetch a glass of water and return to her room, Farzana stepped out onto the balcony to join her sister, making sure to close the sliding door behind her.

"Hand it over," she ordered.

Her sister pulled on the smoke before she passed the cigarette to Farzana, who joined her at the railing, overlooking the impenetrable darkness of densely wooded areas, the clusters of bright lights at plazas and parking lots, and the glowing skyscrapers of the distant Toronto skyline.

Taking a drag from the cigarette, Farzana chuckled to herself. A moment ago, she had been ready to start a search party, ransack Farah's room for the boy's number, and walk over to the adjacent apartment and ring every buzzer until she found Farah.

"What?" Farah asked, taking the smoke back from her sister.

"I thought you'd gone out. To see that boy," Farzana admitted, snatching the cigarette back to finish the last drag.

"Oh," said Farah, and she side-eyed her sister. "Why?"

"Because ... you're you," Farzana answered weakly. "I mean, I thought you ... I don't know. I got scared."

"Don't be. I'm not into him ... like, not anymore, or at least not like ... I'm tired of the bullshit," Farah explained. She furrowed her brows and continued, "Besides, I would've told you I was going. I'm not the one who keeps secrets, remember?"

"What are you talking about?" Farzana asked and immediately regretted giving Farah the opening.

"I'm out in the open, Sis." Farah gave her sister a knowing look. "The one who talks too much, tells too much. I don't hide shit from you."

Farzana didn't like the demanding way that Farah was speaking to her. She was uncomfortable with her younger sister's insinuation that she owed Farah any information about her personal life.

"I have a right to my privacy," Farzana said coolly, keeping her eyes on the view.

Obviously provoked, Farah spun to face Farzana, and replied, "Sure, privacy. But how long are you going to keep secrets? Don't you trust me? I mean, I tell you so much, and you don't even tell me about your boyfriend! You treat me like I'm Mama or Baba."

Now, she was shocked, and she definitely wouldn't face Farah. How had her sister learned about Amir? Quickly, her mind considered various responses to Farah's comments. Having eliminated the least helpful ones, to deny Amir's existence or to persecute Farah for infringing on her privacy, Farzana decided to lead with her heart and address the underlying emotions of the matter.

"I do trust you, Farah," Farzana said, turning to touch her sister's arm. "You're one of my best friends."

"Okay, so," Farah said with a quavering voice, "why do you hide stuff from me?"

"It's not so simple. I'm not really hiding it from you," Farzana continued. "It just takes me ... more time to ... um, get confident, you know, to be able to share myself, with other people."

With a huff, Farah turned to face the city, and snapped, "But I'm not other people. I'm your sister. You should be able to tell me everything."

Farzana sighed and joined Farah in looking out at the night. She wanted to explain that it was difficult to open up to anyone about herself, that every act of sharing required her to fortify herself, bolster her confidence, and invest in her recuperation. It was difficult to trust that others wanted to hear her ideas and opinions. Most of the time, there wasn't enough space for her to be dissatisfied or uncomfortable, or to voice her concerns. The world was dominated by the brash and the boors, and there was no value placed on the contributions of the reticent and no pace set for the reserved.

"I want to tell you a lot. I do. It's just that I'm not like you," Farzana replied.

"Right, not like me," Farah threw back. "The loudmouth, the thug."

"No, not like that," Farzana tried again. "You have confidence, Farah. It's really special, and I know it's not easy for you either. I know you take a lot of flak for ... standing up for yourself, for other people, too. I see that."

Farah turned toward Farzana, who saw that her younger sister was crying. Farzana smiled in return and wiped away the errant tear.

"You are so special, and I am so proud to be your sister," Farzana continued, kissing Farah's wet cheeks.

"Really?" Farah's voice was a thread of itself. "Sometimes I think you're embarrassed of me."

"Fuck yeah," Farzana joked, "sometimes, I am mortified. I mean you chose economics over business. I haven't even told my friends."

Farah chortled, and Farzana took the opportunity to scoot closer, to rub her sister's back.

"Seriously, though," Farzana said, "I'm really proud of you. You have a voice, and I wish I had one, too."

"But you do, I mean, you could say things, too."

"We all have our strengths, right? You have the ability to speak up, and I'm working on it. It just means that I need more time to open up."

"Hm," Farah said, sounding defeated.

"It doesn't mean that I don't want to share things with you, or I don't trust you. I do. I really do," Farzana said. When a moment passed and Farah didn't respond, she nudged her younger sister, "Hm?"

"Hm," Farah grunted and shrugged. Then, as if she caught a second wind, she turned and started, "I don't think you understand how hard it is to be the one who calls them out on their bullshit. I mean, you get to play the good girl and keep everything a secret, and they treat you like a princess, but I'm the one who's being honest and they act like I'm an asshole."

"Well, you didn't have to tell them everything," Farzana snapped back.

Farah's eyes opened wide and she stared at her sister incredulously. She opened her mouth with a rebuke but Farzana interrupted her.

"I take that back. I mean, I don't mean that ... I mean ... I know what you mean. I see what you're saying. I'm sorry. I know that being honest is important to you and I admire that about you. Really."

Farah glowered but she nodded silently, offering Farzana the opportunity to go on.

Farzana exhaled deeply and continued, "I recognize that Mama and Baba treat me differently ..."

At this point, Farah grimaced, and Farzana saw that she needed to be bolder in her word choice.

"Okay, you're right," Farzana conceded. "They are ... easier on me ...because they know less about what's going on with me."

"Yeah, they are." Farah's grimace lifted, and she looked sad. "It's not fair."

"No, it's not fair. I'm sorry, Sis," Farzana said, putting her arm around her sister again.

A few moments passed in silence, and the sisters observed the searchlights in the distance and the red and blue lights of commercial flights crossing the night sky.

"So, did you break up with your boyfriend?" Farah asked tentatively.

Farzana searched inwardly for the answer. It required her to follow a narrow, hidden path that she had rediscovered within herself, one that had existed all along but had overgrown from disuse. She realized that the more often she visited the path, the easier it would be to find and the clearer would be its trail.

At its end, Farzana reached a glorious garden of her desires, each hope and aspiration rooted deeply in her identity, the blossoms and foliage attesting to their fidelity. Like sunshine, her courage and perseverance had nurtured her desires even while she was unable to access the garden. Now, she had found her way back, and she dedicated herself to every blossom that defined her personhood.

"Yes, but it's not a break-up. It's just a break," Farzana answered plainly.

"Is it serious?" asked Farah, blatantly curious but attempting to disguise it by lighting another cigarette.

Farzana didn't need to search for this answer. It came quickly, accompanied by a grin, "Yes."

☽

Charles observed as another employee drove out of the supermarket parking lot, leaving it vacant except for two cars. One was parked near the rear entry of the building, a door that locked automatically and a doorway lit by a single bulb overhead. The second car, his metallic blue sedan, was hidden behind a row of dumpsters, consumed by the shadows cast by the thicket of overhanging trees and within sprinting range of the first vehicle.

Sitting in his car, Charles focused on his breathing, the rise and fall of his chest, to moderate his emotions and ensure that he didn't behave rashly. Equanimity was essential to his success. He must have control of his mind and body in order to achieve his goals.

The store had closed three hours earlier, but he knew that the cleaner, the last employee, wouldn't finish her shift for another quarter-hour. He had studied her movements and he was confident in his timing. Dutifully, he played the waiting game that demanded his undivided attention. Charles prided himself on being a patient man, and he was willing to wait again, like he had with the others.

At the university, he had failed but that had been a tactical mistake, one he wouldn't make twice. He had deviated from his proven strategy, having allowed his overconfidence to lead him to behave recklessly, and he had nearly lost everything.

No more mistakes. Stay on course. Stay in control.

Just then, he caught sight of movement by the poorly lit door at the rear entrance. Using her back, a uniformed woman pushed open the door and stopped to inspect her pockets and handbag one last time before allowing the heavy door to shut. A moment later, she approached the driver's side door, keys in hand. She didn't see Charles as he rushed her from behind, and no one heard her muffled cries as he dragged her into the nearby thicket.

7

Thursday, May 13, 1993

Mustafa reached under the blankets for Maiheen, pulling himself closer to her and wrapping his arm and leg around the length of her warm body. He had been awake for a few minutes and checked the time. The alarm would sound shortly. Maiheen had a habit of sleeping through the alarm and staying in bed long after it was prudent. She'd had the same habit since they first married, and Mustafa had cautioned her against depending on his prodding to wake her. One day, he warned, he might not wake her up for work and she would end up in trouble. Maiheen had brushed off his warning as proof that he was envious of her ability to sleep in.

"*Azziz-am,* my dearest," Mustafa whispered in her ear, nibbling at the lobe when she didn't respond.

"*Khanome Ghasemi,* Mrs. Ghasemi." He tried sweetly announcing her name. "Please come to the front desk. *Khanome Ghasemi,* we have an important package for you."

"Hm," Maiheen moaned, barely stirring.

"Don't miss your chance. It's very important," he cooed and kissed her neck and shoulder.

"I know this package," Maiheen mumbled, nestling her body deeper into her pillow. "It's always available."

"Oh no, madam. This is a special delivery. International shipping," Mustafa purred, pressing his hard cock against her rear.

"Uh-huh," Maiheen said before falling back asleep.

"Maybe you need some incentives to claim this parcel," said Mustafa as he reached around to cup her groin and massage her clitoris.

Maiheen moaned with pleasure, and Mustafa quickened his pace. He loved to hear her enjoy herself, and it had taken years before she permitted him to touch her for the purpose of making her climax. There had been so many reasons why she hadn't wanted him to stimulate her, so many doubts about his desire to please her, so many worries about her taste, her scent, her loss of control and the ejaculate that drenched his chin. He had proven his lust for her folds and her juices, and she had accepted her need for an orgasm. Presently, the lovers began a rhythmic dance which they'd nearly perfected.

Following his shower, Mustafa snuggled up to Maiheen, who had fallen back asleep.

"It's time to wake up. We're leaving soon, remember," he said, rubbing the hair away from her eyes.

"I'm up, just resting," Maiheen replied. She opened one eye and looked at the clock. "What time do we need to leave?"

"Farah said her exam was at nine, so with traffic and everything, we leave here at eight," Mustafa said. "I can drop Farzana off at work after, and Candice knows that I'll be in a bit late."

Maiheen stretched her body and turned to face Mustafa. He touched the impression of pillow creases on her face and kissed the lines.

"Are you okay?" she asked with concern, however groggily.

"Hm," Mustafa said, nuzzling his face into her neck.

He wasn't sure if he wanted to own up to his feelings. He worried that Maiheen might consider him capricious if he admitted to having second thoughts about driving Farah to her exam. Last night at dinner, when he offered to drive Farah, he had recognized the looks of admiration among his wife and daughters. They were surprised, but more so, they were pleased with his decision; they seemed proud of him. It had felt good to be in their esteem, and he was genuinely enthused to be helpful to Farah.

This morning, his overwhelming experience was of apprehension. He wanted to help Farah on her own terms, but driving her to the exam felt irresponsible. How would he justify his actions if anything were to happen to Farah? On the other hand, if he didn't drive her himself, Farah would go to campus in a cab with Maiheen or possibly storm off by herself.

"Are you worried about Farah?" Maiheen intuited.

"Yes, so worried," Mustafa said, somewhat abashed.

Now that he had admitted to feeling uneasy, he needed to say more, to confess his concerns wholly. "Maiheen, what if something happens? How can I face myself if I know I helped her into a dangerous situation? I just don't think I can do this. I want to help her. I really do, but this is going too far. She doesn't realize the kind of danger she's in. She's so stubborn about her decisions and she's stuck in this foolish idea of having to attend this exam. It's one exam. Goodness sake, it's not as important as her safety."

Maiheen listened, and her expression was neutral, void of judgement. However Maiheen felt within herself, when he divulged his anxieties about their daughters, Mustafa knew that she would offer him a safe, non-judgemental space to voice his feelings. Possibly, she recognized how difficult it was for him to admit to feeling uncertain and helpless in his role as a father and provider. Maybe, it was a skill she had intentionally honed once she recognized how much he revealed when she didn't react outwardly. Nevertheless, Mustafa appreciated the chance to share his worries with someone whose judgement he trusted, someone who cared for his daughters as much as he did.

Having voiced his concerns, Mustafa felt relieved and also deflated. It was only the loving and caring expression on Maiheen's face that kept him from feeling hopeless.

"We are going to feel ... uncertain," Maiheen began, searching for the right words. "That's normal. We want to protect her, and that's normal, too."

She adjusted her position so she could run her fingers through his hair as she spoke. He nestled into her body, closed his eyes and allowed her to care and tend to him as no one else did.

"Farah wants us to protect her, still," Maiheen continued. "She wants our help. I know because she accepts it when it suits her."

Mustafa reflected on his wife's assessment, and he realized he agreed; it was true. Sometimes, Farah requested assistance, however tactlessly and without gratitude. Mostly, she refused any advice or interference from her parents. If he tried to help her without being asked, she erupted angrily and accused him of infantilizing her.

He sighed in agreement, and Maiheen continued, all the while stroking his head. "We're still learning how to help her. She's not Farzana, obviously."

They both chuckled at this statement because it was the persistent theme of raising Farah, the comparison to Farzana, and the customary conclusion to every heart-to-heart between her parents.

"She's not afraid like Farzana had been. Remember, the way we had to pull information out of her. We would find her crying about something that had happened days before, something we could have helped her with."

Mustafa nodded at this second truth. He remembered worrying about Farzana's habit of hiding her woes, worrying that he was in the dark about her everyday experiences. He felt that Farzana lived a secret inner life, a mélange of ideas and emotions that never surfaced in his presence. *Why does she do that? Is she trying to protect us? Why is she still hiding herself?*

Maiheen continued, "Farah goes after what she wants. She pushes herself, and she expects resistance, but at least she's loud and clear about her goals."

Mustafa gazed up and added, "And she usually has no back-up plan. She thinks everything will work out on the first go. So naïve, that girl." He nestled back into Maiheen's bosom and sighed with resignation.

"Right," Maiheen continued, "and because she takes on challenges, she needs extra support. Our help, as back-up. Not to lead her. We both know she doesn't need to be led."

Unable to hold back, Mustafa peeled away to say, "But she makes such stupid choices. Like that haircut. How is she going to get a summer job with no hair?"

Maiheen waited for him to resettle into her arms, and she returned to stroking his hair. Once his muscles relaxed, she continued speaking in the gentle soothing voice that he loved.

"Right," she said. "She does make stupid choices, I agree. That's part of her growing up. Farzana made stupid choices, too, but we didn't hear about them until they became major issues."

Mustafa tried to recall the problems caused by Farzana's poor choices as a youth. He must have been holding his breath, or Maiheen intuited that he couldn't recall such an occurrence, because she pulled back to look at him.

"Remember choir?" Maiheen asked pointedly.

Yes, there had been something about Farzana joining the school choir but quitting soon after practice sessions commenced. Mustafa couldn't recall the circumstances, except that they met with the guidance counsellor to discuss the issue.

Maiheen must have sensed that he couldn't completely remember the experience, so she elaborated, "Farzana was being teased by those two girls, the sisters, and she didn't tell us. We didn't even know until the counsellor called us in. Then we found out Farzana had stopped going to practice and she'd been hiding in the library, crying."

It came back to Mustafa, that dreadful feeling of having failed his daughter, and he inhaled sharply for relief. Again, he resettled against Maiheen's body, breathing in her comforting scent to lessen his anxiety.

"Farah counts on us to be her back-up, her reinforcements, when all she needs is a boost or when her plans fail and she hasn't bothered to figure out an alternative. You know, Mustafa, I'm seeing her in a new light."

He was too. Farah was brazen and heavy-handed but she was also brave and upfront. She had survived that monster's attack and returned the next day, determined to write her exam. His youngest was a powerhouse of ambition and dynamism, even in the face of brute violence.

"Mama! Baba! Are you up yet? I have to go!" Farah complained through the closed bedroom door.

Mustafa and Maiheen burst out laughing at her characteristic interjection.

"What do you say?" Maiheen asked, gazing into his eyes.

"Coming!" Mustafa answered Farah's call.

He kissed Maiheen deeply, and then pressed his forehead to hers in a moment of mutual gratitude.

Farzana arrived at work in the nick of time. Out of habit, she turned into the first aisle and began to settle into her usual seat, in front of the glass wall of the supervisors' office, alone. Then, she remembered the new plan, to sit with the other callers, and she collected her belongings. The walk back down the aisle and past the supervisors' office was slow, methodical, as Farzana worked herself up to the task. *This is good. People change seats all the time. This is normal.*

Alternating seats was common among the other callers, but this was Farzana's first time sitting anywhere else in the five months she had worked at the centre. It seemed that her change in routine had attracted the attention of the supervisors, as well. A couple of them stared curiously as she passed their window and headed towards the back of the large room.

Tony, the most senior member of the team, poked his head out of the office and asked, "Everything okay, Farzana?"

She forced herself to smile, though she felt ghastly inside, and replied, "Yes, everything's fine. I'm just moving to the back."

Tony nodded slowly, pausing for more details. When Farzana shrugged, he reciprocated and popped back into the office.

Farzana proceeded past the second aisle, which was occupied by Sandra, another recluse and a good earner who had worked at the centre for several years. The idea to sit with Sandra occurred to Farzana, but she realized that it was a disingenuous attempt at meshing with her coworkers.

She approached the third aisle, which was peopled with a handful of callers, with room to spare. They were chatting casually, and as Farzana passed, a young woman she recognized from smoke breaks, Arista, waved cheerfully. She returned the wave and proceeded to the last aisle, the one that was teeming with callers, each person animated and juggling two conversations at one time. *This is good. This is normal. I'm just finding a seat.*

Her heart was in her throat. The din of people clowning around and speaking over top of each other rattled through her, causing a wave of panic that threatened her composure. Farzana reminded herself that in a few minutes the call centre would quieten as work hours began and callers hustled on the phones to collect donations. *It'll get quieter. Everyone is going to be working. It's not like this all the time.*

While it was true that the social frenzy would subdue, the present clamour was overwhelming Farzana. She took one final step and stood at the end of the last aisle, willing herself to lift her gaze from the carpet to scan for an empty seat. *Come on! You can do this. Take a seat!*

In the brief moment before she looked up to survey the aisle, she searched within herself for that once-hidden path that led to her deepest desires. She walked past the brambles which she had brushed off the path and touched the blossoms on the flourishing flora of her hopes and aspirations. For years, she had dreamed of managing a team, of making a name for herself in business circles, and she refused to waste any more time on the periphery. If she wanted to be one of the leaders, she had to step into the centre of the pack.

Farzana lifted her eyes and scanned the aisle, ready to claim the nearest seat for herself. A familiar face smiled at her, then another, and Farzana smiled back, even managing a wave.

"I think they're all taken back here," said a voice close by.

Farzana recognized Abdullah, a soft-spoken man who had been hired about the same time as her. She smiled at him and shrugged.

"I guess I'll have to come earlier tomorrow," she replied with a smirk.

"I'll save you a seat," he offered graciously and turned to don his headset.

"Thanks," Farzana said as she returned to the more peaceful third aisle.

"Sit here," said Arista, patting the adjacent seat.

"Thanks," replied Farzana just as Tony announced the start of shift, and she beelined for the seat.

"Good luck!" Arista said, putting on her headset.

"Thanks. You, too," Farzana said.

In the seclusion offered by the cubicle's three walls, Farzana exhaled and congratulated herself on taking her first step towards the centre.

Farah began her fourth and final exam, women's studies, with less physical pain and more confidence than she had the previous day.

While she remembered the concepts and principles, she fought to remain focused on answering the questions.

Every sound in the cavernous gymnasium startled her. First, the air conditioner started up with a bang and she dropped her pencil to the floor, a clattering sound that echoed and attracted perturbed looks. Not long after, the student behind her sneezed loudly and Farah yelped in surprise, feeling more than a little embarrassed.

When she hit her stride and became completely engrossed in her writing, hunched over her papers and scribbling furiously, a passing proctor stepped into her peripheral vision and she jolted out of her seat with fright. She whispered apologies to no one in particular and reseated but it was too difficult to regain her momentum.

Afterwards, she felt disappointed in herself, even though her mother assured her that she probably did much better than she imagined. Farah didn't want to discuss the exam, so she remained quiet as the two of them followed the rest of the departing students out through the main doors of the Athletics Building and onto the campus green.

Sadness and anger were building up in her. She considered the reality that her grades wouldn't secure the endorsement of the department head, the scholarship was a lost cause, and she wouldn't be able to move out on her own without being financially bound to her parents. Just two days earlier, it had all seemed like a certainty, attainable and within her grasp. Now, she was haphazardly answering exam questions and preparing herself for a mediocre grade point average. Thinking about her loss agitated her thoroughly, causing her to clench her fists and grit her teeth, which sent bolts of pain through her sore neck and back.

"Farah! Farah!"

A woman called from behind them as Farah and her mother crossed the campus green and headed towards the taxi stand. Farah turned to see Taari rushing through the scattered groups, her carpetbag held to her chest, her long bohemian skirt bunched up in one hand.

Farah motioned for her mother to stop, and she waved shyly at Taari. This was their first chance to talk since Tuesday afternoon when Taari rescued her from the attacker.

From Charles, Farah repeated inwardly.

During the interview with the police officers, she had forced herself to name him and describe his strange behaviour but since then she hadn't referred to him by name aloud. Farah worried that accusing him of being the attacker, when she hadn't seen his face, made her appear paranoid or unreliable. Her intuition told her that it was Charles who had attacked her, but she was concerned that other people would consider her gut feeling to be insubstantial. She didn't want to expose herself to the judgement of others, not when she felt so vulnerable.

When Taari reached her, the two friends stood arm's length apart and exchanged meaningful looks. Then, Taari dropped her bag and threw her arms around Farah. In an instant, Farah began to sob into Taari's bare shoulder, holding her friend tightly and shutting out the rest of the world. They remained in each other's arms for some time, until Farah's crying subsided and she peeled away.

"Sorry about your ..." Farah said, pointing at Taari's wet shoulder.

"It's what best friends are for," Taari replied kindly.

Farah remembered her mother and spun around to see her standing in the same spot, teary-eyed and hugging herself. Farah managed to smile at her mother, to alleviate the sadness which she imagined her mother might be feeling at having witnessed her daughter sobbing. Her mother nodded and smiled back, in a reciprocating attempt to lessen Farah's emotional burden.

Swallowing her pain and tears, Farah introduced Taari to her mother as normally as possible, "Taari, this is my mom. Mrs. Ghasemi, or ..."

Farah stumbled on her introduction. Should she offer her mother's given name? As a teenager, her friends called her mother Mrs. Ghasemi. Now, it seemed unusual for her adult friend to address her mother by her surname. Stumped, Farah shrugged at her mother. This caused her mother to chuckle and smile widely, a pleasant smile that heartened Farah and dispelled the gloom of moments earlier.

"You can call me Maiheen," her mother said to Taari, extending her hand.

Shaking Maiheen's hand, Taari smiled and said, "Nice to meet you, Maiheen. That's a really pretty name."

"Thank you. It's a family name," her mother added. "You also have a beautiful name, Taari."

Impishly, Taari replied, "I think my parents named me after a brand of laundry detergent in Sri Lanka. Or something like that."

"Beautiful all the same," her mother proclaimed. "I really like your handbag. I used to carry a similar one when I was your age."

"Really?" Taari said, delighted. She picked up the carpetbag and held it out for Farah's mother to examine. "I got it at Kensington Market, and now I don't leave home without it. This skirt, too. It's so comfortable."

Farah started to feel self-conscious and a little out of place. Was it possible that Taari had more in common with Farah's mother than with Farah? Both were dressed in colourful outfits, adorned with makeup and jewellery, and sported complicated hairstyles. Farah was in her usual outfit of torn cargo pants and baggy t-shirt, with the same no fuss buzz cut. She hadn't even styled her bangs that morning.

"What do you think, Farah?" Her mother repeated but Farah had lost track of what they were discussing.

"Of?" she asked, looking from Taari to her mother for a clue.

"Of Taari coming to our place," her mother explained, putting an arm around Taari and pulling her closer. "I'd like to thank her with a home-cooked meal, and I'm sure your father would like to thank her in person, too."

"Um, yeah, sure. Now?" Farah asked the two of them, muddled about what had quickly transpired.

"No, not now," her mother answered, and then looking at Taari, "You have an exam, you said?"

"Yes, my last one. It's in ..." said Taari as she checked her watch, "another half-hour. But another time, for sure. I'd like that."

Farah's mother beamed, and as she embraced Taari tightly, Farah heard her say, "Thank you so much for your bravery. I will never forget what you've done for my family. You should be very proud of yourself."

Despite feeling the same sentiment, Farah wasn't confident enough to say as much to Taari. Instead, Farah wished Taari luck on her last exam, and they made plans to meet the following week.

In the cab ride home, Farah didn't snuggle up to her mother as she had on the previous day. Her resentment about performing poorly on the exam had exacerbated her other ill feelings, and she distanced herself by sitting closer to the window and staring at the passing traffic. The envy that had started to bubble when her mother connected with Taari had matured to a rolling boil, and as each jealous thought burst at the surface, it scorched Farah's morale. *She probably wishes I was more like Taari. Pretty and dressed girly. The nice girl who saves her friend. Not the girl who gets ... into trouble.*

At that moment, traffic came to a standstill on the parkway, and Farah pressed her forehead to the car window. This recurring bout of hostility had agitated her since childhood, and long ago she had attributed it to her parents' preferential treatment of Farzana. Why did they treat Farzana like a treasure and her like a rock, jagged and heavy? Why was her mother chattier with Farzana? She was her mother's daughter, too. She performed as well in school and pushed as hard towards success. While it was true that she didn't volunteer to help her mother as often as Farzana did, Farah knew that she was reliable when called upon. She had even heard Yasmeen Khanome describe her as a good daughter. So, why the distance between her and her mother?

An eighteen-wheeler truck slowly pulled up beside the taxi and blocked Farah's view of everything else. She huffed in frustration, imagining that she looked foolish staring out the window at the side of truck. Still, Farah wasn't ready to turn away from the window. To distract herself from her brooding emotions, she examined the muddy tires, the flaps on the underside, the mysterious valves and cylinders that ran the length of the truck, and the company name painted in silver across the semi-trailer, Lanford Logistics. The familiar logo was a stenciled profile of a truck in motion, leaning forward with lines trailing behind.

In a sudden flash, she remembered seeing that logo on Charles's keyring. When he had driven her home on Saturday night, she had been attracted by the furry keyring dangling from the ignition, not realizing it was the severed and hardened paw of a dead animal. Charles had held it out for her to examine the rabbit's foot, but she had also noticed the ornate silver disk that sparkled brilliantly in the lamplight. It was a smooth oval shape, palm-sized, and embossed in its centre was the stencil of the semi-trailer and the company name, Lanford Logistics.

Startled by her recollection, she spun in her seat towards her mother. How could she express her thought without sounding wildly speculative, grasping at straws to identify the attacker?

Her mother must have sensed Farah's urgency because she stared back wide-eyed and asked, "What happened, Farah? What is it?"

☽

Maiheen maintained her composure as Farah described her memory of the keyring. The last thing she wanted to do was to react in some manner that upset Farah, who was likely to shut her out or rush off on her own. They had enjoyed a day of comradery as they prepared for their trip to campus, even though Farah seemed distant and perturbed following her exam, and Maiheen wanted to retain the open line of communication they had established.

Of course, the information that Farah relayed was difficult to absorb. She thought she had identified the attacker's place of employment by a company branded keyring he carried, and she wanted to change their present route, go to the company's headquarters, and demand a list naming their employees.

The naïvety of Farah's plan, its lack of foresight about the obstacles they would surely face and the potential dangers that might result, was taxing Maiheen's practised skill of listening without judgement or sudden reaction. *What is her daughter thinking? Doesn't Farah realize that she can't address such a serious matter without involving the police? How does she imagine this playing out?*

"Driver, take us to ..." ordered Farah, sitting at the edge of her seat and speaking to the cabbie. She stopped midsentence and turned to look out the back window, "I need to see the address on that trailer."

Maiheen looked behind her at the slow moving traffic and spotted the trailer bearing the Lanford Logistics logo. It had lagged farther down the parkway. Horrified at the likely prospect of Farah leaping out of the cab to weave between cars and trucks to get the address, Maiheen improvised her strategy.

"Farah, this is very important information," Maiheen said gravely, trying to hold Farah's darting attention. "If he realizes that we're at his work, he might escape and never been seen again."

Farah, who had been twisting back and forth in her seat, eyeing the trailer, which was falling farther behind, stopped all movement to stare with narrowed lids at Maiheen, as if willing her to speed up her train of thought.

"We need to make sure he doesn't get away. We need people there who can capture him," Maiheen continued authoritatively.

"We must contact the police to meet us there, so they can arrest him."

Maiheen hoped against hope that this line of reasoning would appeal to Farah, to her desire to take immediate action and achieve results. She watched her daughter wring her hands and ponder the idea, her youthful face contorting, at times seeming angry and other times frustrated.

Maiheen longed to embrace Farah, comfort her, and assure her that the feelings of hopelessness and devastation that weighed her down today would pass with time, in this instance and again in the future when hard times returned, as they did for everyone. It would have been the truth but it wouldn't have eased Farah's pain, Maiheen sensed. Her daughter was hurting from the injustice of being stalked and mangled by a predator, treated like an inanimate object, and having survived to receive no assurances of retribution. *Like living in limbo, a perpetual state of trauma. My poor child.*

Even as she grieved for her daughter, Maiheen remained composed and awaited Farah's response.

"How?" Farah asked finally, still at the edge of her seat, wringing her hands, and anxious to move into action. "How do we reach the police?"

"Well," Maiheen replied plainly, "we could call from a payphone, or from home."

At her reference to home, Farah's furrowed her brows, possibly sensing an ulterior motive. Maiheen recognized the cue and proceeded quickly.

"We can take the next exit and find a payphone," she explained. "We can call the police and use the phone book to find the address of the company. It's possible there are several offices in the city. Maybe we can call around to figure out which location he works at?"

Farah didn't answer. Instead, she pivoted in her seat and looked out the front window, most likely to spot the next exit off the parkway.

Without consulting with Maiheen, Farah instructed the driver, "Get off at the next exit and find the nearest payphone."

Maiheen exhaled and leaned back. At least Farah wasn't getting out in traffic to read the address off the back of a truck, but how would she protect her daughter once they reached the payphone? Maiheen hoped that the phone call to the police would hamper Farah's plans. She checked her watch. It was approaching one o'clock, still business hours for logistics companies, so they were bound to answer incoming calls. Could she manage a call to Mustafa, arrange to meet him wherever they wound up?

Gradually, the cab driver changed lanes leftwards and exited the parkway at the next ramp. They arrived in the vibrant district of Greek Town, on the eastern side of the dense urban forests of the Don Valley. The neighbourhood's main road, Danforth Avenue, was jammed with vehicular traffic, and pedestrians spilled onto the road from the sidewalks, dogging cyclists and manoeuvring between cars to cross four lanes to their destinations.

The low-rise brick buildings along the avenue were occupied by delis and bakeries, sidewalk cafés, cobblers and dress shops, travel agencies, and tax accountants. Around an elaborate fountain and at the dispersed park benches, people milled about in the pleasant weather. Years earlier, Maiheen had cleaned offices in this neighbourhood and applied for work at some of the coffee shops.

As Farah peered out the front window, searching blocks ahead for a phone booth, Maiheen devised a plan. She needed to respectfully respond to Farah's anxiety and agency whilst also diminishing the urgency that was propelling her daughter towards a senseless act.

"I know this street, there's a payphone at the next block," Maiheen said.

Her daughter looked over her shoulder at Maiheen and asked, "Where?"

Again, the feeling returned. Maiheen wanted to hold Farah

desperately, to stroke her face and kiss her cheeks, to offer her motherly love when it was evident that her daughter was in anguish. *Not now. It won't work. She doesn't want it.*

"There, you can drop us off at the next lights," Maiheen said to the driver.

"Shouldn't we hold onto the cab?" Farah asked uncertainly.

"It'll be easy to get another one, and it's too expensive to have him wait while we call," Maiheen said, pulling out her purse from her handbag and counting out the fare.

At the next intersection, they disembarked onto the sidewalk, and Maiheen led the way to a coffee shop. Farah paused outside, confused about where they were heading.

"The payphone's inside. It's clean and private. Come," Maiheen said as she held open the door.

The coffee shop was plain, without the frills of the urban cafés, serving coffee, tea, donuts, sandwiches, and not much else. The small place seated about twenty people, but it was nearly empty, and its decor reminded Maiheen of Coffee Express, faded, worn out, and slightly dilapidated.

"The phone is in the back," Maiheen said pointing at the single payphone near the restrooms. "I'll buy something so they don't hassle us."

Farah walked quickly to the payphone, past the server behind the cash register, who watched her cross the room. Maiheen approached the counter and ordered one tea, one carton of chocolate milk, two ham sandwiches, and two custard-filled donuts. Her plan was to feed her daughter into submission. It was an uncomplicated approach, but Maiheen trusted food and its visceral effect on the human body.

She chose a table as close as possible to the payphone and placed upon it the tray of provisions. Farah was hurriedly flipping through the phonebook, which was chained in place. She held its bulk at an odd angle on one thigh while she turned pages awkwardly with her free hand. Correctly guessing that a second phonebook was tucked behind the counter, Maiheen procured it from the server and placed it at their table.

"I have another phone book if that's easier," Maiheen offered from a distance, trying not to overwhelm her careworn daughter.

"Hm?" Farah glanced up at her mother and then in the direction she was pointing. "Oh, uh, okay."

As Farah approached the table, Maiheen obtained a notebook and pen from her handbag, and she held them at the ready. For the next few minutes, she silently recorded addresses and phone numbers that Farah read aloud. First, the three dispersed offices for Lanford Logistics and then the precinct of the constables who had handled the incident. Farah's faltering tone betrayed her diminishing resolve and her growing apprehension. *Dear god, may she realize the absurdity of this plan.*

In her circuitous manner, Maiheen guided Farah towards eating half a sandwich, which led to her drinking the milk and gobbling the donut in three bites. Shortly thereafter, Farah's demeanour changed considerably. Shoulders which had formed peaks up at her ears, had lowered into sloping hills, softened by fatigue and despair. Clenched jaw and furrowed brows were replaced with hooded lids, glassy eyes, and a mournful frown.

Maiheen continued to suppress her desire to hold Farah, to speak gently and offer her sympathy. The girl looked so despondent, so much in need of an arm around her shoulder. Still, Maiheen knew from experience that Farah didn't accept kindness if she suspected it was intended to suppress her will. Her daughter was discerning when it came to sympathy, and Maiheen would need to curb her displays of affection. *That comes later. You've still got a way to go.*

They sat in silence for some time, nibbling at the last morsels. The phonebook lay closed in Farah's lap, and the pen and notepad rested on the table. Farah had her information, and her next step was to call the police and the three offices but she didn't move from her seat or look up from the notepad. Maiheen remained patient and still, anticipating what was to come.

Presently, tears fell onto the phonebook, and Maiheen knew it was time to go home.

☽

Mustafa was double-parked outside Farzana's apartment, awaiting her descent. If traffic wasn't any worse than usual, they would arrive home for six o'clock. He was eager to be home with his family instead of at work fretting over their well-being. Late afternoon, he had called their apartment to check in on Maiheen and Farah, following their trip to campus. His wife had sounded fatigued, explaining that Farah was safe but unwell, and since then Mustafa couldn't focus on any task. Already, he had confused a four-litre bottle of detergent with a degreaser and nearly ruined the car-wash dispensers. Luckily, Afewerk was thinking for both of them and discreetly prevented the disaster.

"*Salaam*, Baba," Farzana said, hopping into the front seat and leaning over to kiss him on both cheeks. "*Chetori?* How are you? How was work?"

"*Salaam, azziz-am*. Hello, my dear," he replied, checking his blind spot.

Mustafa pulled out into traffic as soon as Farzana closed her door and made the first right to take the back streets. He believed he had answered her, but he must have become lost in thought. Farzana was staring at him expectantly, bemused.

"Huh?" he asked. "Oh, uh, good good. And you?"

"It was good. I think things are going better," Farzana answered.

Mustafa imagined that he nodded, but mainly he was focused on navigating the side streets of old Toronto heading to the expressway, which would lead him to the parkway, and then north towards home.

"Is everything okay?" Farzana asked.

The concern in her voice grabbed Mustafa's attention, and he reminded himself that he had two daughters.

"Oh, yeah. I mean, considering everything that's happened," Mustafa said, struggling to calm his nerves and drive at a reasonable speed. "How about you? You said work was good."

"Yes, it was good. I'm making a lot of money in commissions. That's good," Farzana said cheerily.

"Good for you, sweetheart. I'm very proud of you," Mustafa said, and he intentionally smiled and nodded at his eldest.

"*Merci*, Baba," she said. "So … I have good news."

"Oh, I like good news," he said with a glance and a smile, though inwardly he was cursing the car ahead of him for parallel parking during rush hour and blocking the one-way street.

"I don't have to move anymore. My landlord's sorted out something else for his relatives," Farzana explained. "I get to keep my apartment with Soreyah."

"Oh," Mustafa responded less than enthusiastically.

He had continued to hope that she would return home, but at this point Farzana's life seemed stable, and he was disinclined to interfere in her affairs. In fact, since the attack on Farah, he'd been scattered in mind and body, preoccupied with Farah's well-being and unable to focus on any given task. Every day that he went to work he felt treacherous for leaving Farah without protection. Mostly, he wanted to stay by her side even if his working was the best use of his time. If he was being honest with himself, he wasn't interested at all in what was happening in Farzana's life, so long as she was safe.

The car ahead had just finished backing into the parking spot, and Mustafa zoomed past to recoup the few minutes he had lost waiting to proceed. Up ahead, he planned to make a left turn onto the small street that fed into the expressway. He was almost free of the stop-and-go motion of inner city traffic. At the intersection, the light was green but the car in front of him, which was also turning left, waited to allow a pedestrian to cross. Mustafa put on the brakes at the last minute and avoided a fender bender.

"Baba!" Farzana yelped, putting out her hands to stop from colliding with the dashboard. "What's the matter? Why are you rushing?"

Mustafa caught his breath. He was acting like a fool, endangering both of them so that he could arrive home a few minutes sooner. What was he thinking? He had to rethink his tactics and regain control of the game. His daughters needed him to play the long game, think strategically about the future, not fumble on one play after another until time had run out. *Big picture, think big picture. It's about the season, not one game.*

"I'm sorry, honey. I just ..." Mustafa said, taking in a deep breath and shaking off the sense of dread. "You know what? I want to hear about your day. Tell me everything."

Simply having expressed this sentiment felt like the beginning of a better strategy. Maiheen was taking care of Farah, and he was with Farzana, his endearing daughter who was obviously excited about her day. That very morning, Maiheen had reminded him that Farzana was the one who was reluctant to share her experiences with them. Now, Farzana wanted to talk about her work and he needed to be present for this conversation.

"Oh, it's ... I mean, it's not a big deal," Farzana said shyly. "I just think it's going better than before."

"What's it like?" Mustafa asked off the cuff, not certain what he meant.

"The office? It's alright, busy. There's a lot of people," Farzana said. "The manager, Annette, is really hardworking. I mean, she's got a lot of projects on the go, and the call centre is just one of them."

She continued to talk about the office at length, and Mustafa was surprised by the breadth of the World Wildlife Fund's operations.

Somehow, during Farzana's five months of employment, Mustafa hadn't learned about the company's purpose, its international scope, and its multimillion dollar projects. When she had initially described working at the call centre of a charity, he assumed it was a local enterprise with limited financial and human resources.

As she described the organization's initiatives, Mustafa asked more questions about their sources of revenue and their corporate structure. To his surprise, Farzana knew a considerable amount about the various departments and how they contributed to the corporation's international operations. It seemed that Farzana was actively pursuing a career at this organization and she had made some headway with her direct lead.

"*Azziz-am*, my dear, I am very impressed by your initiative. It sounds like your manager's on your side, too," Mustafa said, and he patted her shoulder to communicate his pride.

Modestly, she smiled and nodded, "*Merci*, Baba. I really think I can do well there."

"That's great! They're lucky to have you," he added.

Traffic had backed up along the expressway. Mustafa reminded himself that if they'd reached home already, he wouldn't have learned so much about Farzana's aspirations. He decided to build on his success and see what else came his way.

"So, how about Soreyah? What does she do?" he asked casually.

Farzana faced him surprised, and he realized he had never before asked about her roommate. Was it possible that he had never even said the young woman's name? *She needs me to ask about her life. All this time, she's been waiting for me to ask.*

The car ride home became one of the best hours Mustafa had ever spent with Farzana. Towards the end of the ride, Farzana was speaking rapidly and excitedly, in a manner that he associated with her early childhood. He learned about her friendship with Soreyah, of the young woman's interests and her achievements, as well as a few details about her immediate family. From Farzana's enamoured tone, Mustafa realized that Soreyah was a very important person in his daughter's life, and he made a note to talk to Maiheen about having the young woman over for dinner.

When they approached the Ghasemis' neighbourhood, Farzana stopped chatting and took a notebook and pen out of her overnight bag. Mustafa recalled her taking note of license plate details that morning, furtively in the front seat, out of view of Maiheen and Farah in the back seat. He slowed the car to give her time to survey the side streets and the visitor's parking lot before he drove the car into the underground garage.

"You're a good sister," Mustafa said as the car descended.

"You're a good father," Farzana said, just as earnestly.

8

Sunday, August 1, 1993

Farah descended the two flights of stairs after carrying a second box of books up to her new room at the Cartwright Street rooming house. Despite her early start to avoid the mid-summer heat, the humidity was stifling, clouding her judgement, and twice she had tripped over her own feet climbing the stairs. Farah cursed herself for wearing army boots — her feet felt like heavy bricks — but nothing could wipe the smile from her face.

Her mother was upstairs in the communal kitchen for third-floor residents, cleaning the cupboards assigned to Farah and filling the freezer with individual portions of meals she had prepared. She'd advised Farah against unpacking the cargo until she had thoroughly washed the furnished bedroom, including the baseboards, the window sills, and the drawers. Farah had dismissed the idea as overly domestic but upon closer inspection, she had resigned herself to the task.

It had taken Farah an hour to scrub grime and scrape candle wax from the ledges, remove dust from the crown molding, and wipe the insides of the dresser and desk drawers. Then, she had diligently vacuumed the room, only to discover mouse droppings in a corner behind the bedframe. She had no intention of mentioning her findings to her parents, since they were already displeased by the unclean state of the house.

Farah didn't care that it wasn't up to their standards. It was her place and she was staying put, mice, roaches, or whatever else was crawling inside the walls. She'd buy a trap or poison, or just make do. Mainly, she daydreamed about how gorgeous her bedroom would look once it was decorated, a colour scheme based on the red roses and black stencils of the Red Hot Chili Peppers' album cover. It would be a sultry, edgy design, with black candles and gothic stone sculptures that would impress her guests.

Farah stepped out and gulped in the fresh air, which was only slightly cooler than the temperature in the house but noticeably so. Parked on the quiet street directly in front of the house was the borrowed minivan, which still contained the majority of her belongings, including her mattress and box spring, refurbished bicycle, and several boxes of books, clothes, housewares, and bedding. In the driver's seat, her father was smoking and browsing the sports section. He had refused to lug anything until the entire moving team was present to help.

"Aren't you going to help at all?" Farah complained, hanging on to the open window of the front passenger seat.

"I am going to help when your sister arrives," he explained, smiling at her. "A team needs all its members so that no one person is overly depleted. Yes?"

With that he returned to reading the paper, and Farah spun backward to lean against the side panel of the minivan and check her watch. It was approaching ten o'clock. Who knew when Farzana would crawl out of bed on a Sunday? Farah's irritation lasted a brief moment, and then her wide grin returned as she beheld her new place. To pass the time, she lit a cigarette and calculated her expenses again.

The scholarship hadn't come through, and she wasn't surprised given that she had significantly underperformed on her last two exams. But she was making excellent commission as a telemarketer at the World Wildlife Fund, enough to pay her own living expenses, if not her tuition. It wasn't her ideal job, but the evening hours and the relaxed dress code made it much more suitable than manual labour or flashy sales positions. She planned to reapply for the scholarship next year, and she felt confident that it would come through. Until then, her parents would help with tuition.

"*Salaam!*" Farzana said from down the block. "I'm here."

Farah saw her sister approaching with Soreyah and another friend, a man. Was this Amir? Was she introducing him to their parents? He was certainly dressed like someone who was about to meet his girlfriend's parents, in his collared shirt and pressed pants, clean shaven and hair styled. Farzana and Soreyah looked like their glowing, youthful selves, partly made-up and partly dishevelled.

"Hey! Finally!" Farah greeted Farzana happily, wrapping both arms around her sister. "And you brought reinforcements."

Farah held out her hand to the man, eager to meet him officially, "Hi, I'm Farah, Farzana's sister. Who are you?"

Soreyah guffawed, embracing Farah, and said, "Bold, aren't we? Farah, this is my brother, Amir."

Farah shook hands with Amir and smiled conspiratorially at him. Amir seemed to blush in response, looking at his sister and Farzana for back-up. Farah preferred to play the part of a self-assured, spunky younger sister when she was in the company of Farzana and her friends. She wasn't suited to being meek or mild, and she wasn't confident enough to be herself yet.

"Yes, she's always like this," Farzana assured him.

Farah heard the driver's door open and shut, and then her father was at her side. They faced Farzana, Soreyah, and Amir, who stood shoulder to shoulder in that order. Farah openly examined Farzana's anxious expression and made goofy faces at her older sister to make her laugh. The situation was novel and humorous for Farah, their father meeting a boyfriend, but she could tell from Farzana's body language that her sister was concerned.

"*Salaam, Agha Ghasemi.* Hello, Mr. Ghasemi, nice to see you again," Soreyah said cheerfully, extending her hand.

"Soreyah-*jaan*, dear. Nice to see you too. It's been too long. You should come to dinner again soon, and bring Farzana. She hasn't been home in weeks," her father joked, receiving Soreyah's hand in both of his, and then kissing and embracing Farzana.

"I heard she's quite busy at work. Soon to be president," Soreyah said, nudging Farzana lightly. "And, *Agha Ghasemi*, this is my older brother, Amir. He's studying to be a hotelier."

"*Az ashenayi be shoma khoshvaqt hastam, Agha Ghasemi.* I am pleased to meet you, Mr. Ghasemi," Amir said in a formal tone, holding out his hand somewhat timorously.

"*Az ashenayi tun khoshbakht-am.* Nice to meet you too, Amir," her father replied, using the more casual phrasing as they shook hands.

Farah watched him smile at Amir, then at Soreyah, and finally at Farzana, and she wondered what he gathered by seeing Amir alongside his daughter early on a Sunday morning.

"Managing a hotel is a formidable profession," her father said sagely. "Back in Esfahan, our good friends the Baraghanis owned and operated a three-hundred-bed facility. We used to joke that they raised their kids in the lobby."

Again, her father gazed at Amir, briefly at Soreyah, and then for a moment longer at Farzana. Farah watched her older sister nod solemnly, as if they were discussing the death of a relative.

"*Hatman*, certainly. There is a lot of work involved," Amir agreed. "I enjoy hard work."

Lips pursed and hands wringing, Farzana was wound up with worry. Watching her became intolerable to Farah, and she decided to take matters into her own hands.

In her shameless manner, she grabbed Amir's arm, and said, "Come on, muscles. It's time for you to enjoy hard work."

With that, Farah led him to the rear of the minivan and opened the back door. To his credit, Amir accepted his orders and helped Farah carry the mattress and box spring into the house. They worked well together, navigating the staircase and narrow hallways, and aside from exchanging a few directions and suggestions, they didn't speak.

Upstairs, as they positioned the box spring and mattress in the frame, her mother entered. Farah introduced Amir as Soreyah's brother, and her mother offered her hand and a very charming smile. It occurred to Farah that her mother sensed Amir's relationship to Farzana. Was it the peculiarity of his tagging along with Soreyah to her roommate's family event? Or, had Farzana already informed her mother about their relationship?

"Next time, you should come to dinner with Soreyah," her mother insisted, placing a hand on Amir's forearm.

"*Motshakeram, Khanome Ghasemi.* Thank you, Mrs. Ghasemi," Amir said formally.

"Please, call me Maiheen Khanome," her mother said.

"*Bale.* Yes, Maiheen Khanome," Amir replied, and then he looked nervously about the room and back at Farah's mother. "Great, so I should probably go help the others."

When they were alone, Farah looked at her mother intently, and asked, "What do you know?"

A sly expression appeared on her mother's face, one that dared Farah to reveal more. She didn't want to betray Farzana's confidence, so she held her tongue and tried to communicate as much as possible with her gaze.

"What do I know? What every mother knows," her mother answered cryptically, "how to recognize an intelligent and good-hearted young man. It's my business."

"Uh-huh, okay," Farah replied playfully. "I thought you were going to be a mortgage broker, not a relationship broker."

"I can be both," said her mother, placing her hands on her hips confidently. "Broker mortgages during the week and find my daughter a good husband on the weekends."

"A husband?!" Farah gasped. "What're you talking about? She's not getting married."

The thought of her sister marrying bothered Farah. She wanted Farzana to be happy, to have a boyfriend even, but getting married meant that she was creating a new family, a group distinct from their original foursome.

"Alright, it's alright," her mother assured Farah. "No one's getting married right now."

Farah felt unsettled by the thought of Farzana being annexed by another nucleus, and she tried to distract herself by repositioning the bedframe and quizzing her mother about her new career.

"So, Baba did a one-eighty, huh?" Farah asked, pushing the bedframe closer to the windows.

"It's not good to sleep under a window," criticized her mother, taking a seat at the desk and wiping the tabletop with one finger to check for dust.

"What is that, Iranian superstition?" Farah teased, stepping back to examine the new arrangement.

"No, feng shui. Chinese geomancy," her mother said plainly. "It drains your energy."

"Did you learn that in mortgage class?" Farah stuck out her tongue, feeling antagonistic.

Just as quickly, Farah grew embarrassed by her childishness and her dismissive posturing toward her mother. In the previous months, Farah had frequently felt shamefaced for failing to appreciate her mother's wealth of skills and knowledge. Was it possible that she had been treating her mother poorly all along and she had become aware of her misbehaviour only recently? Certainly, her successful completion of the mortgage brokering course had jarred Farah's impression of her mother's capabilities, especially in the business world. *Why can't I grow up, just have an adult conversation with my mother?!*

"No, I learned about feng shui from Jaleh Khanome. She's a real pro about home décor," her mother clarified as she opened and closed desk drawers, inspecting each for cleanliness. "You know, I could clean these for you."

"I already cleaned them," Farah protested, again hearing her antagonistic tone but feeling hopeless about changing her habit. "Besides, I want to know how you got Baba to change his mind."

"About what?" asked her mother as she bent over to examine a cigarette burn on the carpet.

"Uh, Baba being all fascist about you becoming a broker," Farah said rudely, realizing too late that if she wanted her mother to confide in her about her father then she was making a strategic mistake by disparaging him.

"Your father is a caring and intelligent man. I thought you'd realized that by now. You should reconsider your opinions of him," her mother snapped back, clearly offended.

Farah felt too proud to apologize but she was equally ashamed of herself for maligning her father. Following the attack, he had demonstrated a breadth of compassion, and Farah recognized that not only had the attack changed his attitudes about her and improved his grasp of the adversity she faced, but it had also revealed his unconditional love for her. Her nescient father had transformed into a cognizant man who was committed to nurturing their relationship rather than reshaping her.

Sheepishly, she moved the bed away from the window and back to its original position. From the corner of her eye, she observed her mother thumb through the books in an opened box.

"He is a good dad," Farah said, her back to her mother. "I was being hard on him."

"He wants the best for us, and he tries really hard to help," her mother explained, still bent over and browsing titles.

"So, he's okay with you changing jobs?" Farah asked, sitting on the bare mattress and picking at her nails for somewhere to rest her eyes.

"He understands that I need to pursue my interests," her mother answered, diplomatically. "He doesn't have to like my choices. They are mine. But he does recognize that I know what's best for me."

"Cool, that's good," Farah said, managing to look up and smile.

"Yes, it is, and one day you'll have a husband who ..." her mother began with a beatific smile.

Farah jumped off the bed and interjected, "Oh no! Not more husband talk! I'm out of here."

As she ran downstairs, she heard her mother chuckling, and it made her smile, too.

On the porch, boxes were piled waist-high but none of the quartet was anywhere to be seen. Farah walked to the back of the minivan and found all four of them huddled over the newspaper, which was laid out on the floor of the vehicle.

Jokingly, Farah stood with arms on her hips and asked, "Is this what I'm paying you for?"

For a moment, none of them turned around. Then, her father faced her, looking grave and disturbed. Soreyah and Amir also turned but neither of them looked up. Together, the siblings walked over to the porch, mumbling something about taking boxes upstairs. Farzana was the last to turn away from the newspaper, and she looked at Farah with tears in her eyes.

"Sis," Farzana started, chewing on her lower lip for a moment before she continued, "it's about, um ... about the, uh ... Charles. They've arrested him."

Farah's stomach churned, and just as she lost the strength to stand, her father caught her and seated her on the floor of the minivan. She heard Farzana instruct Soreyah to get a glass of water. She saw her father's face close to hers, looking deeply into her eyes. Moments later, she felt her mother's hand on her own.

The heat of the day made it difficult to recover from hearing the news. Farah always imagined that when the day came that Charles was arrested, she would jump about excitedly, possibly perform cartwheels, and commission a party. She never imagined feeling nauseous or feverish, anxious or frightened.

During her therapy sessions at the sexual assault centre, she'd learned that trauma manifested in strange ways, at unexpected times. Suffering from nightmares and panic attacks, having flashbacks, fearing unfamiliar men, and startling easily all made sense and happened regularly. But why would news about the arrest of her attacker cause her distress? Isn't this what she had been hoping for?

Farah found herself weeping, then sobbing, and pulling up her knees to shield her face from passersby. As panic stricken as she felt, she needed to know the details about the charges against Charles.

Surreptitiously, Farah had already acquired Charles's full name by calling the offices of Lanford Logistics and posing as a potential client. For three months, she had urged the police to investigate David Charles Garrison. Repeatedly, the constables had assured her they were dedicated to the case. Then, they reported that no one else at Taari's house party knew Charles, and they lacked evidence to connect David Charles Garrison with her attack. So, if they had charged him, why hadn't the police notified her ahead of time?

As if coming out of shock, Farah turned to Farzana on her right and requested that she read the article aloud.

"*Azziz-am*, my dear, you don't have to do that now, or today," her mother said softly, patting Farah's left hand.

"Can you just read the article?" Farah insisted, not responding to her mother.

There was only so much effort she could exert to force her will. At that moment, she wanted compliance. She didn't have any patience or interest in negotiating with people who had the luxury of not thinking about being attacked and dragged off to be used like an object.

Farzana's eyes darted from her mother to her father, who stood in front of the seated trio and created a barrier between his family and the world. Then, she retrieved the newspaper and flipped to the article.

Farah stared at her own legs as Farzana read. She needed her family to be present, serving as her providers and protectors, but she didn't want to register their expressions. It wasn't the time for her to offer comfort or assurances; she simply couldn't muster enough sympathy for anyone else. Farah closed her eyes and listened to her sister's quivering voice.

"It's ... uh, it's about ... Well, okay, uh ..." Farzana stammered a little, and then she started with greater resolve. "The title is 'Former T-ball coach charged with twenty-three counts of sexual assault.'"

The words stabbed at Farah, but she fortified herself and waited for Farzana to continue reading.

"A twenty-one-year-old woman who was ... brutally raped and beaten near dawn on Sunday, July 25 ... has provided police with key information that links her attacker with the string of unsolved cases of sexual assaults in Toronto ... David Charles Garrison, a sales manager at Lanford Logistics, was charged Friday with ... twenty-three counts of sexual assault ... as well as assault with a weapon and uttering death threats. The charges are in connection with ... four rapes between 1990 and 1993 in East End Toronto."

Farzana stopped, and Farah looked from her own lap to her sister's and asked, "Is there more?"

"Uh-huh," Farzana said, with a slight whimper.

"*Azziz-am*, my dear, this is ... You don't need to ..." her mother tried to say but Farah interrupted her.

"I want to know," Farah insisted, looking from one lap to another, unable to lift her gaze in case she lost her resolve. "Keep reading. All the way to the end."

Farzana inhaled deeply and continued, "A week ago, a woman met with Metro Toronto police detective Joanne Shelding and provided information linking the ... rapes. Metro Toronto police are also looking into ... nine unsolved sexual assault cases involving young women since 1985 ... Garrison appeared briefly in court Thursday and was remanded in custody to August 12 for a bail hearing."

She paused to wipe away her tears and continued with a trembling voice, "His lawyer Jeffery Keller ... criticized the press ... 'From what I've seen, Mr. Garrison's been already been tried and convicted without having his lawful day in court.' Police refused to identify the young woman who provided the key information that broke the case ... Nor would they say why Garrison was released after being questioned about ... the attack on a young woman which occurred ... on a university campus ... in May 1993."

Immediately, Farah's mother and sister enveloped her in a tight embrace, and she felt her father kneeling at her feet. Her initial impulse was to push them away, to maintain her composure and distinguish herself from her family. But that feeling passed quickly. Crying with them was the greatest gift she could give herself. Under the most difficult circumstances, they had demonstrated their unconditional, nonjudgemental love, and this was her opportunity to accept their compassion and strengthen her spirit.

With heads bowed and crowns touching, Farah cried with her family, trusting that they loved her as much for her brazenness and they did for her fragility.

Acknowledgements

Family and friends, thank you for having confidence in me; it keeps me writing. While I may respond sheepishly, I appreciate your asking about my manuscripts.

Andrew and Maziar, thank you for encouraging me to write, offering sympathy on the bad days, and celebrating that one good day. You have changed me forever, and I am so happy you have.

Katti, thank you for taking me under your wing. You are the other half of my heart, always present in my thoughts.

Meghan and Linda, thank you for the long walks, candid conversations, and popsicles. With friends like you, I can keep the melancholy at bay.

Navneet, thank you for saving me a seat in your life. I feel blessed every time I touch your cheek to mine.

Mary, Jim, Ian, and Kerri, thank you for sustaining my spirits. You are the family I have always needed.

Angelina, thank you for believing in me. You are one of the strongest people I have ever met, and you've taught me so much about resiliency.

Beverley Rach, Fazeela Jiwa and Brenda Conroy at Roseway, thank you for your generosity and dedication. Working with you is a joy that I do not take for granted.